P9-CRR-669

He was her only safe haven in a world that had become her worst nightmare.

For the first time, Torrance got a clear look at her rescuer's face.

"It's you!" she gasped, sounding groggy.

"Shh. Just take it easy," Mason rasped, staring down at her, his expression fierce and brutally hard, with lingering traces of violence and rage. A warm glow burned in his oddly lit gaze. Animal ferocity, predatory and wild, rode the long lines of his body. His eyes smoldered with an intensity that made her feel…uncomfortably sensitive. And suddenly Torrance was aware of being cradled against the strongest chest she'd ever felt.

There was something wrong here, she knew. But she mentally shoved the irritating thought away, her body finding too much enjoyment out of being in his arms. If she thought too hard about things, she would have to move…and that just wouldn't do.

Books by Rhyannon Byrd

Silhouette Nocturne

Last Wolf Standing #35

*Bloodrunners

RHYANNON BYRD

fell in love with a Brit whose accent was just too sexy to resist. Lucky for her, he turned out to be a keeper, so she married him and they now have two precocious children who constantly keep her on her toes. Living in the Southwest, Rhyannon spends her days creating provocative romances with her favorite kind of hero—intense alpha males who cherish their women. When not writing, she loves to travel, lose herself in books and watch as much football as humanly possible with her loud, fun-loving family.

For information on Rhyannon's books and the latest news, you can visit her Web site at www.rhyannonbyrd.com. And be sure to look for new BLOODRUNNERS books coming in April and May.

LAST WOLF STANDING

RHYANNON BYRD

Silhouette Books

nocturne™

If you purchased this book without a cover you should be aware that this book is stolen property. It was reported as "unsold and destroyed" to the publisher, and neither the author nor the publisher has received any payment for this "stripped book."

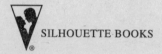

SILHOUETTE BOOKS

ISBN-13: 978-0-373-61782-1
ISBN-10: 0-373-61782-8

LAST WOLF STANDING

Copyright © 2008 by Tabitha Byrd

All rights reserved. Except for use in any review, the reproduction or utilization of this work in whole or in part in any form by any electronic, mechanical or other means, now known or hereafter invented, including xerography, photocopying and recording, or in any information storage or retrieval system, is forbidden without the written permission of the editorial office, Silhouette Books, 233 Broadway, New York, NY 10279 U.S.A.

This is a work of fiction. Names, characters, places and incidents are either the product of the author's imagination or are used fictitiously, and any resemblance to actual persons, living or dead, business establishments, events or locales is entirely coincidental.

This edition published by arrangement with Harlequin Books S.A.

® and TM are trademarks of Harlequin Books S.A., used under license. Trademarks indicated with ® are registered in the United States Patent and Trademark Office, the Canadian Trade Marks Office and in other countries.

www.silhouettenocturne.com

Printed in U.S.A.

Dear Reader,

Dark, deliciously intense alpha males are my favorite kind of hero. I just love their rugged sexuality, rasping growls and fierce possessiveness. As a writer, there's nothing I enjoy more than creating a character who snags your attention, makes you shiver with awareness and, by the end of the story, has captured your heart. What better way to do that than with an alpha—especially one who just so happens to be half werewolf, like Mason Dillinger, the gorgeous, drop-dead sexy hero in *Last Wolf Standing*.

From the opening scene, when Mason walks into a bustling café and catches the scent of his human mate, the primal side of his nature is evident in his every action and thought. And yet despite his intense attraction to her, in true alpha-male fashion, Mason puts up a heck of a fight when it comes to opening his heart and falling in love. But what's so wonderful about this breed of hero is that when they finally give in, they do it with every part of themselves, with all the raw, powerful force of their character. The Bloodrunners may be a wild, wickedly tempting bunch, but it's their complete and utter devotion to their women that I truly love about them.

As the first of my Bloodrunners, Mason will always hold a special place in my heart. I hope you enjoy his story and find him as irresistible as I do.

All the best!

Rhyannon

To my father, Patrick, who has always believed
in my dreams.

Thanks for always being there, Pops! I love you!

I'd like to take a moment to thank all the wonderful
people who have supported me through
the writing of this book:

Deidre Knight, of the Knight Agency,
for making it all possible!

Ann Leslie Tuttle, for her endless patience and
insight. I'm so thrilled to be working with you.

Charles Griemsman, for always being so helpful
and keeping me on track.

Erotic-romance author Madison Hayes,
whose incredible talent never ceases to amaze me.
Thanks for always offering your unconditional
support. I don't know what I'd do without you.

Debbie Hopkins Smart, who keeps me sane
and can always make me laugh, even when
I'm pulling my hair out.

Two of my awesome critique partners,
Patrice Michelle and Shelley Bradley,
whose books I can never get enough of.

And last but not least, my family, who somehow
manage to live with me while I'm under deadline
without killing me. I love you guys!

THE BLOODRUNNERS' LAW

When offspring are born of a union between human and Lycan, the resulting creations may only gain acceptance within their rightful pack by the act of Bloodrunning: the hunting and extermination of rogue Lycans who have taken a desire for human flesh. Thus they prove not only their strength, but their willingness to kill for those they will swear to protect to the death.

The League of Elders will predetermine the Bloodrunner's required number of kills.

Once said number of kills are efficiently accomplished, only then may the Bloodrunner assume a place among their kin, complete with full rights and privileges.

Chapter 1

If not for the bustling noise of the crowd, anyone standing within five feet of Mason Dillinger would have easily heard the two halting, roughly drawled words that slipped slowly past the tightening line of his mouth.

"Oh, shit."

Perhaps not the most erudite of phrases, but what it lacked in eloquence it more than made up for in conviction. In fact, in Mason's opinion it summed the situation up to perfection.

After all, it wasn't every day that one of his kind found his life mate in a throng of jacked-up caffeine addicts. Five seconds ago he'd have sworn that it could never happen—that a woman who had been created as his perfect match, the other half of his self, even existed—but there was no denying what that scent was doing to his head, not to mention his quickly thickening body parts.

"Hell," he muttered under his breath, reaching down with

one hand to rearrange himself, pulling the edge of his flannel shirttail in front of his bulging fly. "I'm screwed."

The second he'd stepped through the doorway into the bustling interior of The Coffee and Croissant, the smell of her had hit him like a fist upside the head, rolling across his tongue like the sweetest sin, the most wicked of temptations. It was something he wanted to sink his teeth into and swallow. Something creamy and entirely *his*. The erotic promise of damp, pink flesh that would be slippery and warm to the lap of his tongue, rich and succulent like a treasure.

He wanted to eat her alive…and he didn't even know who she was.

But he knew *where* she was. She was somewhere in this crowded, pain-in-the-ass, prepped-out joint that his Bloodrunning partner, Jeremy Burns, had insisted they duck into before the entire day had passed them by without eating. With their accelerated metabolisms, it was unhealthy to go too long without sustenance, not to mention dangerous as hell to the general population at large.

Yeah, he knew where she was. And he knew *what* she was, too. She was *his*.

Mason's narrowed eyes quickly scanned his surroundings, taking everything in, and then his head tilted back and he allowed inhuman senses so much sharper than mere sight to take over and read the room. Hot, fresh-baked croissants were just being taken from an industrial oven in the kitchen. To his left, a small, distinct clatter of metal against crockery as a businessman added sugar to his double cappuccino. A toddler fussed in the corner, beside a belligerent, kohl-eyed teenager in black who scowled at her father as he lectured her on the importance of grades. The myriad of sounds and scents assailed him, chaotic and full, and yet she burned through sharp and crisp like a radiant beam of light. Vibrant, breathtaking sunshine on a bone-chilling, cloud-smothered day. Something warm and comforting like home.

Hunger clawed its way up his spine, ripping through his system with such force that he expected to look down and see blood seeping through the thin cotton of his navy T-shirt and dark gray flannel, spreading like death down to the ragged denim of his jeans. Ripping him open quicker than teeth or claws ever could.

His nostrils flared as another soft drift of mouthwatering scent crashed through him. Yes, it was right *there*…lingering on the air, and a hard shudder racked the long length of his body, his skin going hot and damp as a low, unfamiliar burn began in his belly. An animal lust…but different. The unmistakable hunger for hard, grinding, gritty sex, and yet utterly foreign from the driving need he'd known in the past. He'd had his share of women in his lifetime, leaving them quickly, yet always with their well-used bodies heavy with pleasure, steeped in satisfaction—but this was more. Harder. Deeper. A sharp-edged, driving need unlike anything he'd ever experienced, raging and explosive.

He didn't just *want* to bury himself inside her—he *had* to.

But first he had to find her.

"You're growling." The deep voice came low and lazy from just behind him, sounding almost bored, though Mason knew his friend well enough to sense that Jeremy had picked up on his tension, even without the telltale growl rumbling up from his chest.

"Shut up," he muttered silkily, and Jeremy snorted in return, nudging him over as he forced his way in through the door, leaving the bitter wind behind them as the glass monstrosity pulled automatically to a close. A few customers turned their heads to look at them, doing double takes as they took in the sight of two hard, well-muscled men who stood over six feet, their casual clothes in no way disguising the brute strength of their battle-honed bodies. The two Bloodrunners reacted to the attention the same way they always did—they ignored it.

Focused on finding the woman, Mason's nostrils flared, the sound of his heart all but filling his ears as it began a hard, purposeful beat like the pulsing chords of a Goth song. "Don't you smell it?"

"What I smell," Jeremy said, exhaustion weighing his words, "is food, which reminds me we skipped breakfast in order to get a head start on our hunt and we still haven't had lunch. Are we going to stand here in the entrance all day, or actually order something before I have to gnaw someone's arm off?"

"You're not scenting her?" he questioned again, ignoring Jeremy's crude sense of humor, and recognizing the increasing gruffness of his own voice as a clear sign that he was losing control.

Bad timing, considering they were surrounded by the flesh and blood of other customers, but there didn't seem to be a damn thing he could do about it. He wasn't leaving until he found her.

"Which one?" Jeremy muttered, scrubbing one sun-darkened hand over the golden stubble covering his chin as he jerked his hazel gaze left to right, scanning the crowded café. "With all the soaps and lotions women drown themselves in nowadays, flowers are all I can smell in this place, other than the food."

Mason shook his head in frustration. No, not flowers. The evocative scent was different—deeper…earthier…and it was getting stronger.

The smell alone had him tied in knots, his body feeling tight and hot and swollen. It was something succulent and rich that sat on the tip of his tongue like a warm drop of honey. He wanted to roll it around for a deeper taste. Draw it into the cavern of his mouth and bite down on it. Hold it. Keep it and fight for it.

Harsh, lust-thick images in blazing ambers and reds flashed through his hunt-tired mind, revitalizing him, jamming his system, jacking him up and taking him to a bigger high than any substance he'd ever used. Like most cross-breeds, he'd spent his youth searching for a way to fit in and find a measure of peace, but it hadn't taken him long to learn that life held enough chaos without him screwing with it. By the time he was a man, his innocence had long since vanished. He knew what sin tasted like…and this was it. Wicked and yet as sweet as heaven—the most dangerous kind of pleasure.

His keen eyesight scanned the immediate area again, falling on a lush blonde in a skintight spandex workout suit sucking down a coral-colored smoothie, before quickly moving on. Not her. No…this one was *different*. Something sharp and uncomfortable in his gut, an uneasy trepidation, told him far different than anything he was prepared for.

Give him blood and battle and he was right at home. Give him easy and loose, and he could make a woman scream without even trying. But give him a complicated female and he shut down. Too much work and he didn't have the time, the patience or the inclination. Women had always come too easily for him, so why the hell should he work for one?

And this one smelled…complicated.

"Seriously, man," Jeremy growled. "If you don't want me turning to the dark side, we need to get in line and order. I'm hungry enough to do something that we'll both regret."

"You're sick, you know that."

Heaving an exaggerated sigh, Jeremy placed his hand over his heart. "Keep saying things like that and I'll start thinking you don't love me anymore."

Mason opened his mouth, a smart-ass comeback ready to slip free, suitably biting and caustic, when her scent slammed into him so hard he nearly reeled. He spun toward the line that paralleled the one he now stood in, where customers were picking up their stylishly brown-bagged orders. He knew the instant he set eyes on her, though he never would have guessed she'd be the one, had that intoxicating scent not wrapped around him like a vise. But it was her. The innocent-looking little waif with the long auburn braid, her lunch tray tucked up in front of her and a bulky paperback wedged under her right arm, tortoiseshell glasses perched smartly on the bridge of her small nose. She was wearing a deliciously tight white polo shirt with faded blue jeans, a dark red jacket tied around her waist and braided bracelets circling one delicately boned wrist, a slender silver watch on the other. A simple outfit, nothing too provocative, but on her it looked downright sinful, the way it hugged her delicate curves.

A fierce, possessive wave of heat poured through his veins while his mouth watered, and it was only with a conscious effort that Mason controlled the urge to pant like a randy dog. A nice long howl would have felt damn good at the moment, but hardly appropriate, considering their surroundings. Left with no other choice, the animal inside him grumbled its agitation, curling around itself and settling down to quietly seethe, while his human half struggled against the intense need to grab her and run, as far and fast as he could, until he had her all to himself. Not a bad idea, either, except that he'd probably scare her half to death before they got there.

Left with no other option, he waited.

Time seemed to stand still as she walked toward him, his lungs burning while the top of his head felt about ready to come off. Within seconds she was in front of him, without even having glanced in his direction. With an utterly foreign sense of desperation, he did something that he'd never, in all his thirty-three years, thought he would do.

He tripped her.

One moment she was walking past, minding her own business, and in the next his strategically placed scuffed brown hiking boot had her sprawled over the stylish Italian tiled floor, sputtering and cursing quietly under her breath as she came to her knees and struggled to wipe tomato soup off her lenses.

"Are you okay?" he asked, crouching down beside her, wincing at the gruffness of his tone as she turned to him, the biggest pair of dark green eyes he'd ever seen blinking at him in owlish surprise.

"Um, yeah, I think so," she said slowly, then a spark of mischief began to burn in the deep green of her gaze and she laughed a low, throaty sound that slipped down his spine like a woman's mouth, damn near making his eyes cross. "I've never heard of anyone drowning in soup before, so I think I'm safe," she drawled, still laughing, and he felt himself grinning in return, until something seemed to burst into awareness between them and their gazes locked in a powerfully raw, smoldering stare, both of them caught in its hold.

The connection burned like pure energy, crackling and sharp, as if the air between their bodies had been electrically charged, and he all but expected to see sparks skittering on the strange current. As he gazed upon her fey face, unique details began imprinting themselves upon his memory like the timeless grooves worn into stone by the rushing currents of the sea, washing away the women of his past until there was nothing but her. Nothing but the delicate curve of her jaw. The tiny beauty mark perched impishly on the arc of her right cheekbone; the darker green that rimmed the softer shade of her gaze. And then there was that mouth, with sensual lips that looked velvety soft and sweetly shy, their color a natural, blushing rose that no cosmetic could duplicate. The carnal things he wanted to do to that kissable little mouth should have been illegal—hell, in some states they probably were. And on top of everything, all the erotic little details that made his head feel thick and his groin feel thicker, there was that provocative scent, earthy and addictive, drugging him with lust and oddly enough…tenderness.

Her breath quivered, twin spots of color cresting across her beautiful cheekbones, and then she shivered, wrenching herself free of the potent visual hold. She cast a quick glance down at the soup-splattered mess she had made of the floor as her soft pink mouth twisted into a wry smile. "And lucky for me, being a klutz isn't a crime in Maryland, so I don't think they'll kick me outta here."

A low laugh rumbled in his chest. "If they tried, I'd knock their heads together and you could kick them in the ba—*shins*."

Joining his laughter, she reached for her overturned tray at the same time he made a grab for it, and their heads nearly collided. They both pulled back, chuckling softly, the growing sensual connection between them all but sizzling on the air, enveloping them in their own little world. It was something hazy and soft, wrapping them in an oddly comforting warmth— cloudlike and weightless—while the desire twisting through them took on a sharp, dangerous edge, like an animal hunger demanding to be fed. She licked her lower lip in what he strongly suspected was a nervous gesture, though it hit him like a practiced seduction, it was so impossibly sexy. Mason swallowed hard as he tried not to choke on the growl he was fighting down, and then Jeremy, his deep voice rough with surprise, suddenly blurted out, "You tripped her!"

Mason closed his eyes and counted to ten, reminding himself the entire time that he couldn't dismember one of his closest friends, not to mention his Bloodrunning partner, at least not in the middle of a restaurant. The urge to do so was so powerful, however, that he actually felt the tips of his fingers burning as razor-sharp claws pricked impatiently beneath the surface of his skin.

Trying not to snarl, he cut a dark look up at Jeremy, all the while wondering if lightning would strike when he delivered the outright lie. "I think you know me well enough, Burns, to agree that it'd be a cold day in hell before I ever did anything like that." Ten minutes ago that would have been the honest truth, but Mason figured he was smart enough to realize things were rapidly changing on him, and the reason was deliciously wrapped up in white cotton and denim at his side.

"Then hell just froze over," Jeremy snorted, grinning as if he thought it was one of the funniest things he'd ever seen, "because you just did."

"Cut the crap, Jeremy." He gritted through his teeth, not wanting to look at her, wondering with an awful pressure in his chest if she would believe him when he denied it. No way was he actually admitting what he'd done!

"I mean, you normally have women falling all over themselves trying to catch your attention, but I never thought I'd see the day that you actually tripped one to get her on her knees in front of you."

Daring a quick look in her direction, Mason watched as that sparkling laughter faded from her eyes, replaced by a guarded, questioning look. "It was an accident," he muttered, knowing she didn't believe him as she reluctantly let him help her to her feet.

"Yeah, sure," she murmured, looking at the floor, then bending back down for her book.

He wondered if she noticed that he'd copped a feel of one firm, deliciously round breast, letting his hand slide up her side while helping her up the second time, then decided she had when she glared up at him, looking like a pissed-off little librarian with those damn glasses and that braid. That affronted image was all wrong for the molten, fiery passion he could feel bubbling just beneath her smooth surface.

"I swear you smell good enough to eat," he blurted out in a raw, gritty voice, the harsh words all but ripped out of his throat.

He silently cursed, feeling his face go conspicuously hot while she just stared at him in shock. *Where the hell did that come from?*

Jeremy gave him a sharp look, then threw back his head and burst out laughing. "Oh, damn, this is priceless." He wheezed, all but bent over as he struggled to hold in the laughter. "God, Mase, you should see the look on your face."

"Shut. Up. Burns."

"In all the years I've known you, I've never seen you make such an ass of yourself over a broad."

"She isn't a broad," he rasped, his voice sounding husky and thick even to his own ears.

As if a light switch had suddenly been flipped in his head, the humor vanished from Jeremy's face. He cursed roughly under his breath, then cut his sharp hazel gaze from her to him, and back to her again, letting his eyes travel over her in a slow, thorough search from the top of her head down to her cute little sneaker-covered feet. His stunned gaze swung back to Mason, hot with accusation. "I don't friggin' believe it. You can't be serious."

"Leave it alone," he warned, not wanting to have this conversation here, in front of her. God only knew what Jeremy would say.

"She doesn't deserve this," Jeremy argued in a low voice, stepping closer. "Not the kind of crap you'll bring down on her head, and all because you wanna get laid."

Wishing he could gag the son of a bitch before he said anything more, Mason growled, "Last warning, Jeremy. Shut up."

Jeremy stepped closer, unwilling to back down. "Don't mess with her, Mason."

"*Her* does have a name," she suddenly cut in, her slightly husky voice coming through sharp and clear with mounting irritation. Then, as if dismissing them, she turned back to the mess on the floor, crouched down, and began throwing her ruined lunch back onto the tray. She grumbled under her breath about the lack of help from the café's staff, while the growing throng of customers sidestepped the unsightly mess, obviously too rushed or rude to offer any help. Then again, he knew they were probably being given a wide berth on purpose. He'd been told, on more than one occasion, that he and Jeremy were an intimidating pair.

Watching as she finished picking up, Mason felt like an ass when he realized he should have been helping her. She stood up with the trash-laden tray, and looked down at her splattered clothing, shaking her head in disgust, talking to herself as she muttered, "Great, I'm wearing tomato soup. How lovely. Now everyone at work will think I've been ravaged by a bloodsucking vampire."

"You believe in vampires?" Jeremy asked, eyeing her with a skeptical look of suspicion.

"Hardly," she snapped, "but then I'm not the norm around Mic's."

"Who the hell is Mic?" Mason grunted, not liking the questions firing through his brain in rapid succession. Mic, the boyfriend? Mic, the next-door neighbor who tore up her sheets with her on Friday night? Mic, the macho mechanic who made her melt when he smiled at her? Whoever the hell he was, Mason hated him.

"Who's Mic?" she repeated, the corners of her mouth turning down in a tight, irritated frown. "Michaela is my best friend and my boss," she started to explain, before pressing her lips together and shaking her head. "Not that it's any of your business," she added.

"I'm making you my business," he growled softly, stepping closer, crowding into her space.

She took a short step back and stopped, pinning him with a hard glare. "One more move and I'm screaming."

God, what was his problem? He was screwing this damn thing up before it even got started. Hell, no one had told him that discovering his life mate would turn him into a blundering, chest-pounding idiot. He was as bad as a gangly teenager high on raging hormones, unable to think past the red-hazed lust and possessiveness clouding his mind.

And to make matters worse, he actually wanted to…get to know this woman. Learn things about her. Her favorite food. Favorite color. Books, movies, pet peeves and things she did for fun. All of which sounded suspiciously like getting to know her on a level that went far beyond physical intimacy, to something deeper and more meaningful.

That was bad, because Mason didn't have a clue how to handle it. He was a Bloodrunner for God's sake—he didn't have time for conversation and "getting to know" people. Not that he had any choice here. The importance of making a good impression on the woman he was *meant* to spend the rest of his life with wasn't lost on him, and here he was screwing it up with every damn word that came out of his mouth. At least if he'd had Hennessey on hand, he could have asked for some advice from the womanizing Irishman. Then again, maybe having that pretty face around his woman wasn't such a good idea. Burns was available, and he knew Jeremy never had any trouble when it came to women. But his social skills were as pathetic as his own, so there'd be no help coming from that quarter.

Looked like he was on his own. Damn.

Taking a deep breath, Mason strove for a calm, nonthreatening, I'm-just-a-nice-guy kind of tone. "Look, I'm sorry. This has been a hell of a day already. How about you take a seat and I'll get you some more food, okay? That way we can sit and talk." There, that was good, he thought with a brief measure of relief. He'd managed to form four sentences without sounding like a jealous ass or mentioning how badly he wanted her.

But the look on her face told him she wasn't buying it.

Christ. This wasn't going to work. He was going to go up in flames, he realized with no small amount of frustration, dragging the back of his wrist over his damp forehead, wondering if the expression in his eyes mirrored the intensity of his need…or if she simply thought he was nuts.

"Is this," she said after a moment, studying him from beneath the thick fringe of long russet lashes, "some kind of setup?"

Another deep breath, slow and easy, while he struggled to stay in control. "Setup? For what?"

"God only knows. Some radio show? Are you DJs?" she asked suspiciously.

Mason folded his arms across his chest and scowled at her, insulted down to his boots. "Do I look like a damn DJ?"

She shrugged the delicate line of her shoulders, blowing a wayward wisp of curling auburn hair out of her eyes. "I have no idea. Really, I think I should just be on my way now."

He opened his mouth to try and convince her to stay, even though he didn't have a clue what he could say at this point. Unfortunately, Jeremy chose that moment to put in another two cents' worth. "I'm telling you, man, she doesn't deserve this. Leave her the hell alone."

Mason didn't even take his eyes off her as he softly replied, "I don't have a choice."

From the corner of his vision, he watched Jeremy's hazel gaze narrow as the meaning and repercussions of what he was saying—and what he wasn't saying—began to seep in. "Christ, Mase. If that means what I think it means, then you *know* you should walk away. You can't risk it with Simmons more than likely watching us now that we're closing in on him."

"And you should know that walking away isn't an option for me," he shot back, careful to keep his voice low so they didn't draw unwanted attention.

"As fascinating as this is, I'm just going to slink away now myself," she said carefully, obviously freaked out by their conversation and his behavior. Handing her tray to a dour-faced busboy who finally scuffed by, she took several steps away from them. "I'd say thanks for helping me up, but then, you were the one who dumped me on my ass in the first place. Still, thanks."

"Just give me a chance to explain. *Please.* That's all I'm asking. We'll stay right here, at one of the tables," Mason said in a low, urgent rumble, grabbing hold of her arm as she turned, careful not to squeeze too hard. Her bones felt infinitely fragile beneath the inhuman strength of his hand, sending a fierce surge of protectiveness through his blood.

"I need to get back to work," she murmured, trying to break free of his grip, her book tucked up safely under her other arm. "Now let go of me before I pull out my cell phone and call the cops, then start screaming bloody murder."

"I'm sorry, but I can't let you do that," he said quietly, trying to sound reasonable…normal…even though he knew he was going to end up scaring her. "I swear I'm not going to hurt you, okay? But we need to talk, and then I need to get you out of here."

The expression on her face made him wince, an unbearable sense of defeat nearly flooring him as Mason realized she had every intention of ditching him. Not that he blamed her. If their situations were reversed, he'd have thought he sounded crazy, too.

"And just where do you think I'm going to go with you?"

she demanded, the words thick with sarcasm, and he hated the fear he could scent on her—frustrated that he didn't know how to ease it, how to make her understand. You didn't just walk up to a human woman and say, *Hey, I can tell by your scent that you're my life mate, which means we belong to each other for the rest of our lives, and never any other. Oh, and by the way, I'm half werewolf, have a rogue bastard most likely watching me because I'm hunting him down to kill him, and I really, really need to mate with you. Hard. And often. As in damn near all the time.* At least not without getting your face slapped or your balls kicked. From the look in her eyes, he figured both were strong possibilities at this point.

Trying to sound as nonthreatening as possible, Mason kept his voice low as he said, "Anywhere but here. Jeremy's right about this being dangerous. We can't risk keeping you out in the open with him watching us."

She looked at him as if he'd just told her he was Elvis reincarnated by aliens. "Then here's a news flash. Why not try walking away and leaving me alone, before you end up in some serious trouble?"

"Not in this lifetime, sweetheart," he rasped under his breath.

She shook her head in frustration. "Have you recently escaped from a mental institution by chance?"

"Classic," Jeremy snorted under his breath. "As wrong as this is, I can't wait to tell your old man that line. He'll crack a rib from laughing."

"Look, this is just getting too freaky for me. For the last time, you need to let go. Now."

Mason let his hand smooth down her arm, shaken by the softness of her skin, clasping as gently as possible around her wrist. He could feel her pulse racing beneath the pads of his fingers and knew she was scared. He figured she'd have run screaming long before now, if not for the throng of customers filling the café, surrounding them. She'd found a measure of comfort in the crowd, but that feeling was rapidly fading. "I know this sounds weird as hell, but I need you to give me a chance. That's all I'm asking. If you insist on staying here, then at least sit down with me and I'll explain."

"I can't do that." Her green eyes were clear and bright as she tried to pull away from him, the movement jostling the book she'd tucked up under her arm. Mason watched as a small piece of paper fell from between the book's pages, fluttering softly to the floor, and instinct had him covering it with his boot, while he struggled with what to say. There were so many things he wanted to explain, things he needed to make her understand, but all he could come out with was a low, urgent, *"Don't run."*

"Get your hands off me. *Right now,*" she grunted, her voice raised, and the customers closest to them went quiet, all eyes turning toward them. A cold knot of fury…and something that felt strangely like pain twisted Mason's stomach, but he forced his grip to ease, releasing her arm.

She backed away slowly, until she felt the door at her back. Hating the emotions that burned like acid in his gut, Mason watched her turn around and quickly push out into the brisk autumn weather.

She started running the second her feet hit the side-walk…and never looked back.

Chapter 2

Clutching her book to her chest to keep it dry, Torrance Kimberly Watson all but stumbled into the softly lit, subtly incensed interior of Michaela's Muse. Her heart pumped a chaotic beat, while her mind carried on a fierce debate with her grumbling libido—and despite her common sense, it looked as if her sex-deprived inner wild woman was winning.

"Like that should come as a shock," she quietly snickered, groaning at her body's continued reaction to the man she'd left behind in the restaurant. He was certainly a fine specimen of maleness, even if he had been off his rocker. "And not even those last few minutes of rain managed to cool you down, you slut," she jokingly muttered under her breath, slipping out of her damp jacket and tossing it over her arm.

It was a depressing thought, but there was no denying that she'd been a long time without a boyfriend. Heck, she'd been a long time without a simple date. She was in her mid-twenties, meant to be living life to its fullest…and instead she'd practically become a nun. Not that a few short-lived relationships counted for much in the way of past experience, but then she knew she had high expectations when it came to that sort of thing. Expectations she doubted any man could ever meet.

No, Torrance understood the male species for what they were—and, more important, for what they weren't. After dating one too many jerks who were as faithless as they were self-centered and shallow, she'd decided that being alone was better than being used—than settling for something she didn't want—and she still stood by her decision. But, God, it wasn't easy when dealing with the kind of temptation she'd had to endure today.

The guy at lunch had been like something out of her dreams. The really, really naughty ones, she thought with a small, crooked smile.

"Hey, Torry," Michaela called out from the front of the store without looking up, absorbed in her current project.

"Oh, uh…hey, Mic," she called back, suddenly realizing she'd been standing in the doorway, lost in her own little world. With a quick look around the store, Torrance saw that Mic had been busy digging into their latest delivery of new merchandise. A box containing paranormal titles and Tarot decks sat on the floor beside an ornate wooden bookshelf, while another that probably contained scented candles had been placed beside an antique display case.

Torrance had met Michaela Doucet five years ago, at a Tarot demonstration the Cajun was holding at a local bookstore, and they'd become instant, inseparable friends. Two years later, when Mic had opened the specialty shop, Torrance had been right by her side, and together they had made Michaela's Muse an area favorite, with business growing every year.

She loved her job, and felt at home in the warm, soothing atmosphere, surrounded by friends who had become like family to her.

"Torry!" Michaela suddenly gasped in that slow Southern drawl of hers, making Torrance jump. She looked over to see Mic's big, dark blue eyes blinking with surprise as she glanced up from the new Tarot decks she was organizing, getting her first good look at Torrance's ruined shirt. "What happened? You look like you just came from an orgy with one of the undead!"

"Hah!" Torrance laughed out loud, causing Mic to give her a more critical look. "I told them you were going to say something like that when you saw my shirt," she mumbled, feeling strange, as if her body were hot and cold all at once, her skin suddenly too tight for all the chaos going on inside of it. Man, that gorgeous freak-case at the café had really messed with her mind.

"And it wasn't a *what*," she added with a resigned sigh, suddenly giving a wry grin as she tossed her book and jacket on the beautiful bar that served as the store's checkout counter, then stepped around its corner, moving to her customary place behind the gleaming antique. Knowing her tenacious best friend would pry the lunchtime fiasco out of her one way or another, the sanest course of action was to give in gracefully and save what little of her sanity she still had left. "It was a *who*."

Michaela's delicately sloped brows arched high on the smooth perfection of her brow as she moved around the display table draped with sapphire velvet. "Now *that*," she mused, the black mass of her softly curling hair gleaming a deep, dark, midnight-blue, "sounds like something more than just another boring lunch at that corporate zombiefest you can't get enough of."

A steady drizzle of rain began pattering gently upon the roof as the latest storm moved overhead, its pattern soft and fleeting, like the featherlight dance of water fairies. Torrance normally found the sound of early-autumn showers soothing, but today the lilting chorus of raindrops only added to the prickling restlessness shivering beneath the surface of her skin. And it didn't help that she was still reeling from the gorgeous stranger's bizarre effect on her.

Hell, maybe she was coming down with something. Or maybe she was just so desperate for something more out of life, that she was becoming delusional. Had it gotten to the point where she was creating imaginary connections with mouthwatering hunks to make her feel less lonely? How…pathetic.

"Yoohoo, earth to Torry…" Michaela laughed, waving one slim palm in front of her face to get her attention.

"Oh, sorry. Um, I didn't catch that last part."

Mic gave her a quizzical look. "I just said that it sounds like you had an interesting lunch."

"Yeah, it was interesting all right," Torrance softly agreed.

Crossing her slim arms across her bountiful chest, Mic leaned one elbow against the edge of the intricately carved bar. The exquisite piece looked more like it belonged in a high-end antique shop, rather than a mystical haven for lovers of the paranormal. Like several of the store's unusual antiques, the cherrywood bar had come from Mic's grandmother's mysterious Southern estate, buried somewhere deep in the bayou.

It was that bayou upbringing that had given Michaela her comfortable acceptance of the paranormal—an acceptance that Torrance envied. Truth be told, working at the shop had been a test of sorts for her, to see if she could get past her childhood phobias and embrace the paranormal community. And Torrance had done it, kind of like a person with a fear of sharks learning to enjoy the ocean. She loved her job, had a great rapport with their customers, and though it had taken some time, she'd eventually learned not to fear the unknown.

Well, *most* of the unknown. She still had a few phobias, brought on by her nightmares, but she was working to get over them. And Mic and her younger brother, Max, were helping.

"So what was he like?" the grinning brunette asked in a deliberately low whisper, probably meant to keep Max from overhearing.

A dreamy sigh escaped her lips before she could stop it, and Torrance suddenly heard herself saying, "Sex."

Mic's blue eyes went wide, and a throaty chuckle slipped smoothly past the Southerner's rouged mouth. "That hot, huh?"

Torrance didn't think her face could get any redder. Sex! Had she really just said that? Plopping down on her padded stool, she shook her head at the memory of the man who had turned her into a blathering idiot. Though she'd read the phrase a thousand times in romance novels, it had never actually happened to her—but he'd literally knocked her off her feet…and apparently knocked her brains out while he was at it. "Let's just say that there should be a freaking law against men looking that good," she groaned.

Mic's mouth twisted into a sly smile. "Oh, honey, they can *never* look *too* good."

"Well, he looked too good to me." She sighed, remembering that dizzying moment of shock when their eyes had first connected. God, she was still feeling the vibrations from the jolt that had zapped her. Instant lust, something so warm and primitive, she'd barely been able to breathe through it. Heck, she could barely breathe now, just thinking about him. All she'd wanted was to slide up closer to him, then just a little closer, until they were pressed up against each other and she was surrounded by his animal heat—the dangerous, predatory wildness that had pulsed around him like a fiery glow while his deep, chocolate-brown gaze had promised things too tender and intimate to accept from any man, much less from a perfect stranger.

Only…he hadn't felt like a stranger, and that provocative combination of danger and shelter had been too devastating.

So devastating that it'd scared the hell out of her, sending her running faster than all that crazy talk of his could have ever done.

Michaela laughed softly into the charged silence. "That good, eh?"

Torrance nodded her head distractedly, then gave it a quick shake, determined to stop daydreaming about the tall, dark, wickedly handsome stranger. What had his friend called him? Mase? Mason? That was it! A strong, purely male name that fit him to perfection, just like those well-worn jeans that had so easily hugged his powerful thighs and the faded T-shirt deliciously molded to his muscular chest beneath the darker flannel.

Even his hair had been gorgeous. Not black, but a rich, lustrous brown with reddish streaks that turned auburn in the light. It had fallen somewhat shaggy around the strong, rugged angles of his arresting face, as if he didn't get it cut often enough, but hadn't decided to just let it grow. There was the slightest hint of a curl to it, the kind that meant you would snag your fingers a bit when you ran them through the silky mass. With a fierce compulsion, Torrance had wanted to bury her face in those windblown strands and breathe the scent of him into her lungs. It was hot and heady…and animallike. Full of mystery and the wild outdoors, natural and addictive.

Damn it, she was starting to drool just thinking about him, but then, she'd never been affected by a man like that before. In those first moments, she'd thought he was the most beautiful, mesmerizing thing she'd ever seen. Something hot and thick and deliciously wicked *had* passed between them—something Mic would have called a mystical connection—before his friend rained on the parade. She'd wanted to believe it'd been an accident, but something in his eyes had warned her that he wasn't being totally honest about tripping her. Then he'd gone over the top, and she'd hightailed it outta there so fast she'd never even looked back.

Well, okay, so that wasn't totally honest, either. On her way back to work, she'd argued with herself about her decision, uneasy over what felt uncomfortably like an irrevocable loss, as if she'd let something indelibly precious and infinitely significant just slip through her fingers. If things hadn't gone so weird there at the end, she strongly suspected she would have followed the stud to the ends of the earth just to investigate that *thing* between them—to find out what it was really all about.

"Yeah, he was that good," she finally said, "which means he was definitely too good to be true."

Dropping her gaze to Torrance's stained polo, Mic grinned. "So what happened?"

A soft laugh fell past her lips, surprising her, but then it had been funny as hell when the blond one had blurted it out. Well, maybe not funny at the time, but looking back on it, Torrance couldn't help but see the humor in the situation. "He…uh, tripped me."

Her best friend's jaw dropped in shock. "He *what?*"

"He tripped me," she explained with a shrug, knowing it sounded crazy. "I, uh, guess to get my attention."

"Well, I've never heard that one before," Mic admitted dryly, "but I'll give him credit for an original approach."

Feeling the raindrops beaded on her cheeks, Torrance swiped her cool hands over her face, pushing the wayward strands of damp hair back from her forehead. "I didn't know he'd tripped me on purpose until his friend ratted him out. I thought I'd just been clumsy."

"Some friend," Mic snorted, raising her brows.

"Oh, you'd have liked him." Torrance sent the other woman a teasing smile. "He was a total smart-ass."

"Just my kind of guy," the brunette drawled, rolling her eyes.

"Anyway, I swear, Mic, I almost swallowed my tongue when I first set eyes on him. He was…"

Her voice trailed off, and Mic prompted her with an interested, "Yeah?"

She struggled to find the right word, but in the end there was only one that would do. "Beautiful," she said simply.

"As sweet as that is, I need more info," Mic complained with a throaty laugh. "Come on, Shakespeare, and describe him for me. I've got to have a mental picture."

Torrance sent the grinning brunette her best "as if" look. "So you can try to make love dolls of us? Don't think I'm not on to you, Doucet?" she snorted. "I saw you looking through those new voodoo books that came in last week."

Michaela's eyes went wide with a feigned look of innocence. "I wouldn't dream of doing something like that. I'm shocked you could even think it," she muttered, just before she busted up giggling, and Torrance couldn't help but join in with the Cajun's infectious laughter.

"What's all the giggling about?" a deep voice called out. "Did I miss something good?"

Both women looked over to see Max sticking his dark head around the corner of the employees' door, his deep blue eyes dark and hazy, as if they'd disturbed one of his little catnaps. At nineteen, he was determined to pull his weight and help his sister get her fledgling business off the ground. Hurrying back to the shop after morning classes at the nearby community college, he managed the stockroom and updated the accounts in the afternoons, all before working the night shift as a security guard at the local hospital. Torrance got tired just thinking about the poor kid's schedule.

"Hey, Max," she called out over her shoulder, careful to keep her body turned to avoid another round of twenty questions about her clothing. Max took his man-of-the-shop duties seriously, treating Torrance with the same brotherly concern that he showed his sister. "Sorry we woke you up."

"No big." He smiled, running one hand through the rumpled black silk of his hair, his coloring nearly identical to his older sister. "I can catch up on my sleep later. One of the guards at the hospital needed to switch shifts with me, so I've got the night off." He gave them a knowing look, his smile widening. "Guess I'll let you two get back to your gossiping. Later."

"Enjoy your night off," she called back.

Mic waited the five seconds it would take Max to reach the back office, then leaned forward and whispered, "Now back to the gorgeous stud who swept you off your feet." Her blue eyes sparkled with mischief as she waggled her brows. "Any plans for a hot date tonight?"

Knowing what was coming, Torrance shifted uneasily atop the stool. "Uh, no."

The corners of Mic's mouth turned down. "Why not? I know we have plans to catch that lecture at the museum later, but *please* tell me you didn't let that stop you! I'll wring your little redheaded neck if you told that guy no, Torrance! I swear on my...on my—"

Realizing this was only going to get worse, Torrance blurted out, "He never asked me out."

Mic's brows drew together, her gaze piercing. "Well, why not? And why didn't *you* ask *him* out?" Tilting her head to the side, her stare took on that strange, unsettling quality that always gave Torrance the impression her closest friend was reading her mind—even though the Cajun claimed that wasn't in the realm of her powers. "Exactly what happened, Torry?"

"Hey, I said he was gorgeous, not sane," she mumbled, already feeling defensive.

Mic shook her head. "You didn't even give him a chance, did you?" she groaned, her voice rough with frustration and disappointment. Unfortunately, Michaela knew all too well about her penchant for viewing men as fickle creatures; here today…gone tomorrow. It was a natural, knee-jerk reaction, after growing up with a mother who went through lovers like new outfits, always searching for one who would fit—the one who would finally stick around. Torrance had truly liked a few of them, wanting them to stay, though they never did. And some of them…some of them had simply scared the hell out of her. Her mother had died a few years ago in a car accident before ever finding a man who truly loved her, and Torrance had taken the lesson to heart.

"Give me a break, Mic. First his friend starts griping about him hitting on me, warning him about God only knows what, and then the guy starts giving me this crock about how it wasn't safe there and I needed to leave with him! He's lucky I didn't call the cops," she added roughly, hating that he could all too easily recognize the regret in her voice. He may have been one egg short of a dozen, but something about him had felt so uncomfortably…right.

"Damn it, Torrance," Mic hissed, clearly upset. "You can't keep doing this to yourself."

Trying to dispel the burning image of his slow, sinful smile, that wicked look of interest that had all but smoldered in those chocolate-brown eyes, she moaned, "Not now, Mic. Please."

"I hate to see you drying up and wasting away."

"Maybe I'm just tired of wasting my time on relationships that are never going to go anywhere. Been there, done that," she muttered, hopping off the stool to grab her backpack up off the floor. Picking up the book she'd tossed on the bar, she slipped it into the front pouch, ignoring the knowing stare being drilled into her back. She knew Michaela was trying to get a "read" on her emotions. It was a special talent the Cajun possessed but seldom used, since she considered it an invasion of personal privacy. "And you can stop with your mental snooping right now, Mic."

"You do know what's going to happen, don't you, Torry? You're going to end up missing out on the right one, because you're like a little ostrich with your head stuck in the sand. Get up off your rump and get out in the world, *chère*. Because if you don't, life is going to have passed you by and you won't have a clue what happened to it."

"And is that what you're doing?" she demanded, crossing her arms across her soup-splattered chest as she turned back to Michaela. With one hand, she pushed her glasses up on her nose the way a bull might drag his front hooves through the dirt before a charge. "Not to be rude, Mic, but I don't think your social calendar has been any more active than mine recently."

"Our situations are different, Torry, and you know that." The fire slowly faded from Michaela's eyes, her expression all but closing in on itself. "I took a chance on love and it didn't work out," she said flatly, her voice unusually devoid of emotion. "I made a fool of myself, but at least I took the chance. At least I went for what I wanted…or looking back, what I thought I wanted."

"I'm sorry." Torrance sighed, feeling like crap for lashing out at her. "Now I feel like an ass."

"Hey, you're not an ass, you're my best friend." Despite her light tone, Mic's small smile didn't quite reach her eyes. "You know I just want the best for you," she confessed in a soft voice. "If you can find love, then maybe I'll be able to find the courage to give a guy another chance."

"You do know that Ross was an idiot, don't you?" Torrance muttered, experiencing a familiar surge of rage at the thought of what the narcissistic jerk had put Michaela through. "A blind, stupid, raging idiot."

"Of course I do." Mic sent her a playful wink, but Torrance could tell that her friend was still suffering from the humiliating way things had worked out between her and the pretty-faced social climber.

"He's not still calling you, is he?"

She curled her lip. "I keep telling him to leave me alone, only pretty boy can't understand why I'm no longer interested. But enough about him.

"Since the storms will keep things slow in here this afternoon, why don't you go on and head home so that you have time to shower and change," Michaela said, changing the topic. "You *are* going to that lecture with me tonight, and while we're there you're going to tell me everything…*everything*…that happened today. There just might have been more there than you realize, Torry."

Walking to the Tarot table, Michaela went back to work arranging the packs of cards along with a sparkling array of raw crystals, the shallow, rain-dappled light glinting softly against their uncut surfaces in a vivid display of color. "Jennifer is coming in at four for her shift, so I'll be able to get out of here a little early," she explained while Torrance rounded the bar, pulling her jacket on, then slinging her backpack over her right shoulder. "I'll be by to pick you up at five."

"Thanks, Mic," she called back, heading out the front door, the tinkling of the door chimes following her out into the misty gray of the day. The rain had let up enough that it now resembled more of a refreshing mist, and Torrance set off down the street enjoying the cool, damp breeze against her face, the clean smell of the outdoors lingering beneath the more acrid scents of the city. She walked at a steady, energetic pace, her eyes taking in the beauty of the historical architecture in that part of town, the weathered, yet well-kept facades framed by towering willows and oaks, their ancient roots bulging beneath the sidewalk, as if seeking sunshine through the heavy, cracked concrete.

She used the time to clear her mind—or at least tried to—

but two blocks into her four-block walk, it hit her. A strange, unsettling sense of not being alone, which was odd, seeing as how she wasn't. In the garden ahead, an elderly woman in a sun hat knelt among an assortment of perennials, while on the other side of the street a young boy walked his beagle alongside his dad, both of them holding hands and smiling. The sun was beginning to peek briefly through the rain clouds, and up ahead a rainbow formed across the distant silver-blue of the sky, perfect and pristine in its beauty. And yet, something felt…not right. The feeling grew, oddly disturbing, and she nearly tripped on an uneven bit of sidewalk, even though she knew this path well enough to walk it in her sleep.

Clutching her backpack, Torrance sent a furtive look over her shoulder, but there was nothing there. And yet, the feeling wouldn't go away, reminding her of the nightmares that she'd suffered from since childhood. Vivid, terrifying dreams in which monsters stalked her, their warm breath on the back of her neck…before they caught her. The familiar feelings of helplessness, of vulnerability, coated her skin, sinking in through her pores until she felt steeped in them. By the time she reached her apartment building, her lungs hurt from holding her breath and her pulse beat out a hammering tempo that nearly jarred her brain. Moving quickly, she used her key to open her front door. Once inside her apartment, she immediately slid the chain into place.

Leaning her forehead against the cool wood, Torrance let her backpack slip off her shoulder, all the while struggling to get her lungs working properly again. Straightening up, she turned and looked carefully at her living room, seeking comfort in its soothing atmosphere. Mic had helped her to create the perfect ambience, a relaxing blend of bold wood and soft, inviting fabrics, with an old Persian rug covering the dark hardwood floors and scented candles on nearly every surface. Bookshelves lined the walls, while jewel-colored throw pillows covered the oversize love seat and matching chair. Hidden in an oriental-looking cabinet was a small TV set, which she used to indulge her weakness for all the *CSI* shows as well as *Letterman,* while a low table under the window held her speaker system for her iPod and her new laptop.

This was her space, her little getaway, her private corner of the world, and Torrance took a deep breath through her nose…waiting for the panic to ease. She counted the seconds off slowly, willing that feeling of safety that she always found here to come. But there was nothing. Nothing but that bitter lump of fear sitting in the back of her throat, churning her stomach into a knot.

"Get a grip," she muttered, straightening her spine. Damn it, she wasn't going to let her overactive imagination spook her out of her own apartment! Marching like a zealous militant, she went into the kitchen, poured herself a tall glass of sweetened iced tea, and then crossed back through the living room to the single bedroom. Her slightly slanted blinds allowed a narrow glance at the now swollen sky, a sharp crack of resonating thunder heralding the arrival of another storm. Ah, she'd made it just in time, she thought, forcing a small smile.

Walking to her dresser, she studied her pale reflection in the beveled antique mirror on the wall while slipping the clasps free on her small silver hoops, then unfastened her slim watch and slid off her bracelets. A refrain from one of the Celtic CDs Mic played throughout the day in the store found its way into her mind, and she began humming softly, determined to ignore that lingering unease, until she felt a cold, clammy chill crawl over her skin, her palms going damp and hot.

Something's wrong, she thought dully, experiencing the oddest sense of viewing the situation from afar. The feeling tightened, sharpening, until she feared that she wasn't alone, even though she'd seen no one when she'd walked into the room. But on the opposite side of her bed, just behind her, was the closet—and she couldn't remember if the door had been open or closed when she'd entered the room…and was suddenly too afraid to look. Had she remembered to lock all the windows earlier? Damn it, living in a quiet neighborhood had made her careless, because she couldn't remember checking them before she'd left for work that morning!

"There's no such thing as monsters," she muttered, determined to stay calm, but every terrifying scene from every nightmare she'd ever suffered began playing through her mind. A deep, bone-jarring tremor shook her body like a frail, fragile leaf caught in the destructive fury of a storm, and she watched in a numb daze as her hand lifted, reaching toward the surface of her dresser where she kept her mail. Her fingers touched the cold, hard metal of the antique letter opener Mic had given her last Christmas, and as they curled around the silver handle, she heard the telltale creak of a floorboard. A sickening feeling slipped through her, like something sticky and wet sliding over her skin, sending her stomach into a roiling spin. Her breath stopped, suspended, held tight in her lungs as she raised her wide eyes and caught the reflection in the mirror above her dresser.

It was behind her, at the foot of her bed, visible over her left shoulder. Tall, over seven feet at least, with fangs and fur—and a head that resembled the terrifying shape of a wolf.

She opened her mouth to scream, but before the bloodcurdling cry had clawed its way out of her throat, the beast was on her, knocking the dagger-shaped opener to the ground. It twisted her easily, taking her to the floor, where it slowly looked her over out of dark, lifeless eyes that shone as blank and black as a doll's. Despite her frantic struggles, long, lethal-tipped claws took possession of her wrists, lifting her arms up high over her head, stretching her out beneath its hard, oppressively heavy body straddling her thighs. An overpowering combination of animal musk, pine-scented forests and a sharp acidic odor filled her head, and Torrance screamed again, if she'd ever stopped screaming—but she couldn't hear anything over the terrified roaring of her heart, unsure if the sounds of her horror were trapped in her throat or shattering against the walls, drowned out by her heartbeat.

"Well, well, aren't you a tasty little piece?" it drawled in a deep, guttural voice, the words awkward as they made their way past the muzzled shape of its mouth, fangs gleaming whitely in the graying light of her bedroom. It almost looked as if it were smiling at her, and for some reason, that scared her more than anything.

"Who the hell are you?" she sobbed, fear making her own voice sound demonic, deep and rasping and raw.

"My sweet, sweet Little Red," it laughed roughly, its warm breath pelting her in the face, humid and hot and sickly. "Didn't your new half-breed warn you about me?"

"Who? Warn me about what?" she cried, paralyzed within its powerful grip. It held her far too easily, and the cold, painful knowledge of imminent death settled heavily into her gut.

"Don't you know the reason for a Bloodrun, little human?"

"A Bloodrun?" she grunted, so sick with fear she felt nauseous. "What are you talking about?"

"Your new boyfriend tracks down my kind and kills us like animals, simply because we accept what nature meant for us. Because we're not afraid to embrace our natural hungers." It leaned closer, the tip of its dark muzzle all but touching her nose, and this time she knew it was smiling as those black, shiny lips pulled back with malicious humor, its mouthful of razor-sharp teeth promising untold horror. "You're not Dillinger's normal taste when it comes to his playthings," it rasped, tilting its massive head to the side as it studied her out of those emotionless eyes. Leaning closer, she felt the wet roughness of its tongue lick up the side of her throat before curling playfully around the shell of her left ear. She whimpered, hating the pitiful sound, and the monster laughed softly as it whispered in her ear, "No, you're not his usual taste at all. But I think I'll enjoy eating you all the same, honey girl."

Chapter 3

They're real…they're real…they're real…

Torrance chanted the silent refrain over and over within the thick, black haze of terror clouding her mind, while the werewolf's oppressive weight held her down. She knew she should fight, struggle, scream…but after hearing those last words, all she could do was lie there beneath the monster, paralyzed by fear. It spread through her limbs like an intravenous drug, numbing her body while her heart pounded to a painful, resonating beat that threatened to rupture her chest. A lifetime of nightmares, of horrific images of blood and pain, fangs and razor-sharp claws, crept over the surface of her body like a spider, tangling her in its insidious web.

"The more I lick right here," that gruff, garbled voice chuckled with malicious pleasure against her throat, the monster's rank breath meaty and humid as it reached her nose, "the richer the scent of your fear grows."

No. No. No. This can't be happening. Can't be happening. Can't be happening.

Its massive head shifted, muscled, heavily-furred shoulders bunching as the creature moved down her body, dragging its mouth against the upper part of her chest revealed in the now-gaping neck of her shirt, torturing her with the teasing slide of its teeth. "I'll tell you what," it taunted, long, lethal claws clicking ominously against the hardwood floor, heavily padded palms damp with sweat where they gripped her wrists in a biting, bruising hold that numbed her fingers. "Why don't we have a little fun and see just how scared we can get you?"

How scared? She was already filled with terror. The realization that she was a coward burned in her belly like acid, but no matter how fiercely her pride raged against it, Torrance couldn't throw off the smothering wave of fear.

And he knew it.

Smiling, the werewolf cocked his head to the side as he studied her, his nostrils flaring as he breathed in her scent. "So timid, little one. That just isn't going to do. I enjoy it so much more when my meals have a little life in them."

He laughed at his own joke…and Torrance squeezed her eyes shut, silent tears tracking across her skin.

Oh yes, they were real. The monsters from the dark recesses of her mind truly did exist. Not just in her head, but in the flesh. She had often wondered—no, worried—after the things she'd seen and heard around Michaela's Muse, but had never *really* believed. Movies…tabloid headlines…books. The legends were everywhere, for anyone paying attention. And her mother had been one of the biggest believers of all, dragging her daughter off to every horror movie that hit the theaters…always rambling on about mankind's inability to accept the existence of something more powerful than themselves.

As she became older, Torrance began to realize that her

mother had looked to the paranormal as a means of escaping the disappointing realities of life. And in the process, she'd raised her daughter on an unusual diet for a child—one that consisted of vampires and werewolves and witches. But instead of Michaela's healthy understanding of the paranormal culture, Torrance had only known the horror, the Hollywood sensationalism. She had learned to fear early on, and though she'd come to understand so much with Mic's help…there were still some issues she just couldn't shake, no matter how hard she tried.

Her nightmares were one of them.

You should have listened to your dreams. They were telling you the truth, Torrance…warning you…just like Mom told you they were.

All those years spent thinking the poor woman was insane…and she'd been right all along. But Torrance had never allowed herself to believe…and now, on the verge of death, she didn't have any other choice.

Mason cast another hard look at the slip of paper, reading the printed name for the hundredth time.

Torrance Watson.

He ran his thumb over the letters, once…twice, then slipped the wrinkled pay stub back into the pocket of his flannel shirt, sounding out the individual syllables beneath his breath. *Torrance.* An unusual name, but then, she was clearly an unusual woman. The kind of woman who could turn a guy's world upside down. Who could destroy him.

If you were smart, you'd get your ass out of here and forget you ever saw her.

True, and considering he wasn't moving, Mason could only assume he wasn't nearly as clever as he'd thought. Either that or he was thinking with the wrong head.

He slumped in the driver's seat of his Tahoe, a cigarette

pinched between his thumb and forefinger of the hand hanging
out his open window, and turned his attention back to the quaint
Victorian that had been renovated into apartments. After
Torrance had run out on him at the restaurant, he'd sent Jeremy
to get the SUV and followed her on foot to her work, using that
mouthwatering scent to track her, then again as she headed
home. Once there, he'd called Jeremy on his cell and told him
where to find him. Now they sat in the cab of the Tahoe, parked
on her street, watching for any sign of Simmons, while Mason
struggled to figure out what the hell to do next.

He didn't know what he'd been thinking, acting the way he
had when he found her. But he'd been blindsided by too
much…everything. Emotion. Hunger. Possessiveness. The gut-
twisting need to keep her safe—and the knowledge that
Simmons would come after her if he could. All of which had
led to him acting like a cross between a mad stalker and a
complete asshole. No wonder she'd run from him. That he
could understand.

What he couldn't get his head around was why he was here.

If it were simply a matter of safety, Mason knew he could
have called in Pallaton and Reyes, another Bloodrunning team,
and put them on her for protection. But he hadn't done that.
Instead, here he was, playing watchdog for a woman who
should have had him running scared for the simple fact that he
didn't want her.

*Yeah, you just keep telling yourself that, jackass…and
maybe you'll start believing it.*

Muttering a foul, four-letter word, Mason slammed the heel
of his hand against the steering wheel, hating it. All of it. What
kind of sick joke was nature playing on his ass? Anyone who
knew him *knew* the last thing he wanted was a mate. Especially
a small, fragile human one. *Jesus.*

He'd been reminding himself of that fact for the past five

minutes…and yet he couldn't let it go. Couldn't let *her* go. Couldn't make himself turn the bloody key and drive away, while he still had the chance. The past didn't seem to matter. Not the lessons he'd learned or the vows he'd made to never end up in Dean's shoes. Within moments of finding her, the past eight years were obliterated, wiped clean, and Mason found himself as pathetically hooked as the rest of them.

Shit. He scrubbed one hand down his face, then took another long drag on the cigarette while a sharp crack of lightning lit the sky, dark waves of clouds rolling in, smothering out the pale streams of sunlight that had briefly broken through the damp, depressing grayness of the day.

Beside him, Jeremy crossed his arms and let out a loud, jaw-cracking yawn. "What about lunch?" the blond asked. "We still haven't eaten and I'm starving, man."

Mason stared at the apartment building, quietly cursing the thunder that made it impossible to hear—even with his height-ened abilities. And if the rain got heavier, it would ruin his ability to track her scent when she left. "You can take off and grab some fast food," he murmured. "There's got to be some-thing around here within walking distance."

"Great," Jeremy grunted. "Do you know how much fat that stuff contains?"

"We burn more calories than we can ever worry about, so what the hell do you care?"

"It's my arteries I'm thinking about," his partner grumbled. "And what about Simmons? We *are* still on the hunt, man, which means we're supposed to be tracking his sadistic ass down."

Like he needed reminding. They'd been hunting the bastard ever since they found the mutilated body of a young prostitute a few weeks ago, dumped on pack land. Anthony Simmons's foul scent had been all over the victim, and he and Jeremy had been assigned the Bloodrun to kill the Silvercrest werewolf.

Now it was a race against the clock to catch him and eliminate the threat, before Simmons chose yet another victim. The thought twisted his insides. Mason had no doubt the rogue would exploit any vulnerability he could find and use it to strike back at the ones hunting him. His kind always did. And if he'd been watching them today, and witnessed his reaction to Torrance, he now had the perfect opportunity.

Mason couldn't let that happen. To make sure Simmons didn't get near her, he and Jeremy would keep an eye on things here, while Pallaton and Reyes watched the shop where she worked.

"We'll find Simmons," Mason rasped, grinding out his cigarette in the ashtray. "But this takes precedence right now. We have to make sure she stays safe."

Jeremy let his head fall back against the headrest, his hands crossed over his stomach, fingers drumming repetitively against his abs. "You do realize you've probably landed her right in the middle of a Bloodrun, don't you?"

"If he touches her," Mason grunted, his voice rough as he lit up a new smoke and took a deep drag, then slowly exhaled, "he dies. He knows that."

"That's why he's got nothing to lose, Mase. His death sentence has already been signed. His last breath may come tonight or a month from now, but one thing Simmons understands with crystal clarity is that he's already dead. Considering how much he hates you he may think it's worth it, just to screw with your mind."

"If he wants her, he's going to have to get through us first."

"So then we're like a coupla white knights, eh?" Jeremy drawled, snuffling a soft laugh under his breath. "Willing to risk our lives to slay the dragons in order to protect a damsel in distress? It's the stuff of legends, Mason, my boy." The irreverent blond shot him a smart-ass grin. "We should be knighted or made saints or whatever the hell they do for selfless heroes."

Heroes? Not likely. And he sure as hell wasn't a saint.

With a heavy sigh, Mason hunched his shoulders, cast a cautious glance up at the flickering sky…and waited for the lightning to strike.

Another loud, jarring crack of thunder sounded in the distance, lashing against the oppressive silence of the afternoon, heralding the next storm as the now-muggy air became charged with static. The shadows in Torrance's room deepened, creeping into the corners like watchful eyes, enshrouding their bodies in an ominous, desolate gray, while the werewolf did his best to scare her to death. That is, if he didn't just kill her first.

"You have no idea how badly I've been looking forward to this day, Little Red." The hulking head moved closer, the cold tip of his glossy nose touching her own, those black, bottomless eyes staring from only inches away, so close that Torrance could see the short, individual hairs rimming the blackish skin of his eyelids. It was eerie as hell, the way he looked trapped between a wolf's form and that of a man's, his long, heavily muscled length covered in coarse, black fur; arms, legs and wide torso bulging with brutish strength, while his head had taken on the true shape of the animal, complete with terrifying muzzle and fangs. Where once human hands and feet had been, coarse pads now spread over his palms and soles, fingers and toes elongated into gnarled digits that curved into sinister, deadly claws.

"Now that it's here," he mused, rolling his hips against her lower body, "I just can't decide what I'd like to do first. Rip out your tender little throat? Or should I reward myself with a tempting go at this delicate little body instead? One that rips you apart inside—that leaves you broken and bleeding when I'm done with you." He paused for a moment, silent and still, looking as if he were thinking the repulsive idea through, the way a director might visualize a particularly compelling scene within his mind. "Wouldn't that make for some good storytelling when I get around to ending your half-breed's life? I don't imagine Mason likes to share his playthings."

Torrance felt her eyes go wide, unable to believe what he'd just said.

Mason? Mason! The psycho hunk from the café? Oh, no. No way. My luck can't possibly be this bad!

But it was all clicking into place now. That crazy friend of his had said something about putting her in danger. Damn it, she'd known that gorgeous face was too good to be true. And now look at her. Not even her mother had been this unlucky when it came to men!

A new feeling began seeping into her system—a cool, slow-burning fury that filled her from the bottom up, tingling in her fingers and toes, burning at the backs of her eyes. The monster licked a disgusting path up the side of her face, and she jolted, sensation rushing back into her limbs as he pressed his muzzle to her ear. "Yeah, I'm going to enjoy sharing the gory details of our time together with Dillinger," he growled. "Almost as much as I'm going to enjoy making you beg for mercy."

Torrance suddenly heard herself make a tsking sound, her upper lip curling with disgust. "Didn't your mom ever teach you not to play with your food?"

He shifted to stare into her eyes, and grinned at what he found there. "Oh-ho, so there is a little life in her, after all. Goodie."

Oh, God, what the hell was she doing? Before she could figure it out, he leaned closer, pelting her face with his rank breath. "And to answer your question, my mother was a weak bitch who betrayed my father and died in another man's bed." He smiled again, making her cringe as the hazy shafts of light stealing into her room caught the dull gleam of fangs set within pink gums. "The idiots never even saw him coming. Dad told me she was still screaming from her climax when he sliced her throat open."

"Jesus," Torrance croaked hoarsely, knowing the scene he'd just described was going to play front and center in her nightmares from now on—*if* she lived long enough to have another nightmare.

"He took a souvenir to remind him of her, and I'm thinking that maybe I should do the same. Killing Dillinger's new woman is certainly something I'll want to remember. But what should it be?" he murmured, looking her over with slow deliberation. "A lock of hair? A...finger, perhaps? It'll be fun, rubbing it in his smug face that *I* had you. Especially when he wanted you. I could tell. Oh yeah, he wanted you *bad*. But I'm the one who's going to get you."

He lowered his head back over her chest, watching *her* watch *him,* and let his long candy-pink tongue slip toward her breast, swiping at her cloth-covered nipple. Torrance grimaced, squirming, a sickening icy fear fisting in her gut, before settling lower into those deep, inner feminine places, and wrathful frustration surged through her.

She could feel it building...building...and in the next moment a loud, endless roar filled her ears, echoing through her brain...and with a stunning jolt of shock, she realized that it was her! *"Get...off...me!"* she shouted, her rage taking hold, gathering like a coming storm, mounting in her taxed muscles until she felt like she'd explode.

Those black, vapid eyes, empty and cruel like a shark's, narrowed, slick black upper lip curling as he bared long, vicious incisors. "That's it," he whispered with chilling satisfaction, leaning so close that he almost touched her mouth. "But maybe we should keep it down a bit." He stroked the side of her face with one claw-tipped hand, his cold eyes traveling over her features, one by one. "Just think. Even now, he could be out there, watching for a sign of you. He thinks he's so clever, but I got to you first and he doesn't even know it. Now I can have you…then leave you like leftovers for him to find. Sweet, isn't it?"

"You're disgusting." She spat in his face.

"And you're terrified," he said with a soft, guttural laugh. "In case you didn't get it the first time, fear really does it for me, honey. The more frightened you get, the more satisfying this bit of payback is going to be."

"Payback?"

"A long time ago, Dillinger took something from me, and I've been waiting for the chance to return the favor. Now that it's here, I plan to enjoy every moment of it."

Sitting back in a sudden shift of movement, he released her wrists as he straddled her, his brutal claws reaching for her jeans. Rage, sizzling and violent, raced through her blood, and her body instantly went on autopilot as survival instincts finally kicked in. Moving faster than she'd ever thought she could, Torrance bent her knees and planted her feet flat on the ground. Gritting her teeth, she thrust her hips up, hardly moving his solid weight, but jarring him enough to shift his body to the left. She immediately twisted in the opposite direction, lunging to the side as she pulled her right leg free, then struck out, knocking his hips off center. At the same time, Torrance flattened her hand as she slammed it against the floor, frantically searching for the fallen letter opener that he'd knocked from her grip.

Come on…come on…come on… Yes!

The second her fingers touched smooth silver, Torrance grabbed at it, swinging her arm around, aiming for his mangy ruff and sending the cool metal sinking through the tough skin at the side of his throat. An inhuman roar surged up from his chest as she used every ounce of her strength to shove the blade deep. She twisted her wrist, and his body jerked above her, writhing, knocking the breath from her lungs as he fell forward and slammed her back into the hardwood floor. One powerful arm swiped at her face, sending her glasses flying as she jerked to the side, just missing the lethal slash of his claws but smacking the back of her skull hard against the base of her dresser. Stars exploded before her eyes, glittering and bright against the graying edges of her vision.

"Arrrgh," she grunted, gnashing her teeth, using the flat of her palm to push the letter opener deeper, ignoring the impulsive urge to let go when blood began pumping from the wound, pouring over her hand in a slick wash of crimson. Shoving with her leg, Torrance nudged him farther away, the gurgling sounds dripping from his muzzle monstrous and grotesque, like something torn straight from the depths of hell.

"God, just die already," she screamed, the deafening cry drowned out by the harsh, outraged shouts she could suddenly hear coming from the outer hallway.

The wolf's face lifted at the commotion, nostrils flaring as he threw back his head and unleashed an unearthly howl that rattled the doors and windows, the letter opener now fully imbedded in his muscular neck. A crash sounded in the living room, followed by the sound of running feet, heavy and pounding, moving at full speed, and then flashes of a hard, strangely familiar figure as something solid and fast slammed into the beast and sent him hurtling to the side, freeing her. Torrance tried to draw in a huge breath, her lungs burning from lack of oxygen. At the same time she struggled to focus on the chaotic scene, but her head was throbbing and everything was happening too fast.

Curling onto her side, she pulled her legs up into the fetal position and tried again to focus on the blurry shadows crashing around her room. Three twisting figures were fighting with inhuman strength, growling…snarling…biting out virulent curses as they destroyed her furniture. Bodies slammed into one another with preternatural force as they battled for dominance, coarse grunts followed by the sickening sounds of crushed cartilage and tearing flesh. Torrance squinted, certain she had just seen a human arm sporting an amazingly wicked set of claws but couldn't hold the image. A quick, sharp cracking noise, like a snapping bone, came from the other side of her bed, and her stomach churned at the revolting sound.

Then the sound of broken glass hit her ears, followed by a familiar voice shouting into the small alley between her apartment building and the neighboring one. "That's right, run now, but next time we find you, you're dead!"

Torrance blinked against the salty sting of sweat running into her eyes, and for the first time she got a clear look at her rescuer's face as he dropped to his knees beside her, one unsteady, blood-splattered hand reaching out to check her pulse at the side of her throat.

"It's you!" she gasped, sounding groggy, positive she could hear the other one, who had shouted out her window, snickering off somewhere on the other side of the room.

"Shh. Just take it easy," he rasped, staring down at her, his expression fierce and brutally hard with lingering traces of violence and rage, a warm glow burning in his oddly lit gaze. Animal ferocity, predatory and wild, rode the long lines of his body, and there was something different about his eyes, she thought hazily. They seemed more golden than brown, smoldering with a primitive, provocative intensity that made her feel…uncomfortably sensitive—and suddenly Torrance was aware of being cradled against the strongest chest she'd ever felt.

Oh…whoa.

Hot, comforting heat surrounded her, pressing her against solid muscle and strong sinew outlined beneath a sweat-damp

T-shirt. Torrance wanted to moan at the feel of all that hard, unyielding masculinity holding her close, but bit back the sound. Instead, she focused at first on trying not to pass out, and then on the voices, listening to the rich, husky tones, the rhythm and pitch of their speech patterns, so rugged and male. Trying not to groan from the pain in her head, she lay silent as the one named Jeremy spoke to the man holding her within the strong, possessive circle of his arms.

"I took a quick look around the building, but there's not a soul around right now," Jeremy was saying. "Kinda creepy, but at least there won't be any cops on their way, and I've got her door back up on the frame. A good breeze would knock it over, but it will fool anyone who might pass by until we can get outta here."

Strong, infinitely capable fingers pushed her hair back from her face, tucking it behind her ears, her braid a pitiful wreck. "It'll have to do for now," he rasped.

"How's she doing?"

Callused fingertips stroked gently over her forehead, across the tops of her cheekbones, the careful touch so at odds with the raw-edged power she could feel pulsing off him in hot, potent waves. "She's pretty shaken up, but Simmons didn't bite her," he growled, that deep, whispery baritone ragged and hoarse. "The bastard must have been here all along, waiting for her when she got home. How the hell did he track her down so fast?"

"Come on, you know what kind of connections he's got. If she frequents that restaurant often enough, he could have slunk in there after we left and had her name like *that*," the blond argued, snapping his fingers—an unmistakable thread of frustration lacing his words. "Then once Simmons knew who she was, all he'd have to do is hack her information off the Net. The whole thing could have happened in minutes."

Mason made some low, noncommittal sound deep in his

throat, sounding unconvinced as he ran his big, warm hands over her body. Torrance tried to control her shiver and failed, while his delicious scent, like something wicked and sinful that she could almost taste on her tongue, filled her head, crowding out the raw smells of meat and blood and fear.

There was something wrong here, she knew, but she mentally shoved the irritating thought away, her body finding too much enjoyment being in his arms. If she thought too hard about things, she would have to move…and that just wouldn't do.

"There's no such thing as privacy anymore, man." Through her barely parted lashes, Torrance watched Jeremy plant his hands on his hips and glare at Mason. "Who knows what he used. At this point, it doesn't really matter, Mase. We've got a much bigger problem on our hands. It's daylight outside," the blond muttered, gesturing at the pale light beyond the broken window. "He fully changed *without* night. You know what this means?"

"It means this isn't your run-of-the-mill Bloodrun," Mason grunted, still checking her for injuries. A hot, rough palm traveled up her side, feeling her ribs, coming deliciously close to the outer curve of one breast. If it didn't still hurt to breathe, she'd have shifted, just a bit, and gotten that strong hand where she wanted it.

"Yeah, among other things," his friend bit out. "It means there's something a hell of a lot bigger than meat lust going on here, partner. No way in hell should someone Simmons's age be able to dayshift into his full form, even if he is as friggin' pure-blood as they come. And why couldn't we smell him out on the street? If we hadn't heard her scream, we wouldn't have even known he was here and he was practically sitting under our noses."

"I don't know what's going on with his scent. I can smell him in here, but the musk is lighter than it should be and there's something sharp mixed with it that's burning my nose." His hand paused as he turned his head to look toward the blond. "And I don't care when he can change, or how goddamn powerful he is. When we finally get him, he's going to pay for touching her."

Jeremy remained silent for a moment, and then she heard, "Are you going to explain to her what we are?"

What we are? What did that...

In the next instant, forgotten images came rushing back as Torrance suddenly recalled the forgotten piece of the puzzle.

Before Mason could answer Jeremy's question, Torrance scrambled off his lap, her movements awkward and uncoordinated as terror rushed through her, weakening her limbs.

"I already know what you are." The hoarse words left her lips on a soft whoosh of air, barely more than a whisper—and the realization she'd been trying to push away came roaring back, blindsiding her with the force of a kick to the chest.

Mason watched her with a calm intensity as she scooted away on her hands and feet, crab-crawling until her back pressed up against a corner of the room. "Do you now?" he asked quietly, moving with the sleek power of a predator as he gained his feet.

"How did you find me?" She could hear the panic grabbing at her throat, making her voice sound hollow and husky. "What are you doing here?"

At the sound of her fear, his expression closed, like a veil being pulled over a window, filtering out the light. "I doubt you're going to believe me, but I followed you to keep you safe. I was watching the building when I heard you scream."

"I saw claws," Torrance said shakily, pulling her gaze away from him to cast a quick look around the room, unable to believe the destruction. Her once cozy, comfortable bedroom now resembled a slaughterhouse—her white bedding a gory sea of red, a blood-spattered closet door hanging at an odd angle…like a broken limb, window and blinds broken where the monster had made his escape. "You're a goddamn werewolf, aren't you? Just like him!"

His head tilted a fraction as he studied her, dark eyes impossible to read. "Not exactly like him."

"But those were your claws that I saw, right?" she all but shouted, fisting her blood-covered hands at her sides. "When you were fighting off…whatever his name was."

"Simmons. His name is Anthony Simmons. And they could have been either mine or Jeremy's." His broad shoulders lifted in a casual shrug, as if they were discussing nothing more controversial than the weather, when her entire world had just been turned on its head. "That's about all of the change we can manage when it's still daylight. Not even Simmons is meant to be able to fully shift like that during the day."

"They were yours," she stated flatly, remembering the gray flannel shirt. All but shaking apart inside, she sneered, "You guys normally only change at night? Is that supposed to make me feel better?"

Dark heat flared in the rich brown of his eyes as they narrowed, pinning her in place. "I'm not interested in making you feel better. I'm interested in keeping you alive."

A sharp sound of disbelief jerked from her throat. "And I'm supposed to believe that?"

"You would, if you'd just calm down for a moment and listen to what your gut is telling you. I'm not the bad guy here. I'm the only thing that can keep you safe."

"Keep me safe by scaring me to death?" she returned, her voice trembling. "I don't think so."

"I didn't mean to scare you earlier, and it isn't my intention to scare you now, Torrance." He sighed. "I just had to make sure you were going to be okay."

With a little start of surprise, she realized what he'd just said. "How did you learn my name?"

Reaching into the pocket on the front of his flannel shirt, Mason pulled out the pay stub she'd been using as a bookmark, holding it up between his first and second fingers.

Torrance looked from the slip of paper to his face.

"It fell out of your book when you pulled away from me at the café." He watched her for a moment, then quietly said, "You felt it, too, didn't you?"

Torrance shook her head, but she couldn't deny that there was a strange truth to his roughly spoken words. Her gut was telling her…something—but she refused to listen.

Mason stepped forward, his expression turning fierce when he saw her flinch. "Damn it, don't do this. I know you feel it, Torrance. Don't goddamn lie about it."

"You're wrong," she whispered, even though she knew the look in her eyes betrayed her, revealing the intense, almost painful longing that she couldn't hide…couldn't explain or rationalize, considering she was terrified of him. "I'm sorry. Believe me, you have no idea how sorry—but I…I just can't do this."

His head fell forward and he seemed to be staring hard at the floor, lost in thought. Several tense moments passed, and when he looked back toward her, he kept his voice gentle, saying, "Everyone's afraid of werewolves, honey. At first."

"No, you don't understand." Her voice shook, despite her efforts to sound strong. "I'm not just afraid. I'm *terrified*. I've…ever since I was a little girl…nightmares…always. I'm… I can't… I can't do this."

Mason took another step closer to her, stopping when he saw the way her body tensed. "You can't go off on your own again," he said quietly, his tone urgent. "He's not going to stop until he's got you."

"That's crazy."

"Torrance, please listen to me. There's something going on here…a connection between us that's too damn complicated to explain right now. But if Simmons so much as suspects it, he won't give up. He'll keep coming after you."

She blinked, trying hard not to cry. "Why me?"

He stared at her, his gaze moving softly over her face, before settling back on her eyes. She felt as if he could see straight into her—as if he could get into her head and witness firsthand the chaos going on inside. "Because he'll use you to get to me."

Pulling her knees into her chest, she flicked her gaze between him and Jeremy. "And what the hell does he want with you?"

"It's because of who I am. Because of *what* I am," he explained gruffly, hunching down in front of her, his arm resting on his bent knee. "My job is to hunt down and kill Lycans like Simmons. Rogue werewolves. That's what we do. It's called Bloodrunning, and Jeremy is my partner."

"What do you mean rogue werewolves?" she asked, inching farther away from him. He shot a questioning look toward Jeremy, and she could tell from his harsh expression that he didn't want to explain. "Damn it, you got me into this! I deserve to know what's happening."

"Rogues are wolves who have gone over," he told her, breathing out a rough sigh.

Her stomach flipped, making her queasy. "What do mean 'gone over'?"

"They give in to their darker hungers and hunt humans, using them as food. Once they start, the power…the rush they feel from the kill and the feeding is addictive. They have no conscience and they have no fear. Now that Simmons has set his sights on you, he won't stop until he's got you. That's why we need to get you somewhere safe before he comes back. Next time he attacks, you can bet he won't be alone."

Torrance shook her head, a panicked, hysterical laugh bubbling up from her chest. "Somewhere safe? You've got to be joking!"

Mason stood and ran both hands back through his hair, then shoved them deep in his jeans' pockets. Locking his jaw, he said, "Do I look like I'm joking?"

"No, but then you don't look like a…a—"

"Monster?" he supplied helpfully, arching one dark brow at her. Though he tried to cover it, Torrance could see the quick flash of pain that cut through his warm gaze—almost as if she'd somehow hurt him. Leaning against the door frame, Jeremy muttered something foul under his breath, and she felt her cheeks go warm with an uncomfortable wave of shame.

"That's not what I was going to say," she lied, hating the emotional knot in her stomach. "Don't put words in my mouth."

"Why not?" Mason asked, pinning her with a hard, intense stare. "Your thoughts are written plain on your face, Tor. I've never met anyone before who was so easy to read."

She lifted her chin, hating that he could see into her so easily. "You don't know me."

He snorted. "Yeah, and you don't know me. But that isn't stopping you from being judgmental as hell."

He was twisting her words around, confusing her, and it was too hard to think when she was still so terrified. And yet there was something strangely…comforting about the arrogant giant. Again, that odd sense of rightness overtook her, and Torrance struggled to throw off its deceptive allure.

What the hell was wrong with her? Had she lost her mind?

"I need… I think I'm going to be sick," she muttered, pressing her blood-covered hands to her stomach as she surged to her unsteady feet and took off running in the direction of the bathroom. From the corner of her eye, she saw Mason move toward her, but Jeremy reached out and grabbed his arm, holding him back.

"Just give her some time, man. She's been through hell."

"Yeah, fine. Whatever," he grunted, shrugging his arm free of Jeremy's grasp.

Torrance slammed the flimsy bathroom door behind her, flipped the lock…and knew what she had to do.

Chapter 4

Funny, how hard it was to shake off the demons of your past; especially when you'd just discovered they were real. Evening had fallen, the shop had been closed early, and the Doucets had taken Torrance home with them, providing a safe haven in a world that had suddenly become her worst nightmare. Now she sat in their living room, perched on the edge of a love seat, recounting a story that sounded fantastical to her own ears…and she'd just survived it!

God, she could only imagine what they must be thinking.

Without looking at Michaela and Max, who sat across from her on a matching love seat, Torrance stared at the delicate cup of green tea in her hands and finished her explanations. "So I left the water running in the bathroom to cover the sound of the window opening, slipped out into the alley and ran like hell to get back to the shop."

It had taken every ounce of courage Torrance possessed to

climb out of that window. She'd had no idea if Simmons would be waiting for her, but knew she couldn't stay and allow herself to be dragged off to God only knew where with the men who'd chased him off. She'd briefly considered calling the cops as she'd taken the back way to Michaela's Muse, cutting through a maze of alleys and side streets, but quickly decided against it. What would she have told them? That she'd been attacked by a werewolf and then saved by two others? *Right.* She knew customers from Mic's who claimed to have been bitten by vampires and terrorized by Lycanthropes, but she'd never believed them and neither had the authorities. It embarrassed her now to think of how she'd viewed them with equal parts pity and caution, thinking they'd lost their grip on reality.

Now you're one of them, Watson. Welcome to the club.

Stealing a quick look up through her lashes, she saw that both Michaela and Max watched her with expressions that seemed tight with worry, and yet soft with understanding. She took another shaky breath, thankful they hadn't tossed her out on her ear for being off her rocker. Torrance knew their beliefs differed from those of most people—but she still hadn't been sure how they'd take her bizarre accounting of the past few hours.

"I know it sounds impossible," she whispered, "but it's true. Believe me, I wish it wasn't, but it is. Every crazy, psychotic-sounding word."

Michaela leaned forward, her slender hands clasped together atop her skirt-covered knees. "You did the right thing coming to us, *chère.* And there's no such thing as the impossible. You should know that by now."

A shaky wave of relief surged through Torrance, piercing and sweet. "You believe me?"

Sitting beside his sister, Max gave her a reassuring nod that sent a lock of his dark hair falling over his brow, his caring blue gaze urging her to relax. "Of course we do, Torry. You're like family to us. And family sticks together, no matter what."

"But…werewolves? It's like something out of one of those horrible movies." Movies that had scared the pants off her when she was little—lingering images and remembered flashes of sound that still had the power to affect her to this day. Had she sensed, subconsciously, the truth behind the Hollywood theatrics? Had she known, deep down, that the monsters really *were* hiding in the shadows?

Beyond the windows and walls of the house, the bitter autumn wind howled with fury, setting her on edge, to the point she feared she would crack. She clenched her teeth together to keep them from chattering, hoping she could hold it together for just a little bit longer.

"Torry," Mic said gently, cutting into her unsettling thoughts. "You know about our life…about where we come from. The bayou is riddled with tales about vampires and werewolves, ghosts and cat people." Michaela's rouged mouth curved in a wry smile. "The way we were raised, there isn't much Max and I don't believe in. Sometimes you just have to open your mind to the possibilities of things you can't explain."

Setting her rattling cup on the small table in front of her, Torrance ran her damp palms over her jeans. "I wish it was that easy. And most of those things I could handle. You know that. *Anything* but werewolves." Wrapping her arms around her middle, she rocked back and forth, shivering despite the warm air filtering into the cozy room from overhead vents. "God, I'll never be able to just live a normal life after this."

"You're not alone, Torry. Max and I aren't going to abandon you."

An ornate grandfather clock began chiming in the far corner of the room, signaling the hour. Realizing the time, Torrance cast a questioning glance at Max. "Aren't you supposed to be at work right now?"

He shook his head, a small grin playing at the corner of his mouth. "Naw. I've got the night off, remember? Good thing, too, because now I can keep an eye on things around here."

"Oh, God," Torrance groaned, shutting her eyes as a wrenching thought suddenly sliced its way through her brain, battering past her fear. What the hell had she been thinking? She couldn't stay here! If Simmons could find her one time, he could find her again. She was putting both of her closest friends' lives in danger by coming to them for help. Why hadn't she realized that when she'd run to them?

Why? Because you weren't thinking, you brainless, stupid, terrified little idiot!

"What? What's wrong?" Mic asked.

Feeling sick inside, Torrance opened her eyes. "I just realized how stupid it was to come to you. I wasn't thinking straight, and now I've put you both in danger. What if he tracks me here?"

"I'd like to see him try," Max growled, making her blink in startled surprise. It seemed that just yesterday Max had been graduating from high school, but the boy sitting across from her had somehow grown up and become a man without her noticing. One who was tall and broad and lean with muscle. One who looked as if he could handle himself, and would relish the opportunity to get his hands on Simmons. Of course, Torrance wasn't about to let it happen.

She knew she needed to leave, and told them so, but the Doucets weren't having it.

"I don't want to hear another word about it," Michaela ordered, her chin set at that stubborn angle that meant she'd made up her mind and was done listening to arguments. She stood and took the empty teacups into the kitchen, then came back a moment later with a glass of water and two small blue pills on a napkin. "You're staying right here. Now come on and let's get you set up in the guest room. You look like you're about to keel over from exhaustion."

After ten minutes of arguing, and another ten minutes of getting settled in, Torrance found herself standing under a hot, steady stream of water in the guest bathroom. The air was heavy with steam while she let the soothing heat run over her body, washing away the grime of the day, if not the strain. But the sedatives Michaela had insisted she swallow were helping with that, easing the tension as a smooth warmth poured through her veins, relaxing her muscles. Leaning her head forward, the water spilling over her neck and shoulders, Torrance finally admitted to the other, more disturbing reason she had run from her apartment. The one she had refused to think about, until now.

She'd wanted to stay with him.

It seemed illogical, *impossible,* considering the sheer force of her terror, but the desire to go with Mason Dillinger had been frighteningly strong. The very depth of her extraordinary reaction to him had sent her running even more than the panic over what he was—and God only knew that she was terrified by the idea of what he could…*become.* She'd seen those lethal claws firsthand, and knew exactly what they were capable of.

You're losing it, woman, she thought, lifting her face to the spray. *Completely losing it.*

There was no other explanation, because even knowing what he was…Torrance still wanted him.

Hidden within the murky black shadows of the night, Mason rested his back against the rough bark of a giant elm tree and took a deep breath of the crisp autumn air, searching for the scent of Simmons. His keen eyesight zeroed in on the picturesque

house before him—the same house he'd been watching ever
since Pallaton had called him with the address, after following
Torrance from Michaela's Muse. The quaint two-story sat at the
end of a secluded, tree-lined street in an older, historic neighborhood of the city of Covington, surrounded by dense forest
on three sides.

On the surface Mason remained cool and calm, focused on
watching the house to ensure she stayed safe—but on the
inside, he still burned with a cold, relentless fury.

He couldn't believe she'd run out on him. *Again.*

When he discovered that she'd escaped through the
bathroom window, they'd taken off after her on foot, until
Pallaton had called him and said she'd shown up back at
Michaela's Muse. Shortly after that they left the shop, and the
Runners had followed her here to her friend's house. He and
Jeremy had parked the Tahoe several blocks away, then cut
across the woods, until coming up on the back of the house.
Then they'd planted themselves just within the cover of the
forest and settled in for a long, cold night. Around them the
wind surged, brutal and raw, while heavy storm clouds all but
blanketed the glow of the moon, lending an ominous atmosphere to accompany his already crappy mood.

"Man, she's good," Jeremy drawled, leaning his shoulder
against a nearby tree. The blond whistled softly under his
breath as they watched Torrance's silhouette pass a second-
story window in what was probably a guest bedroom. "There
she is, all snuggly and warm in the house, while we're out here
freezing our asses off."

"I still can't believe she tried to ditch me," Mason grunted,
lighting a new cigarette and taking a long drag, welcoming the
burn of the smoke in his lungs, its acrid scent filling his nose.
Yeah, he was pissed at her for bailing, and even more pissed at
himself for ignoring his instincts when he'd allowed her to go

off to the bathroom by herself. But he'd been trying not to spook her, and it had turned around and bitten him on the ass. Hard.

"Forget 'tried,'" Jeremy countered, his grin wry. "Her cute little backside definitely ditched you. Twice in one day. I gotta admit," he confessed with a low chuckle, shoving his hands in the front pockets of his jeans as a brittle breeze whipped through the trees, ruffling their hair, "that I've always wondered what kind of woman would knock you on your arrogant ass."

"Yeah, well," Mason muttered, staring at the window as if he could will her to reappear, "I'm glad I've been able to provide you with some worthy entertainment."

"Hey, what are friends for?"

"Just remember that payback is going to be a bitch, and now the battle lines are drawn."

From the corner of his eye, he watched Jeremy's cocky smirk slip into a scowl. "Meaning?"

"Meaning I'm no longer going out of my way to help you avoid a certain little fair-haired witch."

His partner cursed softly under his breath. "You're such a bastard, Mase. I always knew you played dirty."

"Just don't forget it," he warned, taking another long drag.

Jeremy bent his knees, propping his back against the neighboring elm. After a few moments of silence, he cocked one tawny brow in Mason's direction. "So what's our next move?"

"We wait to see if he shows."

"It's quiet as hell out here," Jeremy murmured, resting his arms on his knees as he leaned his head back against the trunk. "Not even the crickets are chirping. If he gets close, we'll know it, even if we can't pick up his scent."

Mason nodded, moving his gaze over the back of the house. "If he gets close, he's gonna die."

"You hear from Pallaton again?"

"I talked to him while you were running recon on the street.

He and Reyes are combing over the warehouse district here in Covington, checking it out, but nothing's turned up yet. Brody and Cian are still over in Delaine, working on that second murder."

Jeremy lifted his head, his straight brows pulled together in a scowl. "They still trying to finger the rogue?"

"Yeah, and they've got nothing," Mason muttered, running his hand over his jaw, wincing at the sound of his whiskers against his callused skin. He could've used a shower and a shave, but knew he wasn't getting either. At least not anytime soon.

"Nothing they can trace?"

"Hell, there's no trace of Lycan musk for them to even identify, but they mentioned a sharp odor like vinegar all over the place. They tried to track it at both sites, but it messed with their noses, which reminds me too much of what happened with Simmons today. Anyway, they're heading back up to the Alley tomorrow, said they'll bring us up to speed then."

"Good," Jeremy grunted. "Because the killings are too ritualistic to be your average rogue kill. I'm telling you, man, I've got a bad feeling about it."

"Yeah, me, too." Within the past few weeks, two female bodies had been found in wooded areas, not far from the Silvercrest pack's territory. Both of the human victims had been blond and blue-eyed, both were clearly Lycan kills, and both had suffered the macabre fate of having their hearts eaten out of their chests. So far the Runners had been able to keep the grisly killings contained, but Mason knew they needed to settle the matter quickly, not only to ensure there wasn't another victim, but to keep the pack's existence safe from discovery. It was a challenge they constantly faced as Bloodrunners—one that became harder each year.

And then there was the shocking discovery they'd made that

afternoon, its potential consequences along the lines of earth-shattering. Simmons's ability to dayshift was the kind of thing that could prove disastrous not only to the Runners, but the entire Lycan race.

He was making a mental checklist of people he needed to question, when Jeremy suddenly said, "You know, I meant to say something earlier, but everything just started happening and I never got the chance."

Mason sent his partner a wary look. "What is it?"

Jeremy rolled one shoulder in a restless gesture. "I just wanted to make sure that you're handling this okay."

Oh, he knew exactly what Jeremy meant by *this*. Torrance. His mate.

Mason tossed the cigarette on the ground, his voice tight as he asked, "Why wouldn't I be?"

"Come on, Mase," Jeremy snorted, shaking his head. "I'm your partner. Your best friend, man."

"You make it sound like we're going steady," Mason grunted, knowing where this was headed, and not wanting to go there.

"I'm just trying to say that…hell, I know how you've felt about this kind of stuff ever since Dean, and I know you never planned on it happening to you. Now that it has, I just wanted to make sure you were handling it okay."

"Yeah, I'm fine," he stated flatly.

"Are you sure?" Jeremy pressed, clearly unwilling to just let it go.

Blowing out a rough breath of frustration, he growled, "Jesus, Jeremy, what do you want from me?"

A lopsided smile played over Jeremy's mouth, but his eyes burned with a directness that said he was seeing through Mason's bluff. "The truth would be nice."

The truth? Damn, Mason wasn't even sure what the truth

was anymore. All he knew was that he had to keep Torrance safe. After that, he could figure out what the knot in his gut was about. Figure out how to deal with it. Until then he'd keep waiting, watching, making sure she was okay. Didn't matter how long it took, because he knew Simmons. Knew the bastard wouldn't be able to rest until he'd finished what he'd started. And when he made his move, Mason intended to be right there. Torrance Watson was just going to have to learn to deal with it, no matter how she felt about werewolves.

Whether the fiery little redhead wanted him or not—she had him.

"Torry, wake up! Come on, honey. Snap out of it. You're having a dream…"

Torrance could hear the urgent words, their sound muffled as if she were underwater. She struggled to make her way back, thrashing her arms and legs, almost as if swimming up from the sluggish depths of a lake. She could see the distant spark of sunlight, but the dark, grasping shadows of her nightmares still held her with clawing hands that fought to hold her deep beneath the smothering blanket of sleep.

"Should I get some water to throw on her?" she heard Max ask, and she gasped, not sure if the sound managed to make its way past her lips or was still trapped in her throat.

"No, she's coming around," Michaela told her brother, her concern clear in the worried tone of her voice. "That's it, Torry. Come on, honey. Open your eyes for me."

Taking a deep breath, she finally managed to crack one eyelid, wincing when the bright morning sun spilling through the bedroom window nearly split her skull in two. She felt wrecked, her heart racing, mouth dry. But at least she was awake.

"There you are," Mic said softly, smiling down at her, while

Max stared over his sister's shoulder. "We heard you crying out in your sleep, so I'm betting you were having another nightmare. You okay now?"

"Yeah," she croaked, sounding like she'd swallowed a frog.

"I'll be in my room if you need me," Max told them, reaching out to ruffle her tangled hair before heading out of the guest room and giving them some privacy.

"Sorry for being a bother," she mumbled, feeling self-conscious and disoriented, still trying to shake off the heavy layers of sleep. Without her glasses, she couldn't see the clock, but she could tell by the brightness of the sun that she'd slept late. Mic was already dressed, with her long hair curling over her shoulders and wearing a light application of makeup that made her look well rested, even though Torrance knew she had taken turns keeping watch last night with Max. "If you can loan me something to wear, I can hurry and be ready to head into the shop with you in fifteen."

Michaela gave her a startled look of surprise. "Of course I can loan you some stuff, but are you sure you're up for it?"

"Trust me," Torrance said, smoothing her hands over the surface of the quilted comforter, "the last thing I need is to sit around here worrying about everything."

Looking doubtful, Mic crossed her arms over her cappuccino-colored silk shirt. "I really think you should stay here today with Max and take it easy."

"No, that's the last thing I need. The worrying will drive me crazy. Just let me grab a quick shower and I'll head into work with you. It'll do me good," she declared with a grin, trying to sound confident.

"Okay, if you're sure that's what you want," Michaela murmured, still looking concerned as she got up to leave. At the door, she turned back, one hand resting against the frame, her slender silver bangles jangling around her forearm like tiny bells. "You want me to have Max grab a friend and head over to your apartment for some of your things?"

Torrance shook her head, hating the idea of ever having to walk back into her home, knowing the memories would always linger. She loved the building she lived in, loved its character and her colorful neighbors, but she would definitely have to move. When she could finally face going back. And she didn't want Max going anywhere near the place until she knew if it was safe. "Not yet. Let's give it another day or so."

"No worries, honey. But you're staying here with us for as long as you need to, and I don't want to hear anything else about it. You go on and grab your shower, and I'll have some clothes ready for ya when you're done. Oh, and if you're lucky, I'll get Max to whip us up some of his famous French toast before we leave."

With a smile and a wink, Michaela shut the door behind her.

The second Max pushed open the back door to Michaela's Muse, Torrance knew something was wrong. The alarm which should have been beeping persistently, waiting for someone to disengage the system, remained eerily quiet.

"What the hell?" Max muttered, while Michaela pushed past him. Seconds later she rushed into the front room of the shop, a choked sound breaking from her chest that made Torrance feel sick to her stomach.

Sometime in the night, Michaela's Muse had been vandalized.

Bookshelves and display cases covered the floor, broken into pieces, the fine wood finishing marred with long, deep gouges that she was sure had been made by claws. The shop's impressive collection of coffee table books on a variety of paranormal subjects had been shredded, the new shipments of Tarot decks, candles and crystals scattered over the floor, crushed by whoever had stomped over them. Everywhere Torrance looked, something had been mindlessly destroyed.

Silent tears slipped down Michaela's face, Max cursed a foul string of words beneath his breath, and Torrance simply closed her eyes, wishing like hell she could just go back to yesterday morning and start over.

"I'll pay you back," she rasped, her voice rough with emotion. She drew in a deep, shuddering breath, and her stomach churned at the musky scent of animal, ripe and feral, mixing with the rich aroma of perfumed oils whose vials had been smashed to pieces. "I've got some money saved up. We can use it to replace everything that they've ruined."

"Do not make me angry, Torry," Mic snapped, glaring at her. "This is *not* your fault, so don't even start feeling bad about it. You didn't ask that bastard to do this. I will not let you take the blame for it."

"Like hell it isn't," she insisted, furious with herself. "If it weren't for me, this wouldn't have happened!" She gestured at the vengeful destruction that surrounded them.

Crossing her arms, Michaela narrowed her dark blue gaze and in a low, sibilant slide of words, she said, "Did you ask for this to land in your lap?"

"No, but if I had been smart and just left town or something," she groaned, pushing her hair back from her face, "then it wouldn't have landed in yours, as well." God, it would have been so simple! She should have bought a bus ticket and hit the road. The small leather wallet that she used for carrying her check card and ID had been in the pocket of her jeans, so money wouldn't have been a problem. She could have traveled through the night, heading north until she found some sleepy little town with a cozy bed-and-breakfast. No one would have been able to find her…and none of this would have happened!

"Yeah, and you'd probably be dead. Call me crazy," Michaela snorted, "but I'd rather have my best friend alive and breathing and have to deal with a mess, than leave her in the clutches of some psychotic asshole."

"Hey," Max cut in, interrupting them. "I hate to break it up, but you two need to look at this."

Torrance turned toward the sound of his deep voice, painfully aware that what little color was left in her face had just drained away when she saw where he pointed. "Oh, God," she gasped, clutching the edge of the counter with a white-knuckled grip, feeling lightheaded as she read the message that had been scraped into the far wall.

> You can run, Little Red.
> But you can't hide.

"That's what Simmons called me," she whispered in a hoarse voice. "Little Red."

Too nervous to stand still, Torrance turned to pace, picking her way through the heartbreaking destruction while trying to think what her next move should be. Maybe she should just sneak out in the night, leaving a note saying she'd be in touch when she got settled somewhere. They'd be furious with her, but at least they'd be safe. She hoped. Torrance couldn't help but worry that now that she'd drawn them into this, they were stuck in it, whether she stayed or hit the road.

She had just paced her way back toward the front of the store when she glanced through the front window and nearly stumbled over the broken leg of a display table, falling flat on her face. Rushing forward, Torrance peered out through the glass, shaking her head in shocked surprise. "I don't believe it," she whispered, recognizing that familiar dark head and muscular bod.

"What is it?" Michaela asked, hurrying to her side.

"It's him," she whispered. "Mason. The one who saved me. He's out there."

"The guy you ran from?" Max grunted, moving to her other side…and sounding far too protective for her peace of mind as he glared suspiciously outside.

"Um…yeah," she said uncomfortably, feeling her cheeks heat with a telling blush when she realized Mason was staring back at her through the glass, his gaze touching her like a physical caress. He lounged against a black Tahoe, with one shoulder propped against the SUV. His brawny arms were crossed over his chest, biceps bulging beneath the dark cotton of his T-shirt and flannel, a cigarette burning in his right hand, looking every bit the badass.

"Wow," Michaela drawled, "you weren't kidding when you said he was gorgeous."

"I know." Torrance sighed, sounding miserable. She played through a thousand and one scenarios in her mind, then finally said, "I think I should go and talk to him."

"I think so, too," Mic agreed. "But I'm going with you." Turning toward Max, who had fallen into step right behind them, she drawled, "Uh-uh. You stay here and watch through the window. There's already enough testosterone out there. I don't want a fight on my hands."

He scowled, clearly ready to argue, until Michaela added, "It's okay. He's not going to hurt her."

Max cut his sister a sharp, questioning look, muttering, "You're sure?"

"Positive," Torrance thought she heard her best friend say, but she was already pushing through the front door, the silver chimes chattering loudly as the wind caught at the tiny bells. Despite her intention to remain calm, she felt a powerful surge of excitement flutter through her system the moment their eyes connected, dazzling and swift, like a startled school of luminous fish rushing through the water. He stepped away from the Tahoe as she approached, then tossed down the cigarette after taking one last drag, grinding the butt beneath the toe of his boot.

Praying that she wouldn't stammer, Torrance said, "You have a bad habit of following me, don't you, Mr. Dillinger?"

The corner of his mouth twitched, but he didn't smile. He did, however, level an intense stare at her that made her breath catch. "Yeah, and you can thank me for it later. You can also call me Mason."

"Do you know who's responsible for this?" she demanded, gesturing toward the shop.

The rugged lines of his handsome face settled into a hard scowl. "You know who it was, Torrance."

She nodded, that sick feeling twisting through her stomach again, and his dark eyes narrowed in concern, the wind blowing the thick strands of his hair across his brow. "Are you holding up okay?" he asked in that whiskey-rough voice she'd spent a good portion of the morning trying to convince herself wasn't nearly as sexy as she'd remembered.

She'd been wrong. It was even better.

Giving another jerky nod in answer to his question, Torrance found herself drowning in rich, velvety brown ringed by the thick border of his ebony lashes. No man had ever looked at her the way *he* did, and it hit her on a level that went beyond the physical, to something deeper, darker…more intimate.

Despite the chill in the air, she felt hot beneath the skin, mesmerized by his presence, even though he looked scruffy as hell. Dark stubble shadowed the strong line of his jaw. His eyes were tired…clothes wrinkled. In fact, he was still in the same jeans and shirt he'd been wearing yesterday, and she suddenly wondered if he'd slept at all since she'd last seen him.

Almost in answer to her unspoken question, he jerked his chin toward the shop. "I was outside your friend's house last night, watching, staying close. That's probably why he decided to come here instead."

"He left her a message inside," Michaela blurted, and

Torrance turned to find the brunette standing near her side, staring at Mason out of narrowed, piercing blue eyes.

"Michaela!" she groaned, wondering what the hell the woman was up to.

"What's it say?" Mason asked in a silky rasp, shoving his hands in the front pockets of his jeans. She got the feeling he was trying to look and sound nonthreatening, but she could see the tightening of his jaw, the flare of fury in his eyes, and the telltale pulsing of a vein in his temple.

He was pissed—because she'd been threatened.

"It says that she can run," Michaela told him, "but she can't hide."

His gaze cut back to Torrance, and he squinted against a shaft of late-morning sunlight breaking through the heavy cloud cover, the corners of his eyes crinkling in a way that only made him look better. As if he needed to look any better. "You know what you have to do, Torrance."

She was beginning to suspect he was right—but that didn't mean she had to like it. "Is that so?"

"If you want to keep your friends safe. If you don't care about dragging them into this, then…" He shrugged his broad shoulders as his voice trailed off, but his meaning came through loud and clear.

Michaela arched one slim brow in his direction. "She's not going to be guilted into going anywhere. You're—"

"Not above doing whatever it takes to keep her alive," he finished in a low, hard tone, cutting her off.

Her best friend watched him for a moment longer in that intense way she had when trying to read someone and then grabbed Torrance's arm, pulling her farther into the parking lot. "Give us a minute, okay?"

He gave her a short nod, and Torrance felt like stamping her foot, feeling like they were having some silent conversation over her head. They walked about twenty feet, before Michaela released her arm and turned to face her, a small smile playing across her mouth. "Oh, man, honey, that guy is something else."

"I told you," Torrance groaned, flicking a quick look at him over Michaela's shoulder. He was talking to his partner, who she hadn't even noticed until that moment. But then Mason tended to overwhelm her, taking all her attention.

"Could you read him?" she asked Michaela, ripping her gaze away from him.

"You could say that," her best friend offered with a throaty chuckle. "His feelings toward you are incredibly powerful," she murmured, blue eyes shimmering with satisfaction. "The guy wants you bad, Torry. But more than that, he wants to keep you safe."

Torrance sent a second glance over Michaela's shoulder, and found Mason watching her with another dark, breathtaking stare. Softly, with her pulse racing, she said, "I can't stay here, Mic."

Her best friend reached out and gently touched her shoulder. "I'm not trying to get rid of you, Torry. You're welcome to stay if that's what you want. You know that."

"I'm worried about you and Max," she admitted, her voice cracking.

"Hey, Max and I can take care of ourselves. You're the one I'm worried about."

She stared out over the neighboring storefronts, taking comfort from the familiar sights and sounds. It would be so easy to stay, taking refuge in that familiarity, but she knew that it wasn't the road she was meant to travel. For whatever reason, fate had set her on a path that led to something strange and new, with the mystifying…unsettling promise of something…*special,* and though she was afraid, her instincts told her it was the right choice. "I'll go with him," she stated quietly, the wind nearly drowning out her huskily spoken words.

A gentle smile played over Michaela's mouth, her blue eyes dark with acceptance and a softer, perceptive look of understanding. "I don't know how to explain it, but it feels right to me, honey. He'll be able to keep you safe. And I think it'll be good for you, too. There's something powerful between the two of you. Something that needs to be looked at more closely, if you know what I'm saying."

"I'm not sure about all of that," she mumbled, unwilling to admit to what she was feeling. "But I think he's my best shot at making it through this without anyone else getting hurt."

"You better promise me you'll be careful." Mic gave her a big, crushing hug, whispering in her ear, "And I expect you to call me every day with all the delicious details, woman. And I mean *all* of them."

"You're crazy," Torrance quietly laughed as Mic released her, and they both sniffled, determined not to get emotional.

"You better not forget to call," Michaela called out, quickly walking back toward the shop. When she had one hand on the door, she turned toward Mason, pointing one slim finger at him, looking like a prim schoolteacher getting ready to reprimand a disobedient student. "And you had better take good care of her."

Michaela disappeared inside, and Torrance watched as Mason said something to Jeremy, then started toward her. When he stood no more than an arm's length away, she asked, "Can you keep them safe?"

He thrust his hands into his front pockets again, his gaze direct, as if he were looking right into her. "I already have a team of Runners assigned to them."

"Knowing Mic and Max," she told him, "they won't like it."

He nodded in understanding, while the breeze swirled around them, carrying his warm, masculine scent to her nose, and she bit back a telling moan, thinking he already looked far too sure of himself…and her. "They don't have to know. Pallaton and Reyes are good at staying out of sight."

"Where were they last night?" she demanded, sending an angry look toward the shop.

The corner of his mouth twitched at her tone. "Once I had the lot of you under watch at the house, I sent them to search for Simmons."

"Did they find anything?" she asked, pulling her lower lip through her teeth.

"Not yet," he grunted, staring at her mouth, at the precise point where her teeth pressed into her lip, before pulling his gaze back up to her eyes. "But we will. Once I get you settled."

She wrapped her arms over her front, as much to hold herself together as to keep warm. "I can't believe this is happening."

"I swear you'll be safe, Tor." He pulled one hand out of his pocket, rubbing at the back of his neck, and she almost flinched at the flood of awareness that rushed through her, violent and shattering. The image was intoxicating, a purely male stance, with the way he held his tall body, head angled slightly down while he looked at her through his thick lashes, powerful arm bent and lifted so that the muscles bulged, his expression…earnest, strong, *hungry.* "I won't let anything happen to you."

"Safe from Simmons, maybe," she whispered, blinking rapidly as she stared into his warm brown eyes. And in the next moment she heard herself saying, "But what about from you?"

Something silent and powerful passed through his gaze; something that reverberated through her, touching her deep inside, where she felt it in her blood and tissues and organs, pulsing in the very core of her body. "I'd never hurt you, Torrance," he finally said, and there was no mistaking the conviction in those simple words. "And I'm sorry as hell I've landed you in the middle of all this."

"It's not like you meant for any of it to happen," she muttered, ignoring what her name on his lips did to her heart rate.

His eyes narrowed, the molten brown barely visible through the thick, lush line of his lashes. "I should have just ignored you in that damn café and walked away. But I couldn't."

Since she didn't know what to say to *that,* she kept silent. Another chilling blast of wind surged around them, whipping her hair around her shoulders, and Torrance shivered as she grasped at the windblown strands, then rubbed her palms together, trying to work some heat back into her numb fingers. She jumped with a start of surprise when he lowered his arm and reached toward her, but he merely grabbed her hand, running his thumb across the fragile bones, warming her skin.

Feeling disoriented and off balance from his unexpected touch, Torrance eyed the powerful width of his chest beneath the flannel shirt and fought the bizarre urge to step closer and nuzzle the strong, tanned column of his throat with her cold nose. He had the warmest skin she'd ever felt, as if he were burning inside with an inner fire that heated his body like a fever. She sighed, watching his large hand engulf her own, his thumb rubbing across the small vein beneath her skin in a soothing gesture that struck her as breathtakingly intimate, though the touch was innocent.

But it didn't *feel* innocent.

"You're going to have to come with me, Torrance." His dark gaze—full of primitive, provocative intent—was piercingly direct as he stared down at her.

Her throat quivered, tongue flicking nervously at her bottom lip. She was so afraid, and yet, despite her fear, Torrance couldn't deny that she was drawn to him. "I really don't have any choice, do I?"

"Not if you want to live," he answered in a low, husky rumble that trembled through her system.

She swallowed hard, her words shaky and soft. "Where will you take me?"

That powerful stare, so warm and chocolatey brown, impossibly...vividly sexy, slipped from the top of her head, down to her toes in a long, thorough sweep, then repeated the same path until he was once again staring into her eyes, making her world spin. "We'll go home. Up to the mountains. To my cabin."

Chapter 5

She seemed to take a moment to absorb his answer, then finally nodded. The breath Mason hadn't even realized he'd been holding released on a low, shaky sigh, at the same time a raw, powerful rush of anticipation surged through him. There was no denying that he wanted her—that his body craved her. But it was *more* than that. And the more was making him nervous as hell.

Releasing her hand, Mason reached into the pocket of his flannel shirt, took out her glasses, then handed them to her. "Here, I picked these up for you at your apartment."

"Thanks." She took the glasses, her cheeks flushed as she used the hem of her pale gray sweater to clean the lenses. Finally, after what seemed like a torturous, jaw-grinding eternity, she slipped them on and looked back up at him. "What will happen when we get there?"

Mason tried to control it, but he knew the smile curving his mouth had more than a little of his wolf in it. "Let's just get you there in one piece," he rasped in a low, uneven tone that had her beautiful, wary eyes going wide. "Then we can figure out what comes next, Tor."

"I like the way you call me that," she murmured, looking surprised by her admission. "Nobody's ever called me Tor before," she added awkwardly, running one hand through her hair in a nervous gesture that drew his eye. Yesterday, her hair had been braided, but today the lustrous tresses fell past her shoulders in a wild, silken mass of deep, dark red. He wanted to see her hair like that when she was under him, the fiery locks flowing over his pillows like a silken wash of crimson that caught every shimmering shift of light, while her eyes went heavy, clouded with pleasure—the image so erotic, it nearly took his breath. His mouth twisted with a wry grin, and Mason shook his head at his unprecedented reaction to her. "You do know that this is going to be hell on me, don't you?"

"What is?"

His gaze rolled down the delicate lines of her body, lingering over the precious, provocative details, while his pulse roared in his ears. "Being near you."

"Oh," she breathed out softly. Mason could hear her fear in that single word, as well as caution…but there was also a touch of satisfaction, of *interest*.

He hoped to God he could control himself, because it was that last part that was going to kill him.

She was on the petite side, making him feel like a damn giant beside her, but for some reason it only upped his excitement. Since the day he'd first satisfied his body's need for sexual release, Mason had adamantly avoided women her size, always feeling clumsy around them, too aware of how much bigger he was, how easy it would be to get too rough with them.

But not this time.

No, the primitive, wild side of his nature was raising its head and howling with feral anticipation, breathtaking fantasies burning like molten, flame-red embers through his mind, until she made a small, nervous sound in the back of her throat.

Before he could say something to reassure her, Jeremy walked over, flicking a quick look at the sturdy silver watch on his wrist. "It's getting late. If you two are ready, we should hit the road."

"Yeah," he agreed, knowing they needed to make the mountains before nightfall. "Let's get out of here."

A minute later they were packed up in a rugged black Tahoe, the mud caked on its bumpers and wheels attesting to the mountain cabin Mason had mentioned. The interior smelled of luxurious leather and warm, male musk, as well as the earthy scents of the forest, making Torrance want to draw the heady mix into her lungs and hold it, enjoying something that was so elementally appealing—and yet so different from anything she'd known in life. Jeremy had offered to drive, snuffling a soft laugh under his breath when Mason readily accepted the offer and climbed into the backseat with her, making the large space seem almost cramped with his long legs and broad shoulders, not to mention the warm, vibrant energy that surrounded him.

"How long will the drive take?" she asked as they headed west, toward the mountains that ran through western Maryland and eastern Virginia. A steady case of nerves jittered through her system, and she found herself rubbing her damp palms across the tops of her thighs, toes curling girlishly within her shoes.

"Shouldn't take more than a couple of hours, but it depends on traffic." Mason sat with one arm braced along the door, dark eyes scanning the street, probably watching to see if they were being followed. He looked dark and dangerous, as if he could handle whatever life threw at him, reminding Torrance of how thoroughly opposite they were from each other. Yet she couldn't deny that being close to him felt impossibly right. The fear was still there, she knew—but her powerful, breathtaking attraction to him continued to battle against it, demanding her focus.

Noticing the dark circles under his eyes, as well as the lines of strain that bracketed his sculpted mouth, she said, "You look tired."

Another wry grin tipped the corner of his lips as he laid his head back against the seat. "Not sleeping for two days will do that to you."

"You stayed up all night watching the house?"

"Yeah," he rumbled, and then, as if he wanted to change the subject, he said, "Do you have any family? Anyone who will want to know where you are?"

"No, my mother died when I was twenty. There's an aunt and uncle somewhere, but we've never kept in touch. I haven't seen them in more than a decade."

"Friends?"

"Only ones through work, and Mic will let them know that I've…gone out of town. What about my apartment?"

"I've sent a crew in to clean up," he explained. "I asked them to pack up some clothes for you, so they should show up sometime tomorrow."

"That'll be good. Michaela loaned me these for today, but they're all I've got." And they obviously didn't fit right. Mic had a killer figure…while the growth spurt Torrance had always hoped would round out her hips and chest had never arrived. Still, she loved the outfit Mic had let her borrow, the flowing skirt and soft cashmere sweater making her feel like a gypsy.

"You should have your stuff tomorrow by noon, at the latest."

She nodded, and a softly charged silence settled between them, while they stared across the short space separating their bodies in the backseat. The country music Jeremy had turned on played softly in the background, and time just seemed to slip away. Torrance didn't know how long she just looked at him, soaking up the mouthwatering, masculine view that made her feel all hot and hectic inside, while his heavy-lidded eyes moved over her face, before finally settling on her mouth. The longer he stared, the more her lips tingled.

"You should get some rest," he finally murmured. The low, scratchy sound of his whiskey-rough voice shivered across her skin, melting through her senses, giving her that hot-beneath-the-skin feeling again. "The last two days have been hard on you."

She laid her head against the seat and closed her eyes, willing herself to relax—but she could still feel Mason's dark eyes watching her, taking in the rise of her chest, every slow, calculated breath that she forced herself to take. Knowing that she wouldn't sleep, she finally opened her eyes and said, "Do you mind if I ask some questions?"

Mason lifted his brows, looking somewhat cautious, while Jeremy called out from the front seat, "Let's hear 'em, doll face."

She rolled her eyes at the outrageous nickname, but couldn't help grinning. "Well, you said yesterday that you were different from Simmons. Other than the obvious—I mean, he's a total creep and you guys seem relatively sane—how are you different from him?"

With his elbow propped on the door, Mason rubbed his long, scarred fingers across his mouth and stared out the window as he explained. "We're wolves—werewolves, like him—but we've never been part of our birth pack. Before Simmons went rogue, he was a full-fledged member of the Silvercrest Lycans."

Something in his tone warned her that this was…shaky ground, but Torrance didn't back down. No, she needed to get as good a handle as she could on what she was dealing with here. "Why aren't you members?"

Jeremy steered the SUV onto a two-lane highway, then spoke up before Mason could answer. "Because we're half-breeds, meaning one of our parents is human and one is Lycan, or werewolf. In mine and Mason's case, our mothers are human and our fathers are wolf."

"So your werewolf fathers married human women?"

"Yeah," Mason replied, his voice mild despite the tension riding his big, powerful body.

Shocked by this bit of news, Torrance took a moment to simply watch him, appreciating the way the afternoon sun shone through his shaded window, putting him in a soft, natural spot-light. She liked the way his ragged jeans hugged the hard, thick muscles of his thighs. Liked the way the soft flannel he wore fit across those wide shoulders and the rigid biceps in his powerful arms. Heck, despite her fear of what he was, she'd be lying if she said she didn't like it all, the whole unbelievable package.

Realizing she was staring at him again, she jerked her gaze back to her lap. "Your mothers must be pretty amazing."

"They are definitely that," Jeremy agreed, sending her a lopsided grin in the rearview mirror when she looked up at the sound of his voice.

Glancing at Mason, she asked, "So what are your parents like?"

"Attached at the hip," he snorted, turning his head back toward the window after a fleeting look in her direction. A golden streak of vibrant sunshine cut briefly through the now quiet storm clouds, setting the deep auburn tones of his hair alight. Her fingers tingled with the blossoming desire to reach out and run her fingers through the windblown strands; feel their warm, silken heat against her skin. A heady, erotic vision of wrapping her fingers in that gorgeous hair and pulling him down for a hot, wet, openmouthed kiss burned through her mind, until his next words pulled her back to reality. "They're so wrapped up in each other, so in love, it's damn near disgusting."

Whoa. Something sharp and disturbing skittered through her system at his muttered words—and from the front seat, she heard Jeremy rasp a soft curse under his breath. Carefully, without inflection, she said, "You think love is disgusting?"

"Naw," he grunted, looking frustrated as he cut her a quick look from beneath his lashes, as if he wished he could take back the uncomfortably revealing words. "That's not what I mean."

"Then what is it about your parents' relationship that makes you…" Her voice trailed off, not knowing quite how to phrase her question. Despite the strange connection between them, he was still essentially a stranger to her.

"I love them. I think they're great," he explained quietly, his low voice barely audible over the heavy sound of the tires upon the road. His left hand flexed and fisted where it rested atop the hard-muscled length of his left thigh, revealing his obvious tension. There was something here, something important, but Torrance couldn't put her finger on it. "They're the best parents a kid could have ever had, and believe me, I gave them their share of grief."

Running the tip of her finger over a crease in the natural leather of the seat, Torrance followed the meandering line while trying to follow the path of his thoughts, reading the meaning behind both what he said…and what he didn't say. "So you love them, but something about them makes you uncomfortable?"

"Yeah, I guess it does," he admitted, blowing out a rough breath. "I think if one of them died, the other would just lie down and follow. It's like they…breathe life from each other."

She watched his hand slide from his thigh, lying re-laxed…and yet somehow expectantly on the seat between them…and her breath held, wondering if he would reach out and clasp her fingers, twining them together. Her heart lurched, feeling tight and heavy in her chest, her pulse fluttering like a schoolgirl's at the thought of holding hands with him—but she was honest enough with herself to admit that she wanted it. That she wanted this hard, rough warrior to reach out for her and simply hold her hand within the strength of his own, sharing his heat, his touch, the way he had in the parking lot. "I imagine growing up and witnessing that kind of commitment could lead to a person feeling one of two ways."

"Yeah?" She could feel his gaze on her finger, watching as she followed the crease in the leather.

"Hmm. You either crave the same kind of connection for yourself…or spend your life swearing that you'll never let yourself become so vulnerable."

He gave a low grunt, which she supposed was all the reply she was going to get, then crossed his arms and turned his attention back to the repetitive line of trees beyond his window.

Wrapping her arms around her middle, Torrance stared out her own window, at her lap, the back of Jeremy's blond head, wondering what to say next, thankful when he hit the indicator and began pulling off the highway.

"We're going to need to stop and fill the tank in this baby before we go any farther."

They pulled into a station attached to a roadside diner, and Mason immediately opened his door, giving the impression he was making an escape. "I'll grab us some coffee. Sit tight." And just like that, he was gone.

Torrance chewed on her lower lip as she thought about their odd conversation, and as if they had a will of their own, her eyes tracked his progress across the small lot, following his long, masculine movements with an avid, hungry absorption. She loved the thick muscles that flexed against his jeans as he moved, the shape of that incredible ass, and the bulge of his bicep as he pulled open the door. Loved the way the wind blew the dark strands of his hair around his head. Loved the rugged cut of his jaw and the sharp profile of his nose.

"If you weren't such a scaredy cat, you'd be throwing yourself at him, enjoying him for as long as you could have him," she whispered under her breath, fully aware that it was true…and hating it. The guy could have *any* woman he wanted—hell, he probably *did* have any woman he wanted—probably had them morning, noon and night. Yet here he was, with her.

It didn't make any sense, because if she'd learned anything in life, it was that a handsome face didn't stay for the long run. With a sharp pang in her chest, she remembered Clint, one of the few men her mom had dated whom she'd liked having around. He'd been so sweet and attentive, playing games with her, taking them on outings—but eventually he'd left, just like the rest of them. No matter how much they'd seemed to enjoy her charismatic mother, in the end they'd all moved on. Every single one of them. And Torrance had learned from the lesson.

Men didn't stay.

If she got past her fear and became involved with Mason Dillinger, there was every chance she'd end up with her heart broken. She knew it. He'd grow bored with her, and then he'd wander. She'd seen it happen so many times as a child, she knew the routine by heart.

It didn't matter that he ignored the perky blondielocks behind the counter of the diner who kept swishing her double Ds in his face. And damn it, why was she even thinking about it? It's not like she…wanted him. Right?

And if you're buying that one, Watson, then you're a gullible idiot…as well as a liar.

Not enjoying that train of thought, Torrance focused on listening to Jeremy hook the nozzle of the pump into the gas tank, then nearly jumped out of her skin when his fingers rapped on the passenger-side window. She reached across the seat, lowered the glass and he crossed his arms inside the frame, one golden brow arching when he caught her strained expression. "Something wrong?"

She made a low sound of disgust, jerking her head toward the diner's front window, where Mason stood waiting for their order while the blonde made eyes at him. "Do women always melt over him like that?"

Jeremy's chest rumbled with a soft laugh. "Yeah, but don't let it bother you, Torry. None of them have ever mattered to him, and Mason isn't the type to fall in love and then wander."

"Jeez, Jeremy," she wheezed, completely stunned. "Who said anything about falling in love? I don't believe in love at first sight. And he doesn't even *know* me."

"Oh, he *knows* you." His hazel gaze sparkled with humor, smile lines crinkling sexily at the corners of those mischief-filled eyes. "If you don't believe in love at first sight, then call it good ol'-fashioned *lust at first sight*. But it's more than that. Finding a mate isn't like being randy or having a bad case of the hots, though there's no doubt that the hunger is there. It's more…*intense* than that. Now that he's found you, it's not a matter of another woman turning his head—because she won't." He paused for a moment, as if carefully weighing his next words. "He could take another woman, but it wouldn't be because he wanted her. He'd have to make himself do it, and in doing so, know that he was destroying the bonds he'd made with you—and that would be like ripping his heart out."

Something in his voice was too personal, as if he spoke from experience, but he didn't offer an explanation…and Torrance wasn't about to pry.

"So, um, what exactly do you mean by 'mate'?" she asked, feeling dazed by his strange words.

He gave her an odd, piercing look, rubbing his hand over his gold-stubbled chin. "I thought Mason might have explained that back at the shop, while you two were chatting in the parking lot."

She shook her head, whispering, "Must have escaped his mind."

The blond's mouth twisted into a boyish smile. "Well, in our world, each male and female has a perfect other half, a life mate, who…completes them, as corny as that sounds. There are still those who believe that humans can't really be mates to wolves, but they're full of shit. I've seen too many successful unions not to believe that species doesn't matter. All that matters is what's inside."

"And you think that Mason believes I'm his…mate?" she croaked, swallowing an uncomfortable lump of surprise.

"I don't *think* it, Torrance. I *know* it. You *are* his—which is why Simmons will be so intent on having you. The bastard suspects you're special, because Mason wouldn't risk putting a woman in the middle of a Bloodrun unless he had no choice. In this case, he doesn't."

Her laugh sounded nervous and fragile even to her own ears. "I guess we'll have to see about that."

"Trust me, honey, he wouldn't have pulled you into all this if he wasn't completely convinced. It'll all work out in the end. Just take a deep breath and take it one step at a time."

"That may be easier said than done," she muttered.

"I don't know," he drawled. "Something tells me you're the kind of woman who can do anything she sets her mind to."

Hah! Little did he know. Right now she felt like a woman who wanted to go and hide under her covers for about the next…say, twenty years. Needing to pull her mind off Mason and mates and masochistic werewolves who were trying to kill her, she said, "Can you tell me more about a Bloodrun?"

Jeremy nodded, the look in his eyes warning that he knew she was changing the subject but was going to let her get away with it for now. "Like Mason told you before, Bloodruns are what we do. If we want the chance to become a part of the Silvercrest pack, we have to kill a given number of rogue Lycans. When we reach that assigned number of kills, we can quit Bloodrunning, or hunting, and become members of the pack."

Her brow furrowed as she asked, "And so you're still trying to reach your given number?"

"Naw." He grinned, flashing her his killer smile. "We both completed our required kills a long time ago." His shoulders lifted in a casual shrug. "This is what we do. We were raised with the pack, so we know exactly what they're like. Even when we were kids, they treated us like something to be ashamed of and swept under the rug. We couldn't care less about becoming a part of Silvercrest."

Torrance wondered if that was true—and despite the terror that filled her at the thought of an actual werewolf pack, her heart broke for the two boys who had been excluded because of some stupid, idiotic prejudice. She wanted to ask more, but Mason came through the door of the diner, carrying a drink holder that held three paper cups of coffee in one hand and a paper bag in the other.

"Nothing fancy," he rasped in his whispery baritone when he reached the Tahoe, climbing into the backseat. "But I grabbed us some doughnuts to go with the coffee since we've missed lunch."

"Thanks." He handed her one of the sticky pastries and a cup, and she took a cautious sip, careful since she knew it was hot. "Oh, man," she moaned. "I really needed this."

"Yeah, me, too," he said, wiping a smear of glaze off his lip with the back of his hand.

Too on edge to sit in silence with him while Jeremy replaced the fuel pump—especially after everything she'd just learned— Torrance searched for something to say. "So, is your cabin near your pack?"

He paused in the middle of taking a bite, saying, "They're *not* my pack."

Despite the mildness of his tone, his bitterness rang through loud and clear. "You really don't like them at all, do you?"

"I'm nothing as far as they're concerned."

"Then why do you keep Bloodrunning for them?"

Raising his brows, he cut her a questioning look. "How do you know that I do?"

Torrance took a bite of the doughnut, surprised at how good it was, the sugary glaze melting over her tongue. "Simmons said as much yesterday, and I had an insightful talk with Jeremy while you were getting the coffee."

"I'll just bet you did," he grunted, making another one of those totally male snorting sounds.

"I can guess he probably has a pretty sordid reputation when it comes to women," she drawled, grinning. "But to be honest, he was a perfect gentleman."

"Especially with you keeping your eagle eye on us," Jeremy laughed, sliding his long body back into the driver's seat. "I'd be willing to bet my favorite body parts that he had one eye on us the whole damn time he was in there, Torry." Jeremy sent her a smug grin in the rearview mirror. "Mason doesn't trust me as far as he could throw me."

"Shut up and drink your coffee, you ass."

The blond snickered, taking a sip of the steaming brew, before changing the radio to a soft rock station.

They merged back onto the highway while "Sweet Home Alabama" played quietly from the speakers, and Torrance waited before saying anything else. They finished up the doughnuts and sipped from the huge cups of coffee for a while, but when the lag in conversation seemed to thicken, a sense of uneasiness overcame her. Was he just the strong, silent type? Or was he irritated over the questions she'd asked about his parents? She didn't know how to read him or his moods, but she wasn't going to just sit there with nothing but her nerves for company.

"So this Simmons guy," she blurted out, more sharply than she meant to. "He really hates you, doesn't he?" Torrance winced a little on the inside, thinking that she really needed to work on her conversational skills. Talk about rusty!

"The feeling's mutual," Mason drawled with a hard smile.

"You're enemies. You're the hunter—he's the one being hunted. I get the whole dynamic, but…"

"But what?"

She shrugged, trying to put her finger on it. "His hatred seemed more personal than that."

"Death is a pretty personal thing, Tor. Simmons knows that Jeremy and I have been hot on his trail. His time's running out. If I hadn't been more concerned with making sure you were okay yesterday, I'd have gone after him then and ended it."

"Still, I think there's more to it."

His head tilted a bit to the side, gaze shadowed by long lashes that most women would have killed for, but looked perfectly masculine on him, giving his gaze a sexy, decadent look. "What are you asking?"

She thought about it for a moment, trying to follow the niggling thread in her mind. "He hated you before this Bloodrun, didn't he?"

He nodded, waiting for her to continue, while Jeremy pulled off the highway, taking the Tahoe onto a rural, private road that cut through the forest, and they started to climb the mountain.

Pulling her lower lip through her teeth, she said, "He told

me that you took something from him, and now he was going to take something from you."

His dark eyes cut back to the window, tension all but pouring off him in waves. "Five years ago, I killed his younger brother."

"Oh." A stupid response, but that wasn't really what she'd been expecting. She'd thought, at the time, that maybe Simmons had been referring to a stolen girlfriend, a job…a prime piece of real estate. She hadn't been expecting a dead family member.

Mason blew out a harsh breath, then explained. "As Bloodrunners, our main focus is on rogues, those who turn dark—who begin using humans as a food source. But, we're also charged with keeping the Lycans' existence secret. Simmons had a brother whose tastes ran to the…extreme. He hadn't gone completely rogue, but the bastard started picking up underage humans, boys and girls…and *treating* himself to them. We hunted him, tracked him down, and caught him in the act. He fought back. Resisted our attempts to take him back to the pack for punishment."

"The jackass wasn't willing to take what the pack would've dished out," Jeremy added. "So he attacked Mason."

"And you killed him," she concluded. "In self-defense."

He took another long, slow sip of his coffee. "I sure as hell did, and enjoyed every minute of it. That sadistic asshole had it coming for what he'd done to those kids."

Torrance went over the story in her head, looking at it from different angles. "So," she murmured, "that's probably why Simmons went rogue."

"Huh?" He jerked so hard, his coffee sloshed out onto his thigh, making him curse.

Turning in her seat, Torrance curled her right leg underneath her body as she faced him. "He not only holds you responsible for his brother's death, but he probably blames humans for his brother's weakness, for getting him in trouble to begin with. Over time, that blame turned to hate…and the hate could have led to…what he's become. Not to mention the messed-up stuff he told me about his parents. No wonder he and his brother turned out like they did. That is one messed-up family."

He didn't respond. Just stared at her, like he was trying to figure her out, solve a puzzle, unravel a code.

"Don't you ever question why one of your kind turns?" she asked, unsettled and a bit embarrassed by his intense scrutiny.

"Why?" His broad shoulders lifted in a stiff shrug. "It wouldn't change their fate. They turn, they die."

"But it could help to understand their motivations," she explained in a soft voice. "Even if they're inherently evil, like Simmons. Or insane…like Simmons. It could help to make sense of things, see them for what they really are."

"It could help, yeah—but the end is still the same."

"It can't be easy," she murmured, wanting to keep delving deeper, uncovering his secrets, discovering more as she peeled back the layers one by one. But she knew he wouldn't make it easy. "The constant hunting must wear you down."

Another sip of coffee, followed by a roll of one shoulder. "Most end quickly."

"I imagine they do. You're…intense about your job."

His hand stroked his jaw with a lazy motion as he stared at her from beneath his thick lashes, a strange, dazzling mixture of humor and lust suddenly spreading over his "dark angel" face. "I'm intense about a lot of things." He sent a slow smile to keep company with the provocative words, and Torrance felt that smile deep inside with a physical jolt.

Then he reached out and covered her hand with his, curling his long fingers into her palm and rubbing his callused thumb over her knuckles.

Her breath caught, and something inside her melted at his

touch. She didn't know if she believed in all that mate talk, but she knew she didn't want to turn away from this before seeing exactly where it would lead. She just had to find the courage to see it through.

"You're worrying too much. And you're staring," he said with a boyishly crooked grin, his tone deep and dark and low. He drew in a slow, uneven breath, then another, and she knew he was pulling her scent into his lungs, savoring it. The eroticism of the act made her tremble, while her palm went damp around the heat of the coffee cup she still held in her other hand. "It's going to be okay, Torrance. I won't let anything happen to you. And I won't hurt you."

"It's not that. It's just that…even though I'm a bundle of nerves, I can't deny that I like looking at you." She was surprised at her bold admission, but lifted her left shoulder in a shrug that said *so there*.

It was a nice, warm, fuzzy kind of feeling to see his eyes flare with surprise at her words, his rugged face taking on a hard, hungry cast that told her just how badly he wanted to be alone with her—and she knew she should have been terrified. But she wasn't. Mesmerized? Definitely. But for some reason, she wasn't afraid. The sensual line of his mouth parted the barest fraction for the evocative rush of his breath, and his fingers squeezed hers tighter, drawing her eyes. "You have the most beautiful hands," she murmured, meaning it.

Strong, rugged hands that led into powerful wrists. He'd pushed up the sleeves of his flannel and she could see that even his forearms were beautiful, with thick, healthy veins running between hard muscles and dark, golden, hair-dusted skin.

"They're scarred and used," he muttered roughly, and she couldn't help but smile at the tone of his voice. She'd embarrassed him, the sharp crest of his cheekbones flushed a dull red, and it charmed her clear down to her toes.

"That's part of what makes them beautiful," she whispered, setting down her coffee, then running the tip of her index finger along an angry-looking scratch that slashed across the back of his fist, where a heavy vein had thickened, cutting a dark line beneath his sun-darkened skin. She turned his palm over, rubbing her thumb across his lifeline, and his body vibrated with a fine tremor as he sat beside her, the sinew and tendons in his forearm going rigid, as if he were struggling to hold himself in check.

Casting a quick glance from beneath her lashes, Torrance glimpsed a hard expression etched with hunger, his eyes dark... almost wild, lips parted for the harsh force of his breathing.

He was turned on. By the touch of her fingers upon his hand.

A sense of wonder spilled through her, like a comet rushing across the sky, vibrant and shimmering against the infinite blackness of space.

He started to say something, but whatever he would have said was drowned out by some sort of guttural cry. Or had it been a howl? It was eerie...terrifyingly stark. The kind of thing that made your stomach flip and every hair on your body lift in alarm—reminiscent of childhood fears and things that went bump in the night.

Mason tensed at the demonic sound, and from the front seat she heard Jeremy mutter a low, foul, four-letter word.

The same coarse word repeating itself over and over in her mind.

"Mason," she whispered, clutching on to his fingers so hard she imagined them turning white within her grip, and he set down his coffee. "Wh-what the hell was that?"

"Sounds like our pal Simmons is paying us another visit," he rasped in a low, lethal slide of words, at the same time the forest filled with an entire range of those earsplitting, bone-chilling cries. "And this time, he's brought friends."

Chapter 6

Jeremy hit the gas and the SUV roared ahead, but they couldn't outrun the guttural, demonic howls. The bestial sounds kept pace with the speeding Tahoe, following from the shelter of the trees bordering the private road as it grew steeper, meandering its way through the thickening, sun-dappled woods.

Torrance jerked hard to the side, slamming against her door as Jeremy took a bend too fast. Mason cursed hoarsely as he reached out, pinning her back with a rigid, muscled arm, holding her in place. She tried to brace herself, when an ear-splitting crash boomed up ahead, and Jeremy slammed on the brakes. They came to a jarring, metal-screeching stop that had her seat belt cutting across her shoulder and abdomen, knocking the air from her lungs as her body lurched forward, then jerked back against the seat.

"Goddamn tree in the road," Jeremy muttered, jamming the

flat of his hand against the steering wheel. He turned in his seat, looking past them, through the back window of the Tahoe. "There's another tree down a few hundred yards behind us," he growled. "We're going to have to fight our way outta here."

"Looks like it," the man sitting at her side agreed, his voice lower, more guttural than before, with something dark and violent roughening the edges of his speech.

Another howl echoed sharply through the dense, enclosing woods, sounding far too close for comfort. The wind surged, blowing low-hanging branches against the roof like sinister claws, scraping Torrance raw with fear—and she knew Mason could scent it. With a low rumble, he pulled her into his side and pressed a hard, quick kiss against her mouth. "I want you to get down on the floor, Tor, and no matter what you hear, you are *not* to get out of this car."

The touch of his mouth left her reeling, but she managed to stammer, "Wh-what… What are those things out there?"

She didn't know what she expected him to say. Torrance *knew* what they were. But in some illogical corner of her mind, she thought maybe she'd hoped he would tell her something like killer bunny rabbits…or even rabid chipmunks. Something small and relatively nonthreatening. Something you could shoo away with your foot if they got too close.

She just wasn't ready to accept the fact that they were being slowly surrounded by howling, meat-eating werewolves—ripped straight from her nightmares.

Blowing out a rough breath, Mason brushed back a curling wisp of hair that had stuck to her cheek, the tight smile jerking at the corner of his mouth somehow comforting her, even though she was breaking apart inside. "There's nothing out there that Jeremy and I can't handle, I promise you. I only just found you, Torrance. No way in hell am I going to let anything happen to you."

She tried to smile at that, but only managed to wobble her mouth. "What should I do?"

His dark eyes scanned the surrounding trees beyond the windows of the SUV. "Exactly what I said. Stay down and keep quiet."

"Can't you call someone to come and help us?"

"No time for that," he answered grimly.

"C-can I have a gun?"

"I never take guns into the city with me, and it won't do you any good anyway, angel." He looked back at her, rubbing his knuckles under her chin in a tender gesture so at odds with the banked fury etched into the rugged features of his face. "Bullets may slow one of us down, but they can't kill us. We can bleed out if cut up enough, but the only way to really make sure we won't heal from our wounds is to snap our spinal columns or separate our heads from our shoulders. Just in case you were wondering how to get rid of me," he added lightly, giving her a playful wink.

"I'll keep that in mind," she laughed shakily, caught off guard by his unexpected teasing. He turned to open his door then, and she clutched at his arm, grabbing on to the firm bicep beneath the soft flannel of his shirt. "Mase?"

He looked back at her over his broad shoulder. "Yeah?"

The words tumbled past her lips, soft and fast. "Is it too late to go back?"

"Back home?" His dark brows drew together as he stared at her, waiting for an answer.

Torrance shook her head, trying to stay calm, but perfectly aware that she was terrified beyond belief. What was so amazing, though, was that most of her fear centered on the man in front of her, who was about to leave the shelter of the Tahoe and put his life in danger to battle against the monsters. She still didn't understand the connection between them, the unsettling mixture of fear and hunger that drew her to him—but she knew without a shadow of a doubt that she didn't want to lose him. "Back to the beginning," she whispered, her voice trembling. "Before this started happening."

He grunted under his breath. "If not today, it would have landed in your lap sooner or later, Tor. Nature would have brought us together, no matter how hard we tried to fight it or avoid it."

Her fingers tightened, nails biting into rigid muscle. "It's not the two of us finding each other that's bothering me! It's the thought of something happening to you—of you getting out of this damn vehicle and never getting back into it again!"

"You're not going to lose me. Just let me get us home alive," he rasped, leaning over and stamping another hard, searing kiss across her trembling mouth that would have been delicious if she wasn't sick with fear. "Then I'll show you that there *is* something good about all of this. That having me in your life isn't going to be all blood and battle."

She nodded numbly.

"I want you stay down and out of sight." Long fingers grabbed her chin, forcing her to hold his hard stare. "Do you understand me?"

"Okay, okay. Just…"

"Yeah?"

"Don't make me wait too long."

He gave her a hard grin, and then he was gone, the door slamming with a dull thud of finality that made her wince. Then the shivering began deep inside her body, before rushing through her, until her teeth were chattering so hard she sounded like a set of castanets.

The forest had grown eerily quiet, but Torrance knew the monsters were out there, watching them like vipers camouflaged in the leafy floor, lying in wait before striking. Beyond the dark windows of the SUV, she could see the shimmering shades of dusk, streaks of purple and pink splashed like water-colors across the canvas of the sky, and her breath caught at the brilliant display of beauty. How could a moment so awe-inspiring be filled with so much terror? How had a week that started out so ordinary, so routine, end up containing the most amazing hours of her life?

She didn't know, didn't understand, didn't have the answers. All she knew was that she wanted the chance to figure it out. To discover the truth of what had happened to her, and what it all meant. What it would take to get over her fear, if such a thing could be done—and what the dark, outrageously intense Mason Dillinger really wanted from her.

And if they made it out of this alive, Torrance had every intention of finding out.

Forcing himself to stay calm, Mason watched through the SUV's window to make sure Torrance followed his orders. Having been through this drill before, he and Jeremy took their stations, Mason on the passenger's side, Jeremy on the driver's. They braced their legs, then flexed their long arms out at their sides, allowing their hands to transform. Bones cracked and snapped into position as they length-ened, skin molding itself to the new structure, while long, lethally sharp claws pierced through their fingertips with a slick, sibilant hiss.

He was ready. Ready to kill. Ready to protect what was his. Then he would get his mate to immediate safety. He knew he needed to stay levelheaded and cool, but the icy claws of fear were digging into his gut, and there didn't seem to be any way to shake the sheer "emotion" of the situation. Always before, he'd operated, functioned, on pure instinct and training. Emotion didn't weigh into his fighting. Emotion didn't weigh into *anything* in his life. And now his goddamn claws were rattling at his sides, fury pounding hard and swift through his system, making him want to tear something apart.

You're screwed, Dillinger.

Yeah, on a personal front, he was in some deep shit. But as the branches began swaying off to his left, he knew he was about to be offered the perfect outlet for his rage.

"Come on, you sons of bitches," he grunted under his breath. "Let's get this over with."

His lips curved in a grim smile of anticipation, as the first one came at him in a blur of dark, midnight-black, leaping from the dense foliage that swallowed the lower portion of the tree trunks. His body relaxed at the same time his instincts sharpened, and he countered the first volley of slashing claws with an ease that told him Simmons's lackeys had yet to be properly trained. They were also young.

It was the lack of training and experience that made them easy takedowns. Even when in human form, the Bloodrunners possessed preternatural strength—and they were trained with deadly skill in physical combat. Without proper training, not even the fully shifted Lycans' impressive height and mass could ensure them victory in battle against the Runners.

Mason took the first wolf down with a hard kick to its gut. It lurched to its knees, and he wasted no time grabbing its furry skull and jerking the beast's head sharply to the right, breaking its neck in a clean, fast strike.

Before the werewolf had even hit the ground, the second assailant rushed him from his right, swiping long, curling claws at his head. He growled as the creature lunged for his throat, its jaws gaping, and spun his body, striking back with a side kick that smashed the wolf's genitals. It was a dirty move, but then so was attacking in full wolf form when the sun had yet to set. Simmons obviously wasn't the only Lycan dayshifting who shouldn't be, and the implications were enough to make Mason's blood run cold.

"These bastards are really starting to piss me off," Jeremy shouted from the other side of the Tahoe, fighting off his own set of attackers, as it became increasingly obvious they were outnumbered. In the past Mason had always thrived on challenges such as this, but not this time. Not today. Not when his human life mate was hiding in the Tahoe, terrified out of her mind.

His eyes scanned the trees, looking for the next attack, and he saw a familiar mangy ruff of ginger fur just before his third assailant rushed him in a head-on assault.

Oh, man, he should have expected this. Alan Curry, one of Simmons's longtime pals and partners in crime.

"Shit," he snarled, knowing damn well that Curry was going to be a bitch to take down.

The werewolf threw his entire body at him, crushing him into the front passenger's side door, and it took every ounce of strength Mason possessed to throw him off. Then the asshole moved in again, landing a round kick to his chest that knocked the wind out of him, really pissing him off. He kicked back, slamming Curry on his hairy ass, and smiled coldly, drawing from the anger burning through his veins. Curry gained his feet quickly, but Mason was already on the offensive, striking with his claws again and again, following him as he retreated toward the back of the SUV. The massive werewolf lunged for his side, but he swiveled on the balls of his feet, and the beast's strike missed its mark, long claws screeching ominously across the sleek black metal of the Tahoe's back door.

"Let's put an end to this thing, Burns!" he roared, disliking the fact that both sets of doors were now unprotected, with his partner fighting at the front of the vehicle and him at the back. Curry made another lunge for his gut, and he countered with a front kick that sent the wolf stumbling back on its hind legs.

"What the hell do you think I'm doing? Playing Parcheesi?" Jeremy snarled a moment later, sounding outraged as he came around the back of the Tahoe from the driver's side. "I just put the last of mine out of its misery and ran off two more." Coming to a stop by the left taillight, Jeremy whistled under his breath when he saw who Mason was faced off against. "Well if it isn't Simmons's little gofer boy," his partner snickered. "I should've known that foul odor belonged to you, Alan." Sniffing the air, Jeremy shook his head with disgust. "You bathing in vinegar nowadays to cover your stink or what?"

The ginger werewolf growled in response, watching him with a cold black gaze, its massive chest heaving as it slowly backstepped while Mason advanced. They'd been waiting for Curry to turn rogue for months now, and it looked as if their wait had finally come to an end. He recognized that dead look in the wolf's eyes all too well.

"Did you get Simmons?" he asked his partner, keeping his eyes on Curry.

"Get him? I haven't even seen him," Jeremy grunted, just before a powerful wall of dark red fur sprang from the trees, slamming the blond into the side of the SUV. At the same time, Curry rushed Mason, taking him to the ground. From the corner of his eye, he saw a golden wolf join in the fight against Jeremy, while Curry fought to get his long claws around his neck. Planting his feet in Curry's gut, Mason flipped the massive werewolf over his body, sending him flying through the air.

A low noise came from the Tahoe, and Curry lifted his muzzle in interest as he sluggishly gained his feet, sniffing at the air. He drew in a slow, deep breath, then flashed his signature sadistic smile. "Are you hiding your little bitch in there, Dillinger?" he asked, making a smacking sound of anticipation. "Simmons said she's all mine if I can get my hands on her— and I'm gonna make it last, bite by bite."

"Come on, Curry," he rasped, flexing his claws at his sides. "I've been waiting to take your head off for years."

The werewolf came at him hard and fast this time, throwing a roundhouse that landed in the center of his chest, sending him flying backward until he slammed into the trunk of a towering pine. Mason hit the ground hard, on his knees, pissed that he'd let the bastard get in such a good shot. Aware that Jeremy still had his hands full with the other two wolves, he knew he needed to work fast and take Curry out of the equation. He took a step forward, planning his attack, when the engine cranked, roaring to life, and the Tahoe reared back. Its wheels screeched as it slammed into Curry's massive body and knocked the Lycan twenty feet through the air, until he finally landed with a dull thud in the middle of the road.

What the…?

For a moment, Mason just stared in shock, unable to believe that Torrance had disobeyed him. He wanted to drag her out from behind the wheel and turn her over his knee, but he didn't have the time. He needed to get to Curry—who lay slumped in the road, silent and still—and break the bastard's neck, but Jeremy was in too much trouble. The wolves had come at him hard, the side of his shirt already covered in blood from where he'd been savagely clawed. Growling low in his throat, Mason lunged for the red wolf, taking him to the ground, then quickly twisted its massive head until he heard the final snap of its spinal column, like a sharp, resonating crack.

Getting back to his feet, he swiped the back of his arm across his forehead, wiping away the salty sting of sweat running into his eyes, and watched the impressive sight of Jeremy striking claws with the remaining golden wolf. Mason was ready to tell his partner to put an end to it, when he heard metal screech, and turned just in time to see a burly charcoal-colored wolf perch on the roof of the Tahoe, one claw-tipped arm battering at the windshield.

"Torrance," he rasped, feeling the angry rush of blood drain from his face.

Everything that happened after that seemed to move in excruciatingly slow motion. With wild eyes, he watched Torrance throw open the driver's door just as the reinforced windshield groaned under the hammering force of the Lycan's fist. She stumbled over one of the fallen bodies, her terrified eyes burning a deep green in the paleness of her face. Mason's legs were already running in her direction, but Jeremy was closer. His partner quickly slammed the golden wolf against the nearest tree, then lunged for Torrance.

They were both within a few feet of reaching her when Curry smashed into Mason's side, at the same time the bastard from the roof leaped onto Jeremy, taking a sharp bite from his throat. Jeremy staggered to his knees, his expression stunned while blood poured down the side of his neck, soaking into his T-shirt.

"Torrance!" Mason roared, fighting off Curry while a terror unlike anything he'd ever known ripped through him, sizzling and sharp, scraping him raw. "Get back in the goddamn truck!"

But she didn't seem to hear him. She stared at the gray wolf standing over Jeremy, and the next thing he knew, she'd picked up a fallen branch near her feet, rushed forward and whacked the Lycan in the back of his skull like a ballplayer swinging at a pitch. Mason shook his head, unable to believe his eyes, and knew he was going to kill her when he got his hands on her— if the bastard didn't get to her first.

Fighting off Curry's slashing claws, he bellowed a bloodcurdling sound of fury as he watched the gray wolf turn away from his wounded partner…and leap onto Torrance, catching her in a roll that ended with the mangy beast on top of her, pinning her to the ground. She screamed, bucking beneath the were-wolf's body, the branch falling from her hands, and Mason felt the fury of his own beast struggle to break free, despite the golden smear of the sun still hovering low on the horizon.

"No!" he growled in a savage roar, power surging through him like a rising wave building across the surface of the ocean. His fangs burned in his gums as he threw Curry off, wrapping his claws around the bastard's throat and twisting so hard, his head actually ended up parallel to his shoulders. Still roaring, Mason threw off Curry's heavy weight, ready to leap on the gray wolf pinning Torrance to the ground, when the golden Lycan Jeremy had thrown aside sprang forward, taking the gray wolf with him as they rolled end over end across the road.

Mason rushed toward Torrance, who'd already scrambled to her feet, her expression dazed as she stared at his claw-tipped hands. "What the hell were you doing?" he snarled, wanting to shake some sense into her at the same time he wanted to kiss her senseless.

"Trying to help," she offered weakly, staring with a mixture of awe and utter terror between the fighting Lycans and his claws. The look of horror on her face was so wrenching, that for a split second he almost allowed his hands to reform. But just as quickly, he squelched the knee-jerk reaction. Protecting her was more important than scaring the hell out of her—and deep down, he refused to be ashamed of what he was. If they had any chance at all for a future together, she was going to have to learn to deal with his dual nature, which meant claws and fangs and fur, as well as a vicious need to protect what was his.

Mason wrapped her in his arms, ignoring the way she flinched, going rigid against his body, and lifted her off the ground as the two werewolves rolled over the hard asphalt, slashing and snapping at each other. They were too evenly matched, until the one who'd attacked Torrance reached out for one of the small boulders that lined the rustic road and slammed it into the temple of his golden opponent. The younger wolf slumped to the ground, knocked unconscious, as the other stood up on his hind legs, turning to look at them with a malicious snarl curving his muzzled mouth. Mason lifted his upper lip and growled, backwalking toward the Tahoe, while keeping one eye on their remaining threat. When he felt the door at his back, he set Torrance on the ground, opened it and snarled, "Do not get out of this goddamn car!" as he tossed her up into the backseat.

"I'm going to enjoy having a go at that one, after I tear your head off, Dillinger."

Mason stared at the gray wolf without bothering to make a response. It had been a close call with Torrance—too close—and he still didn't know how badly Jeremy had been injured.

This bastard really needed to be dealt with quickly.

Moving with a speed and strength that had come from years of training, he leaped through the air, landing two feet in front of the wolf, then immediately kicked out with his right leg, wiping the beast's legs out from under its towering body. The werewolf landed on its back, but was already springing up when Mason twisted with a powerful roundhouse, knocking his booted heel into the muzzled jaw, grinning with stark satisfaction when he heard the sickening crack of bone. The creature howled, a sharp, garbling sound, its bottom jaw hanging crooked and bleeding, eyes wide with shock as Mason reached for its head and twisted its neck, separating its spinal column and ending its life in the blink of an eye. Before the warm body had even hit the ground, Mason was moving toward Jeremy, who'd managed to prop himself against the bark-covered trunk of a majestic maple.

He allowed his claws to transform back to their human shape, and crouched down next to his scowling partner. "What's the damage?"

"I'm more pissed than anything," Jeremy muttered, his voice rough with disgust. Gritting his teeth, he pulled his shredded shirt away from his bleeding ribs. "It was stupid to let that bastard get a bite of me."

"I owe you one," he admitted gruffly, fully aware that Jeremy had risked his own safety in trying to get to Torrance.

"Hell, you owe me more than one," Jeremy drawled with a low, shaky laugh.

Lifting his nose to the wind, Mason took a long, deep breath, searching for that strong vinegar smell that had been on the wolves. "Everything we didn't kill has hightailed it outta here. But we need to clear the scene as quickly as possible."

Wincing, Jeremy pulled his shirt off over his head, revealing ribs that had been slashed on his right side. Balling the ragged fabric into a wad, he pressed it against the bloody wounds in the side of his throat. "Yeah, and then let's get the hell home. I'm in serious need of some of your secret stash of Lagavulin. After this shit, I've earned it."

Mason gave him a long, critical look of assessment. "I guess you're feeling better than you look, if you can be thinking about raiding my best Scotch."

"Aw, it's just a flesh wound," Jeremy shot back in the crisp tones of a proper British accent, repeating the classic line from his favorite Monty Python movie.

Mason's chest rumbled with a rough laugh, his relief sharp that the jackass felt good enough to crack a joke. It was going to take a few days before he was a hundred percent, but with their rapid-healing traits, he knew Jeremy would be back in fighting shape in no time.

Unfortunately, Mason wasn't so sure about Torrance. Wondering how he was going to go about soothing his fragile little human life mate, he headed toward the Tahoe.

Mason hadn't taken more than three steps when the back door opened and Torrance slid out of the backseat, her dark green eyes roaming the ground, pinging from one downed body to another. Once dead, a Lycan returned to its human form—and her surprise at seeing naked human corpses in place of the dead werewolves was evident in her stark, stunned expression.

Then she looked their way, and a sharp cry fell from her lips as she started running toward them. Mason opened his arms, ready to catch her, when she sailed right past him, falling to her knees beside a grinning Jeremy. *"Ohmygod,"* she gasped, her small hands fluttering in front of her, as if she didn't know where to touch him without hurting him. "Are you okay?"

"I'm fine, honey," Jeremy replied with a warm smile, making Mason roll his eyes.

"Are you sure?"

"If he can flirt with you," Mason muttered dryly, "I'd say that's a pretty good indication that he'll make it, Torrance."

Whispering loudly enough for him to overhear, she leaned closer to his partner and said, "Is he always such a grouch after he wins a fight?"

Hazel eyes glittering with humor, Jeremy somehow managed to both laugh and wince at the same time. "I think he's about to bust a jealousy gasket, so go easy on him, Torry."

She cast a quick look up at his scowling face, giving him a critical once-over, a flash of relief filling her expression when she eyed his human hands. "I think you may be right," she murmured, regaining her feet and moving a little closer to where he stood. "Thanks for—" her hand gestured over the horrific scene "—everything."

Mason studied the hectic color in her cheeks, the way she nibbled at the corner of her lower lip, and just like that, he nearly staggered beneath the torrent of hard, provocative images swimming through his head.

Aw, hell. Wiping at the sweat streaming down the side of his hot face, he wondered what kind of bastard it made him, seeing as how he was rock hard in the middle of so many corpses. Huh. Probably a really a sick one…with a *really* dirty mind.

He cleared his throat, trying to get past the uncomfortable lump of lust that was nearly choking him. "Are you okay?" The growl that rumbled with those words sounded thoroughly pissed, and he winced at the rough sound.

"Yeah, he didn't even scratch me," she told him with a wobbly grin. "So I won't be going furry anytime soon."

He still felt shaken, but managed to smile down at her with a crooked twist of his lips. "That's only if you're bitten, Tor."

"Really?" she asked with obvious surprise.

"Yeah," he drawled, shaking his head at her stunned expression. "Not everything you see in the movies is real, honey."

"Well, even though all of it nearly scared me to death, I'm fine, thanks to you." She gave him a shy smile, then looked him over from head to toe. "I can't believe it, but you don't even look like you got a scratch."

"I'll be feeling it tomorrow," he confessed with a deep sigh, knowing his body would feel battered and bruised. "Trust me."

She took a step forward, looking as if there was something else she wanted to say, when Jeremy pulled himself to his feet and joined them. "Looks like Simmons has been building his own little gang, and now he's got an army of head cases following him," the blond snorted, still pressing the balled up shirt against his neck, the cuts across his side streaming with crimson color, until the warm spill of blood met the waistband of his jeans, darkening the faded denim. "This must have been his goon squad demonstration."

"You sure you're gonna be okay?" Mason asked, eyeing the wash of red running down Jeremy's side. Generally, loss of blood from these kinds of injuries couldn't kill them, but it could make them sick as hell, sapping their strength. "Do you want me to call some meds down from Shadow Peak?"

"Naw, I'll live. Let's just wrap this up, get in the Tahoe, and get the hell outta here."

At the mention of the SUV, everything suddenly came rushing back at him, and Mason turned to stare down at the woman who'd managed to turn his entire life on its head and damn near give him heart failure, all within the mere span of twenty-four hours. God only knew what kind of havoc she'd end up creating by the end of the week, not to mention over the course of his lifetime. Her gaze flicked from him to Jeremy, then back again, and he smiled with grim satisfaction the second she caught his furious expression. "I thought I told you *not* to get out of the Tahoe," he rasped, trying to control the tremor of fury that settled into his throat at the thought of what she'd done.

"You didn't say anything about driving it, Mason," she pointed out calmly, blinking up at him with those big green eyes, making him want to throttle her for putting her life in danger. At the same time he wanted to slide his mouth over hers, tangle his tongue with her own in a deliciously wet, carnal act of dominance and possession, and kiss her rebellious little backside into submission.

He drew in a deep breath, tall body shuddering with anger and the lingering traces of abject terror at the knowledge that something could have happened to her. "At this moment," he stated in a silky murmur, "are you or are you not in the SUV, Torrance?"

Despite the lingering fear he could scent on her skin, her expression turned mulish and she crossed her arms, all but glaring at him while her toe began to tap against the road. "I didn't get out of the damn thing until they started breaking their way into it! Should I have just stayed there and let them eat me?"

He took a step closer to her, invading her personal space, but she didn't budge—and he couldn't help but admit that he was proud of the way she was standing up to him. Proud...but still pissed. "If you had stayed down, like I told you to do, then I would have gotten to them before they could reach you."

He paused to take a deep breath, getting ready to launch into her about the damn branch and the Lycan she'd used for batting practice, but she made a soft, feminine sound of irritation and muttered, "Why don't you just stop being an ass and say, 'Gee, that was really swell of you to try and help out, Torrance. Without you, I could have had my head chewed off.'"

Jeremy wheezed under his breath, trying to stifle his laughter—not out of any sort of loyalty to him, Mason knew, but because it hurt like hell. "I was *not* about to have my head chewed off," he said grittily, insulted that she'd thought Curry and those other runts could get the best of him.

"That wasn't what it looked like from my point of view," she countered, her tone just as grim as his had been. "It looked—"

"Okay, kids, we need to save this delightfully entertaining...disagreement for later," Jeremy cut in, pushing his blond hair off his forehead. "Right now we need to clear as much of this off the road as we can, call for some cleanup, then get the hell home."

"I'll get Brody," Mason grunted, turning away to put in the call.

A few minutes later, when he'd finished on the phone and turned back around, he found Torrance moving in a slow circle, looking over the gruesome scene with a calm strength that astounded him, considering her fears. Then she came to a hard stop as she stared at the human body of the golden wolf who had, for some bizarre reason, apparently tried to save her.

"Ohmygod, I think he's still alive," she gasped in a hoarse rush, moving closer to the long, lean body that lay curled on its side, the chest moving slowly in and out. "He's still breathing!"

"What do we do with him, Mase?" Jeremy muttered under his breath.

"Hell if I know. We don't—"

"You can't do anything but take him back and make sure he's okay," his little redheaded hellion announced with firm conviction, dropping to her knees beside the young Lycan's body and checking his pulse. Her other hand lifted, brushing the thick chestnut locks back from a face that looked too innocent to belong to a killer—but Mason knew better than to take things at face value.

"Get the hell away from him, Torrance."

She cut a sharp look up at him, slim brows pulled together in a frown. "He's just a kid, Mason."

"He's also a killer," he barked, ready to reach out and pull her away. "And a monster, remember? One of the things you hate."

Anger washed over her features in a warm wave of crimson heat. "Hating and fearing are two different things. And he's not a killer," she argued, refusing to back down. "He saved me, and you're going to help him."

Mason snorted a harsh sound of disgust. "Says who?"

"Says me."

He arched both brows high on his forehead, wondering how a woman could be so full of contradictions. She was fascinating, obviously—but Mason had a grim feeling she'd spend the rest of her life keeping him on his toes, if not running him through the emotional wringer. "And if I don't?"

"Then I'll help him on my own," she vowed, crossing her arms over her chest as she glared back at him.

"I knew it," he rasped, planting his hands on his hips and shooting her a baleful glare through narrowed eyes. "I damn well knew you were going to be trouble. The second I caught your scent in that damn café, I knew you'd end up *complicating* everything!"

"Me?" she gasped in outrage, surging to her feet so that she could poke him in the chest with one pointed finger. "You insufferable jerk! Since meeting you, I've been attacked twice, had my apartment trashed, my workplace vandalized, my friends terrorized and been forced to put up with your mercurial mood swings."

Jeremy made a rough, choking noise at her back, as Mason's irritation escalated. "I do *not* have mood swings."

Torrance snorted. "Hah! Tell that to anyone who knows you!"

"She's got a point, Mase," the blond drawled.

"You want me to leave you out here to bleed to death?" he snarled, glowering at his grinning partner.

"Don't listen to him, Jeremy. He's just...cranky."

"Oh, damn," Jeremy snickered, the low laughter quickly turning into a groaning sound of pain as he clutched at his side. "Stop making me laugh, woman! I'm in shreds over here."

"Will you both just shut up?" he muttered, and then, in a softer tone, he stared down at her and said, "You know, you're awfully lippy for someone who's supposed to be afraid of me, Tor."

Her mouth compressed into a hard line as she continued to glare at him. "I'm too irritated to worry about being afraid right now."

He wanted to say more, but his cell phone began buzzing on his hip. "Dillinger," he clipped out, after flipping open the phone.

"Hello, Mason." The connection was crap, crackling and

weak, but he knew it was Simmons. "Did your little honey girl enjoy her mountain welcoming party?"

"Yeah, it was a blast," he drawled, mouthing the bastard's name to Jeremy and Torrance, who were both watching him closely.

"I just wanted to make sure she knew what she was getting into with you. And, of course, it's fun putting you in my place. How's it feel to be the hunted one?"

"You can only hunt something that runs, Simmons. You want me, you know where to find me. Unlike you, I'm not chickenshit enough to hide like a coward."

"Ah-ah-ah," Simmons scolded. "Make me angry, and I'll do more than just kill your little redheaded plaything the next time I get my hands on her. I'll give her a taste of what a real man is like. Then eat her while she's still warm from coming."

His fingers tightened to the point that the phone made a metallic groaning kind of noise, grinding and sharp, but he forced himself to remain calm. "I'm afraid we've thinned out the numbers of your new little psycho party of assholes. Looks like you've been a busy boy lately, Simmons. What's the problem? Can't find a woman who will put out for a useless piece of dick like yourself, so you've decided to play gang leader?"

Despite the poor connection, he could easily hear the harsh blast of Simmons's angry panting. "My followers embrace the truth, Dillinger."

"And what's that?" he drawled, keeping his tone cocky. "The fact you're a pathetic bastard who tries to make himself feel like a man by preying on those weaker than himself? Yeah, you're some hero," he snorted.

"That we should become what we were destined to be," the rogue snarled, the words tremoring with his rage.

"Monsters?" he laughed, purposefully goading him.

"Gods!" Simmons roared, and there was no mistaking the madness in his maniacal tone. "The deliverers of death."

"We're men, you ignorant jackass. The only one with a God complex is you, and you're screwed in the head."

"We are the beasts," Simmons countered in a calmer tone, obviously striving for control. "The kings. And they are nothing more than a petty food supply. Human nature is weak, Dillinger. How long did you think it would hold us back from realizing *our* true nature? From what we crave?"

"We'll see how kingly you feel when you're tracked down like the dog you've become," Mason promised in a quiet rasp. "And in case you're too thick to fully understand what I'm saying, I'll spell it out for you. I'm coming for you, Simmons, and when I get you, you're dead."

"You may have taken down my foot soldiers, but not even you and Burns together managed to kill me, Dillinger. I'm not afraid of you."

Mason smiled, the hard curve of his mouth almost cruel. His hatred for the rogue was strong enough that he could feel its ugly presence weighing heavily in his gut; the kind of hate that could poison your soul. "Then that's your second mistake."

Simmons chuckled softly. "Oh, yeah? And what's my first?"

"Daring to touch my woman."

With those parting words, he disconnected the call.

Chapter 7

After the bodies had been hidden in the woods, where Mason explained a second set of Runners would later deal with the remains, he used a heavy chain and the Tahoe's powerful engine to drag the fallen trees off to the side of the road. Then they'd loaded the unconscious Lycan into the backseat with Jeremy, and Torrance had ridden up front with Mason while he drove the rest of the way up the mountain. It didn't take them long to reach what he called Bloodrunner Alley, where he and the other Runners lived. Mason had described the Alley as a secluded, slightly sloping glade, surrounded by the wild, natural beauty of the forest, housing only the Runners' individual residences, since they lived separately from the Silvercrest. There were ten cabins in all, though not all of them were currently being used. And despite the fact they had to go into human civilization to stock up on goods (refusing to buy them from the pack), they had all the modern amenities, from power to hot water and high-speed Internet access, just like the Silvercrests' town of Shadow Peak, built higher up the mountain.

According to Mason, to an unsuspecting human eye, Shadow Peak looked like any other small mountain community. Only the inhabitants knew the truth about the locals, and they seldom encountered unwanted visitors. Still, as a precaution, there were scouts posted for the town throughout the forest, to alert them to any humans who came near, traveling the mountain roads. When she'd asked if the Alley had scouts, as well, he'd said no, explaining that they were so well hidden, they didn't need them.

He'd also explained that both the Alley and the town itself were built on private land that had belonged to the eldest pack families for centuries, with access only by private roads that were clearly marked. And even when they left the mountains, the Lycans and Bloodrunners blended well into the human world, complete with driver's licenses and Social Security numbers. Even their genetic makeup cloaked their true identities, as there was nothing in their DNA to alert the medical world of their species. The only real threat to their existence came from the rogue wolves, who threw the laws which kept the Lycan world safe by the wayside in order to satisfy their baser hungers.

Her curiosity getting the better of her, Torrance had hoped for a clear view of the Alley, but by the time they arrived, the sun had long since dropped behind the treetops. All she could make out was the outline of several large, rustic-looking cabins.

They parked in front of the nearest one, and while Mason carried the teenager downstairs, Torrance took the opportunity to look around the spacious, high-ceilinged room.

The inside of the rustic dwelling fit its owner to perfection. Rugged and intensely beautiful, with a masculine flavor that sported two sturdy leather sofas situated before a rock-walled fireplace, and handwoven rugs in deep shades of burgundy and gray scattered over the deep, luminous gleam of hardwood floors so dark, they looked black. Recessed lighting cast a low, golden glow over the warm interior, an invitation to snuggle up on one of the deep sofas before a roaring fire and enjoy the soothing atmosphere. A faint scent of cedar and wood polish hung on the air, combined with the earthier scents of the forest beyond the wide windows.

The cabin spoke of both taste and necessity, rugged and natural like the surrounding woods, but with a rich, masculine edge to it, invoking a comfortable state of luxury.

Bloodrunning was apparently more lucrative than she would have thought. Torrance grimaced a little on the inside at the knowledge that Mason Dillinger had both looks and money—which seemed to set an even greater divide between them. Even if things somehow worked out between them, she knew that trying to keep him would be like trying to lasso the moon or reach up and touch the shimmering sparkle of a star. Unattainable, always hovering beyond your reach—and yet something you couldn't keep yourself from wanting.

"It's beautiful," she murmured when she heard the men coming back into the room, their heavy boots thudding against the wooden floor. She ran her fingertips over the rich brown leather of the nearest sofa, enjoying its buttery-soft texture.

"Would you like me to make you something to eat, or grab you a drink?" Mason asked, his deep voice raspy, roughened around the edges, and she could feel the heat of his body at her back. "The tour can wait until tomorrow."

"Wow, be still my heart," Jeremy laughed, and Torrance looked sideways to see the battered blond leaning back against the wall beside an open door, a stairway lying within the shadowed recess. "An offer of both food and drink before you whisk her away. You really know how to lay it on, Mase. I don't think I've ever seen you this charming before, bro."

"This is his charming act?" she gasped, trying to pull off an expression of shocked surprise.

Jeremy winked at her, earning a low, rumbling growl from the man still standing just behind her. "It's sad, I know, but for Mason, damn. Usually he just grunts at a woman and she'll follow after him like an adoring puppy."

"Just what I wanted to know," she drawled, her voice dry.

He lifted his broad shoulders in an unrepentant shrug, hazel eyes shining with laughter. "Like I said, he wasn't exactly Prince Charming before meeting you. I gotta admit that it's refreshing to see the new Mason. Though I'm sure his sense of humor is still warped as hell."

"And yours isn't?" Mason muttered with a sharp snort of disgust.

"Naw." Jeremy grinned, waggling his brows at Torrance. "I'm an angel in disguise. All pleasure...and no bite. Unless, of course, a woman wants me to bite her."

A hard, heavily muscled arm wrapped around her waist, pulling her back against the intense heat and strength of Mason's body. Torrance automatically stiffened at the contact, but he didn't release her. He just held her there, trapped at his front, with his body warm and solid against her back. "Stop flirting with her, you idiot."

Jeremy whistled softly under his breath, eyeing the arm banding her middle with a speculative gleam in those smoky hazel eyes. "I forgot to add *possessive* to that stellar list of personality traits he's acquiring."

Torrance looked over her shoulder to see Mason send his teasing partner a sharp look of warning. "Now that I think about it, Burns, maybe I should give our little Jillian a call. Your neck looks pretty bad."

"Who's Jillian?" she asked.

"The pack's Spirit Walker," Mason replied in a lazy drawl. "She's a holy woman of sorts, and their healer."

And something more, she'd be willing to bet, based on the closed look that crept over Jeremy's golden face at the mere mention of the woman's name, leaving his once-laughing countenance hard and shadowed.

"I'll live," the blond grated under his breath.

"You sure about that?"

Ignoring the taunting question, Jeremy moved away from the wall. "I'm heading down to bunk with the boy wonder," he muttered, before his teeth flashed in a teasing smile. "You two little lovebirds have fun." He pulled the door shut behind him, whistling a tune that sounded suspiciously like *The Love Boat*'s theme song.

Torrance stared at the door until the whistling became too faint to hear. "Man, he's subtle, huh?"

"As a freight train," Mason grunted under his breath.

And just like that, they were alone, standing silent and still in the softly lit room, with only the ticking of the clock on the far wall to note the passage of time. A thousand thoughts and emotions swirled through her mind, urgent and soft—strangely, disturbingly intense—but all she could think to say was, "Do they have enough room down there?"

He gave her a quick squeeze, then released her. "When I moved in here, I made the basement into a small guest apartment for out-of-state Runners when they're in the area." He punched in a series of numbers on the illuminated alarm panel beside the front door. A short beep signaled the alarm had set, and he turned toward her, propping his shoulder against the wall, watching her through heavy-lidded eyes. "Jeremy's got restraints in the bag he carried in, so he'll be able to keep the kid where he wants him."

She shifted nervously beneath the intensity of his stare, unsure of what to do with her hands. "I hope he'll be okay."

Mason made a noncommittal gesture with one shoulder, then turned and headed through one of the archways, toward what Torrance assumed would be the kitchen. Before she could decide whether or not to follow him, he'd come back in, carrying two bottles of beer. He handed her one, the bottle cool and damp against her palm, a white frosted vapor rising from the open neck. "Come on," he rumbled, inclining his head toward the shadowed hallway at the far end of the room. "If you're not interested in food right now, I'll go ahead and let you get settled in."

Torrance hesitated, running the tip of one finger over a dog-eared copy of Patterson's latest Alex Cross novel that lay on one of the wide, wooden end tables. "I, um…wanted to apologize for losing my temper earlier," she told him. "And if I forgot to say it before, thank you for not letting them have me."

"No thanks required." His mouth kicked up a little at one corner, easing some of the red-tinged rage left over from the fight, the hot emotion still casting that hard, fury-darkened shadow over his features. As if trying to appear nonthreatening, he leaned his shoulders back against the wall and took a long swallow of his beer. With the thumb of his empty hand hooked in the front pocket of his jeans, he made the perfect visual for the ultimate bad boy. Rugged and tough and mean, with a breathtaking edge of masculine beauty, a body that would make any hot-blooded woman melt on sight, and eyes that revealed a dangerous, predatory sexuality. And then, to top it all off, there was that wicked, mischief-made smile that did breathless, naughty little things to her insides.

She shook her head at her contrary, amazing reaction to him. "Well, I meant it. Most men wouldn't have risked their life that way for a stranger."

She could see the arguments that he wanted to make in the brown depths of his eyes, the words bitten back, left unsaid: He wasn't most men; he didn't consider her a stranger; and it was because of him that Simmons was after her in the first place. He seemed to struggle for a moment, and then, sending her a devil's grin, he finally said, "Why don't you come a little closer and show me just how *grateful* you feel right now?"

"I'm not *that* grateful," she retorted in a slow drawl, amazed that she could enjoy this easy banter with him, even knowing what he was.

Knowing he was one of the things she feared most.

And yet…she felt safe. Felt as if she was where she was supposed to be, which made no sense at all.

"Can't blame a guy for trying," he replied with a low, husky chuckle, moving to her side and herding her toward the hallway with his warm hand on the small of her back. As if sensing her resistance to go with him, he moved in front of her, taking her empty hand to pull her along behind him.

"Mason…"

He spoke without looking at her. "You're thinking too hard, Torrance."

"I hope you have more than one bedroom back here," she breathed out in a choppy rush, "because I'm not having sex with you. And I'm not sleeping in the same room with you, either."

He stopped in front of her so quickly, she plowed into his back, smacking into a solid wall of warm, firm muscle and sending beer splashing over the rim of the amber bottle.

"Why?" he asked gruffly, his eyes burning oddly bright in the deep shadows of the hallway as he turned toward her. She had a vague impression of closed doors farther along the walls, and a wide bay window at the far end, covered by long, sheer swaths of muslin. "Because of what I am?"

Torrance swallowed, her throat dry while her mouth watered at the sight of him standing there, proud and strong in the moonlight, wearing a hard expression that didn't quite manage to conceal a surprising edge of vulnerability. "Th-that's part of it."

"Bullshit."

She blinked. "Excuse me?"

He stared at her with a heavy-lidded gaze, then slowly nodded his head, as if coming to some sort of realization. "You heard me," he said, the words soft.

Torrance returned his intense stare with wide eyes, not a clue what to say.

"You know what I think?" he asked silkily, stalking closer to her, his dark eyes burning in the thick shadows. "I think you want me, and that scares you more than knowing what I am. I'm beginning to think you're not all that afraid of me. And even if you're not ready to have sex with me, I think you should get in that bed with me and let me show you just how much you *do* trust me, Tor."

Something trembled through her. Something that felt entirely too much like need—and she struggled to smash it down into submission. "You actually think sl-sleeping in the same b-bed tonight is a good idea?" she stammered.

Mason gave her a slow, arrogant nod, the intense look of determination stamped across his rugged features daring her to argue. "I think it's the best damn idea I've ever had."

Rolling her shoulder, she tried to hide how nervous she was—how tempted. She took a deep breath, and his scent enveloped her, like warm, summer sunshine and a deep green forest, all earthy and rugged and clean—even though he was still a little hot and sweaty from the fight with the rogues. "I'm sorry. I…can't."

A rough, quiet sound jerked from his throat. "You know, you weren't this nervous around me on the drive here."

"That's because we were in a car," she muttered under her breath. "Not heading to your bedroom."

His eyes, so dark and rich and full of life, glittered with sinful intensity. "Honey," he rumbled with a low chuckle, "I hate to shatter your illusions, but there's nothing I can do in a bed that can't be done in a car."

Her lips parted, but words seemed to fail her, dissolving on her tongue like snowflakes.

"Stunned you into silence with that, huh?" He laughed, studying her as he rubbed one hand against his whiskery jaw. Finally he blew out a rough breath and said, "Look, believe it or not, I like my bed partners to be a little more willing. You don't wanna have sex? Fine. I can respect that. But you're *still* sleeping with me, in *my* bed. I can't protect you otherwise."

Oh, yeah. Torrance seriously doubted that *willing* was ever a problem for a guy like him. "I just… This is all… It's just that my head is spinning, trying to understand everything that's happened since yesterday," she tried to explain. "I still don't even really know what you want from me."

"All I want is to keep you safe. Come on." He sighed, and she followed him down the hallway and around a corner. They stepped through a door into what was clearly his bedroom, where she caught a shadowed impression of a beautiful, massive sleigh bed and sturdy wooden furniture. He turned on a low light and turned back toward her. "All you need to do is trust me a little, Tor," he said quietly, as if trying not to spook her. "Do you think you can do that?"

The second she stopped fidgeting and nodded her head, Mason took a step closer, feeling a pull from the middle of his chest that made him want to keep going until he had her plastered against him, all warm and soft and willing. He could see the questions in her eyes as her gaze got trapped in his stare—

and he knew she felt it, too. Knew that she was caught by the same glowing force that wrapped around his heart.

"Are you sure this is just for protection?" she asked softly. "You're not afraid that I'll try to run out on you again, are you?"

"You can try, but it won't work," he told her, fighting back a rough bark of laughter at her disgruntled expression.

"Would you trip me again?" she asked, lifting her brows.

A slow, wry grin tugged at his mouth. "I'll never live that down, will I?"

"Not in this lifetime," she told him with a crooked smile.

He gave a gruff chuckle at her drawled words, then sobered, watching her for a moment—thoroughly enjoying the view. "Yeah, well," he rasped, wondering if she could feel the brutal heat, the sheer savage possessiveness of the hungry stare he spread across her skin, "I wasn't letting you get away." The air between them thickened, swollen with expectation, like the next wave of thunderstorms he could hear building in the distance. "And if you tried to run—"

Exasperation quirked the soft curve of her lips. "Honestly, Mason, do you really think I'm stupid enough to run, now that I know the score?"

"Torrance, you barely even understand the game," he countered, his voice full of gravel and gentle bite, "and I'm not giving you the chance to bail on me again when things get…"

Russet lashes lowered over smoky green. "Scary?"

"I was going to say *complicated*."

"Oh." She laughed, and he watched as a soft wash of color crept over her face. "Sorry."

Reaching out, unable to help himself, Mason ran the back of his knuckles against the softness of her cheek, wishing he could put her at ease. When she didn't pull away, he brushed his thumb over the crest of pink in her cheeks, marveling at the exquisite silkiness of her skin, the beautiful arc of her cheek-bones and that provocative beauty mark that he wanted to touch with his tongue. He breathed deeply and found more of her earthy scent on the air, rising with the heat of her body. It surrounded him, easing into his pores until he felt steeped in her, drunk on the hunger.

Aware that he was shaking apart inside, he lifted his other hand and ran his thumbs over the fine arching slopes of her brows, the fragile skin beneath her eyes, the corners of her trembling mouth, before cradling her throat in his palms. Slowly, giving her time to tell him no, if that's what she wanted, he leaned down and feathered his mouth across hers. And that was all it took. She moaned against his lips, lifting her hands to clutch at the thickness of his wrists, and he was lost. The awareness of just how dangerous this was slammed through him, and he knew one kiss wasn't going to be enough. He needed *more*. Needed all of it. All of her.

"Torrance," he growled, and what started out as a slow, damp slide of lips and shared, soughing breaths, sharpened instantly into something wild and explosive. Her taste hit his system like a life-altering drug, making him tremor as he struggled to stay in control. With a rough sound of craving, Mason thrust his way into the moist, delicate silk of her mouth and tasted. Her palate. The smooth inner curve of her cheeks. Her tongue and the slick enamel of her teeth.

With the need to penetrate her in every possible way crawling up his spine, biting at him with insistence, he claimed her mouth with tender aggression, feasting on the succulent flavor, capturing her tongue when she dipped into his, sucking on it. Raw, scraping sounds of demand vibrated in his throat, while the waves of lust battered through him like the stormy surge of the tide against the fragile shoreline of a beach, reshaping him into something unfamiliar and different.

Had any woman ever felt this soft against him? This warm and vibrant and alive? This deliciously addictive, such that he craved her with every cell of his body? As if he'd never get enough of her?

"Son of a bitch," he cursed thickly, his hands still clutching at her throat, holding her in a gentle trap, her body vibrating against his with a low, erotic frequency that nearly brought him to his knees. "It's too good. You taste so sweet, Tor." She moaned in response to his growled words, and he took one last hungry stroke at the slick, inner surface of her lower lip. Then slowly, because it hurt like hell to deny himself something he wanted so badly, Mason put his hands on her shoulders and took a step back. She released his wrists, and his head lowered, hanging forward, while he struggled to get a grip on himself.

Air rushed from his lungs in a jagged rhythm, like he'd just finished a long, grueling run through the forest. Putting a mental chokehold on the hungry need burning in his gut, Mason jerked his head toward the connecting bathroom door. "Why don't you go on and grab the first shower."

She pulled her lower lip through her teeth in that sexy way she had of doing, the look in her eyes warm and mysterious. "Okay. I'll just…um—"

"Hold on a sec." From the top drawer of his dresser, he pulled out an old concert T-shirt that had grown baby soft from countless washings and offered it to her. "Here, you can put this on to sleep in."

"Thank you. I hadn't even thought about that. Are you sure you don't mind?" she asked, sounding cautious, as if he'd just offered her a ring instead of a shirt.

Shaking his head at her hesitation, Mason choked back a laugh. "Go ahead and wear it, Tor. I swear it isn't some secret werewolf ritual that means you're stuck with me forever or anything."

* * *

Reaching out to take the shirt from him, Torrance grinned at his teasing comment and turned toward the bathroom, only to spin back around, and the question just fell from her lips, surprising her as much as him. "What does it mean, being a life mate?"

He paused in the act of pulling off his T-shirt, a stunned look in his dark eyes. "Where did you hear that?"

She lifted her brows at his disgruntled tone. "Where do you think?"

His breath made a soft, whistling sound through his teeth as he pulled the shirt over his head. "Jesus. I need to muzzle that jackass."

"Don't you think *you* should have told me?" she asked, trying not to drool over the sight of his naked chest—but damn. He was, without a doubt, the most breathtaking thing she'd ever seen. Harshly, ruggedly beautiful, his body reminded her of an ancient Celtic warrior, scarred and bronzed, rippling with muscles and power, formidable in size and strength. He simply stole her breath.

"I was going to tell you," he said through gritted teeth, looking adorably irritated…and maybe even a little bit embarrassed. He lifted one arm to rub at the back of his neck, muscles bunching, and her mouth went dry, while a hazy, sumptuous swirl of desire poured through her belly and limbs, making her all quivery and warm. She was melting inside, like taffy left out in the scorching heat of the noonday sun. "But I'm still trying to figure out how to explain it."

He sounded nervous, which made her want to smile. "Can you at least try? I mean, what are we supposed to do? What happens to us? Is it just based on a physical attraction or is it more than that?" She paused, working up the courage, then softly asked, "Are we meant to fall in love eventually?"

"We stay together, forever. Get married, have a family. But it's a chemical thing. Metaphysical. Whatever you want to call it," he muttered, blowing out a harsh breath, clearly uneasy with the conversation as he emptied his pockets, dumping the contents on top of his dresser before sitting down on the side of the bed. "Love has nothing to do with it, which is just as well, since I'm not wired for it, anyway."

Torrance didn't understand why those words held such destructive force for her, but they did, slamming into her stomach with a heavy weight of disappointment. "Right," she murmured, pulling her gaze away from him. "I guess I should have expected that from a guy like you."

"What's that supposed to mean?"

"Just that we're strangers thrown together because our bodies like each other," she offered with a small shrug, wishing she'd never started the conversation. She'd have been better off not knowing. "I don't know why I thought it would get…emotional. Just forget I said it, okay?"

"Not likely," he grunted under his breath.

She ignored that, and though she meant to turn around and get the hell out of there, she heard herself say, "So it's supposed to affect both of us?"

"Are you trying to say you don't feel it?" he snorted, the rude sound grating on her last nerve.

"No." She sighed, wondering why these things kept flying out of her mouth and at the same time trying to ignore the effect of his half-naked bod on her pulse rate. She was trying like hell not to ogle him, but it wasn't easy. "I'm just saying that if it's a Lycan thing, why is it affecting me? I'm not a…"

"Monster?" he supplied, the cut of his mouth grim as she jerked her gaze back to his. He looked hard. A little angry. Vulnerable? Which made no sense, since he had all the power here. Didn't he?

"I wasn't going to say that," she whispered, hating the vicious tangle of emotions winding her into knots.

"Just because you're human doesn't give you an escape route," he said, turning his attention to unlacing his boots. "Believe it or not, we're more the same than we're different. The same way it hits me, it hits you. You just don't know how to read the signs as well. Your sense of smell isn't as sensitive or highly developed. But, you're still going to feel the effects, Torrance. And the longer you fight it, the more you'll suffer."

Yeah, she could believe that. She was suffering right now—breathtaking swells of desire rolling through her, sizzling and sharp. With wide, avid eyes Torrance gave in and moved her greedy stare down the strong column of his throat, across the broad, beautiful expanse of his chest. Oh, man, talk about a delicious visual exploration. She felt like a glutton seated at a Roman banquet. Her gaze kept going, discovering the rugged scars that slashed across the dark perfection of his skin, hating that he'd been hurt, the pain that he'd suffered…but profoundly proud of the signs of his courage and valor. He led the hard, brutal life of a warrior, and yet, he could be tender, too, and the combination was devastating to her senses.

"So…when you…I mean…" she stammered awkwardly, until she finally just made herself say, "Do you…have sex… like…"

He choked back a coarse laugh under his breath, his broad shoulders shaking. "Like normal people?"

"I didn't mean it like that." She frowned, her frustration mounting as she lifted her gaze from his chest to glare at him. "Stop putting words in my mouth."

He held her stare for a moment, looking as if he was carrying on an internal debate, then finally said, "Sex *can* be dangerous, which is why a Lycan has to learn control. It's hardest for a pure-blood. Their beasts are more…feral. Less easily managed. Not a problem when sleeping with another wolf, but it can be tricky with a human partner. If he's too rough and she bleeds, the beast can awaken…and bad things can happen. So, you learn to control it."

"How did you learn to control yourself?" she asked in a hoarse whisper.

"My older brother and my dad," he rumbled with a low laugh, as if he were recalling a funny memory. "I swear they lectured me until I thought my head would explode, but I listened."

He slipped off the boots, bent to pull off his socks, then turned his head to stare at her through the thick fringe of his dark lashes, a reddish brown hank of hair falling over his forehead. She wanted to walk over to him, reach out and brush it back, just so she could touch him. "Have you ever had trouble controlling—"

"Naw, I'm a half-breed, remember?" he cut in. "I have better control than most Lycans."

Control. Right. Torrance figured she could probably use some of that at the moment, since her gaze had fallen back to the mouthwatering territory of his six-pack abs. She licked her bottom lip, spellbound, unable to look away. Bombs could have started falling from the sky, a modern-day blitzkrieg in the mountains, and she'd have still stood right there. Heck, she probably wouldn't have even flinched.

"Torrance."

"Yeah?" she rasped, forcing herself to drag her focus back up to his face. She got there just in time to see the corner of his mouth twitch. "I'm trying to respect your no-sex policy here, but if I'm going to keep my hands off you, then you've gotta stop looking at me like that."

"I'm trying," she whispered honestly, making his shoulders shake with a quiet laugh, followed by a groan that was low and throaty…and sexy as hell. "I'll just go, um, grab my shower."

"You do that," he grunted, falling back to the bed as he

threw one perfectly muscled arm over his eyes…and she could have sworn she heard him chuckling as she hurried toward the bathroom.

Torrance opened her eyes to the moonlit darkness, a stifled scream burning in her throat—and found herself lost in warm, chocolate-brown, a stare so hot, so possessive, her breath caught with a little hitch.

"Why are you holding me?" she demanded hoarsely, aware that she was wrapped up in the unyielding strength of Mason's arms.

"Damn it, don't look at me like that," he growled under his breath. "I'm not going to hurt you. You've been asleep for a few hours but started having a nightmare. When I tried to wake you up, you latched on to me. I wasn't trying to grope you in your sleep."

"Sorry," she whispered, suddenly realizing that she had her nails imbedded in his biceps. His powerful arms, capable of so much strength, held her carefully, his hands stroking softly against her back in an offer of comfort.

"You okay?" he asked, his deep voice gentle with concern.

"I… I don't know," she answered honestly, shivering not from fear, but the slow burn of desire in those mesmerizing eyes. Uncomfortable with precisely *how* comfortable she felt in his arms, she tried to move, shifting away from his body, but he tightened his hold and kept her in place.

"Shh…" he whispered, "don't pull away from me, Tor. I won't hurt you."

"I know. I'm sorry," she said thickly. "It's just an automatic response. The dream…" She closed her eyes, remembering the horror of her nightmare—Simmons's heavy weight holding her trapped, his meaty breath in her face—and her lashes grew damp with silent tears.

"Don't cry, baby," Mason groaned, the words rough as he pressed the warmth of his mouth against the corner of her eye, kissing away the tears. "These nightmares of yours, will you tell me why you have them?"

"Why do you want to know?"

He tipped her chin up with the edge of his fist in time for her to see the deep look of tenderness that melted into his eyes. "Because I want to know you. Understand where you're coming from."

"I don't think it's from any one event, just a bunch of things all thrown together," she finally told him after a still moment of silence. "My mom had this thing about dragging her little girl off to gruesome horror movies so that she wouldn't have to go alone, whenever she was in between boyfriends, which was often. All she had to do was flash a smile, and they would let her take me in with her. I started getting easily frightened, and a few of her boyfriends thought it was funny. They got a kick out of trying to scare me. One of them even went so far as to make clawing sounds on my door at night, growling and snarling and making these eerie howling noises. He'd think it was hilarious when I freaked out, and my mom would yell at him. But she never kicked him out for it."

"These boyfriends," he rasped, a savage look of fury etched into his features, "they didn't…I mean none of them ever…"

She gave a little shake of her head. "No. Nothing like that. They just enjoyed scaring me. And I was so jumpy, it was easy to do. By the time I was a teenager, I thought having nightmares was just…normal."

"I'd like to get my hands on them. Give 'em a taste of their own medicine."

"Oh, man, I'd pay to see that." A small bubble of laughter broke free from the tightness in her chest, and he smiled at her. And just like that, Torrance felt a hunger for him unlike anything she'd ever known. There was a distant voice in her head warning her that this wasn't a smart move—but she didn't want to listen. She didn't want to hear any reasons why following through with this piercing urgency to get close to him wasn't a good idea. Shoving that irritating voice into the back of her mind, Torrance slammed a door on it and gave herself up to the desire rushing through her veins.

Feeling as if she was falling into another dream—this one urgent and sweet and intense—Torrance pressed her palms flat against the firm, scorching-hot surface of his chest. His heartbeat vibrated beneath her touch, healthy and strong, while his ribs expanded with his slow, deep breaths. She flexed her fingers, enjoying his sharp intake of air, the way he went silent and still beneath her touch, savoring her effect on him, marveling at its existence. There was hardly any give at all to the resilient muscles under her trembling fingers, and her body hummed with pure feminine appreciation.

Pushing a wavy strand of hair back from her cheek, Mason cuddled the side of her face in his rough palm, a tremor shivering through his hand that made her breath catch. She lifted her gaze and absorbed the stark, masculine beauty of his features in the ethereal beams of moonlight spilling through the bedroom windows—from the sensual, evocative shape of his mouth and the high cut of his cheekbones, to the sexy creases that crinkled at the corners of those mesmerizing eyes.

His body rustled against the soft, sleep-warm sheets as he propped himself up on one forearm and stared down at her, his thick bicep bulging beneath his dark skin, her head cradled in the crook of his arm. "If you don't want me to kiss you again," he warned her in a silken, seductive rasp, rubbing his thumb along the edge of her jaw, "then you need to tell me now, baby."

Torrance curved her hand around the back of his strong neck in answer, his skin hot to the touch, and with a deep, husky moan, his mouth touched hers. Like a match set to gasoline, the attraction between them burst into an explosion of hunger and need.

Mason pressed her back against the bed, covering her with the decadent warmth of his upper body, his mouth hovering over hers, so close…so deliciously close, it made her writhe with the urgent hunger twisting beneath her skin. She wanted him so badly that she ached. Wanted more of his heat—more of the heady, beautiful taste of his mouth that made everything deep inside pull tight…tighter. It was too much—and not nearly enough.

"More," she moaned, blinking in surprise at the breathy demand as it spilled past her lips, urgently aware of the impossibly hard, thick erection pressing against her thigh, the thin cotton boxer shorts he wore all that separated her skin from his.

He lowered his head and his low laugh rumbled against her cotton-covered nipple, sexy and rugged—full of pure raw, male desire. "Don't rush me, Tor. I want to take my time savoring you," he whispered, exploring her ribs as he pushed the shirt out of his way, stroking a thumb over the velvety indentation of her navel.

"Mmm," she purred, rubbing her skin against his, loving the contrasting textures, how hard and hot and big he was. Muscles rippled as he shifted closer, his heat pouring over her, that rich, musky scent filling her head. She gasped, the breathless cry melting into a long, husky moan as he nipped at the tender underside of her breast, his warm breath fanning her skin.

A thin, feathery sound filled her ears, and Torrance realized it was the rapid thread of her breathing, shallow and fast. Then his warm, large hand slid inside her panties, and she forgot to breathe altogether. His callus-tipped fingers dipped between her legs, finding her swollen and hot, embarrassingly wet—and a gruff, animal sound jerked from his throat.

"Th-that's not kissing," she gasped, shivering at the scorching, intimate touch.

"Yeah, I know," he whispered with a ghost of a smile, his whiskey-rough voice melting her from the inside out, while the touch of his hand made her burn. "Just go with it, sweetheart. I won't hurt you, I swear."

"Mason," she moaned, whimpering…writhing, undone by the wealth of need pouring through her, hot and relentless.

He cupped her sex in a warm, possessive hold while his breath rushed from his lungs, heavy and rough with lust as he nuzzled the shirt out of his way and lowered his mouth to her breast, flicking his tongue against the swollen tip, making her cry out. "I can't get enough of you," he growled softly, tasting her with long, slow laps and sharp, suckling pulls that arched her back like a bow.

"*Mase,*" she hissed, arching her back higher, pushing her nipple against the velvet roughness of his mouth, his breath warm and evocative against her tingling skin. The texture of his lips undid her, so damp and soft, when the rest of him was so brutally hard.

"Relax," he breathed against her trembling lips as he shifted higher, nibbling at her mouth, his taste filling her with so much hunger, so much craving, Torrance didn't know how to hold it all inside. It felt like it would shatter out of her, breaking her apart, too violent and strong to contain.

She held his stare, loving the dark, savage heat in his eyes as he urged her legs farther apart with his muscular thigh. Torrance made a choked sound in her throat as he teased the rough tip of his middle finger around the tender, slippery entrance to her body. His gaze burned into her, glittering with primitive hunger, his face flushed, lips parted, while that diabolical finger just kept stroking…and stroking. She shivered, twisting against his body, anxious for more…for everything.

One second she was writhing, and in the next, Torrance found herself stunned into a violent stillness as he buried that thick middle finger deep inside of her. She moaned a low, deep shivery sound, deliciously aware of her body clutching greedily around him.

"Damn." He flexed his finger, and her inner muscles squeezed down on him even harder. "You're so small. Hot and wet and tight." A second finger pushed into her with ruthless insistence, stretching her, making her gasp, and Mason pressed his mouth to hers. "That's it, honey. You can take them," he growled, breathing the words against her lips. Then he pushed deeper, curling the long digits, rubbing against a dark, sweet spot inside of her that made choked sobbing sounds vibrate in her throat.

Fear and danger and nightmares were all forgotten beneath the intensity of such violent, consuming pleasure. Like an erotic master, Mason plied her body, his tongue sweeping hungrily into her mouth, thumb grinding wetly against her swollen, softly pulsing clit, thick fingers thrusting heavily into her slick heat…and she crashed over the edge. Crying out with the swift, molten rush of ecstasy erupting through her, tingling in her fingers and toes, blooming beneath her skin like tiny pinpricks—Torrance felt her world shatter apart. It went on and on, destroying her, until she finally slumped back against the bed, harsh bursts of air jerking painfully from her lungs.

She heard Mason whispering soft, husky, *urgent* words into her hair, but before she could answer, she drifted into sleep, wrapped in his arms…her cheek pressed to the heavy, violent pounding of his heart.

Chapter 8

"Mmm. I thought I smelled coffee."

Jeremy turned away from the bay window, where he'd been staring out at the forest, clearly lost in thought, and grinned at the sound of her voice. "You're so easy, Torry," he teased, those hazel eyes moving over her freshly scrubbed face in a slow, thorough look of male appreciation. "All it takes is the promise of a little caffeine, and you come running."

"You've found my weakness," she sighed, making him laugh as he moved to pour her a cup.

When she'd awakened, alone in the bed, she'd found three suitcases and four boxes full of her personal things stacked in a corner of the bedroom. Glad that her stuff had made it there so quickly, she'd pulled out a pair of faded jeans and a dark blue sweater, gotten dressed and decided to venture out of the bedroom.

The smell of freshly brewed coffee coming from the kitchen had lured her like the promise of honey to a ravenous bear.

"You take cream and sugar?" he asked, glancing over his shoulder.

Feeling chilled, she curled her sock-covered toes against the warm tiles of the kitchen floor. "A little of both would be great, please."

"Ya know, I'm thinking I won't mention this caffeine addiction of yours to Mason," he told her as he pulled the cream out of the fridge. "Not that I don't love him like a brother, but it'll be more fun watching him figure out his way to your heart all on his own."

Torrance winced at the mention of the man's heart, thankful that Jeremy's back was to her as he moved around the kitchen. She recalled all too clearly Mason's earlier explanation of how things would work between them. He'd made it perfectly clear that he'd share his body...and nothing more.

God, she'd been so stupid.

If she'd listened to the voice of reason whispering in her head last night, she'd have realized that with such a powerful connection between them, she wouldn't be able to separate her emotions from the physical hunger. Having his hands and mouth on her body had only intensified her feelings—and now her lust had already evolved into something *deeper.*

"Is he here?" she asked, trying to keep her tone neutral as Jeremy handed over a heavy mug and she took a seat at the table.

"Yeah, Mason's in his office," he told her, while he went about putting on a fresh pot of coffee, since they'd emptied the old one, "checking to see if we've had any leads come in from Covington. We've got a whole network of informants who're keeping an eye out for Simmons."

She asked about the boy, and Jeremy filled her in while he finished with the coffee. "He's been coming around slowly, so we're keeping a close eye on him. Mason's desperate as hell

to get something out of the kid. Something that we can go on."
Taking in her troubled expression as he sat down across from
her at the gleaming pine breakfast table, he sent her a gentle
smile. "Not to be a jerk and stick my nose where it doesn't
belong, honey, but I can't help but notice the look on your face
every time I mention Mase's name. Why do I get the feeling
that things didn't go all that well last night?"

"No, everything's fine," she started to lie, but something in
his earnest expression made her say, "That is, I asked him
about us being…about that whole mate thing you mentioned.
And he explained how it works." *Before blowing my mind with
the most breathtaking orgasm I've ever experienced.*

"I'll just bet he did," the blond snorted, shaking his head.
"God knows if anyone could butcher a talk like that, it's Mason.
I'm not sure I even want to know what he said."

"He actually didn't say much," she admitted with a small
smile, finding the laid-back Runner amazingly easy to talk to.
"I think the gist of his explanation was that he intends for us
to share a physical connection, but I shouldn't go getting my
hopes up that he'll ever fall in love with me. According to
Mason, he's not *wired* that way."

"Oh, shit," he groaned, flashing her an apologetic smile.
"I'm sorry, honey, but only Mason could screw that speech up
so bad. I love the guy like a brother, but he can be such a bull-
headed ass."

"Why is he so dead set against caring for someone?" she
asked, folding her cold hands around the sturdy mug to capture
its warmth. She wanted—no, *needed*—to understand. Needed
to understand what was going on in his head, so that maybe it
could help her get a grip on her own jumbled, chaotic emotions.

Jeremy's usually carefree grin bled into a small frown at her
question, the splash of sunshine beyond the window casting his
shaggy hair in a pale-golden glow, his hazel eyes turning

thoughtful beneath his straight, tawny brows. "I think a lot of it comes from how we grew up. God knows it affected us all, some in the same ways, some different. I guess we all thumb our noses at the pack for their refusal to accept us for who we are, and that's bled into how we live. We're always on guard. Always wary. Knowing Mase the way I do, I think he's terrified of what he could feel for you, if he gave himself the chance. And that's before you take into account what happened to his brother."

A cold knot of dread settled in the pit of her stomach at his words. "What happened to his brother?"

"Dean committed suicide eight years ago," Jeremy admitted quietly, staring into his coffee.

"Wh-why?"

The Runner blew out a harsh breath, then leaned back in his chair, tipping it back so that he balanced on the rear legs, his hands folded over his hard stomach, the wounds in his throat already showing remarkable signs of healing. "Dean had been mated and married for almost three years when his wife was killed in an accident. When one half of a bonded mating pair is killed, the sudden severing of the connection can drag their mate into a living hell. Usually they simply lose the will to live and slowly fade away—but in some cases, the rage over their loss consumes them, destroying who they were. When Dean lost Lori, he found himself so filled with fury that he worried over what he might become. To keep it from happening, he took his own life."

"He was worried that the grief could turn him, making him go rogue, wasn't he?" she asked, her voice quiet, her head and her heart hurting for what Mason and his family must have gone through. "He didn't want to harm anyone, and he didn't want Mason to have to track him down and kill him."

"Yeah," Jeremy rasped, shaking his head. "And Mason was

the one who found him. Since that day, he's sworn that he'll never end up like Dean did."

"So that's why he's so determined to keep his emotions under lockdown," she said shakily, thankful that Jeremy had shared the story. It made it easier to understand where Mason was coming from, though it was still hard to accept. Especially when she feared she was already falling in love with him. "No matter what, after going through something like that, he'll keep his distance to protect himself."

The same as she intended to do. God, they were such a pair.

"He can try, but it ain't gonna work," Jeremy argued with a husky chuckle. "I have a feeling that if anyone can get under Mason's skin, it's you, Torry. The guy can't keep his eyes or his mind off you. You're just going to have to trust him and give the big dolt some time to sort it all out in his head."

"That may be easier said than done."

His smile was crooked as he tilted his head. "But unfortunately true. You just need to be patient with the man."

"Well, I guess we'll have to see," she said quickly, needing to change the subject before the understanding in those smoky hazel eyes broke her down. She took a slow sip of her coffee, then asked, "So how many Runners live here in the Alley?"

"Including me and Mase, we have six right now. We're a tight group, so you'll get to know everyone really well."

If I'm here long enough. "You sound close, like a family."

"Yeah, I guess we are. God knows we fight like one," he laughed. "You'll like the others when you meet them, but you had better watch out for Hennessey. That womanizing Irishman has worked hard to earn his sordid reputation."

Torrance smiled off his playful warning, finding it hard to believe that all their reputations weren't sordid when it came to the ladies. "Don't you have any female Runners?"

"We only have one right now, but she's down in Covington. In fact, she's working with her partner, keeping an eye on your friends."

"Pallaton?" she asked, remembering Mason mentioning that name during their conversation in the parking lot. Was that only yesterday? It seemed impossible, a world away, a lifetime ago.

Jeremy shook his head. "Carla Reyes. We've had others, but they've all mated and settled down."

Torrance took another sip of her coffee, but despite the caffeine hitting her system, she had to cover her mouth when she yawned. "Sorry, I don't know what's wrong with me. Coffee usually wakes me right up."

"You're still exhausted," he told her, grinning. "God knows yesterday was enough to wear anyone down. Why don't you go and grab a bit more sleep, and then I'll throw together an early lunch."

Since she was already yawning again, she didn't argue. "I think that's probably a good idea. And thanks for the talk. It's a lot to take in, but it helps to understand."

"I'm here whenever you need me, sweetheart," he drawled, sending her a teasing wink as she walked out of the room. Torrance shook her head at the guy's irreverent flirting, knowing he didn't mean anything by it. Walking past the room she assumed was the office, she could hear Mason's low voice, probably on a phone call, and a flurry of butterflies took flight in her belly. Oh, man. Not good. For a split second she debated knocking on the door and just getting the embarrassing "morning after" confrontation out of the way, then decided against it as she headed toward the bedroom. She needed time to think over everything Jeremy had told her; but when she walked into the room and saw the massive sleigh bed, memories from the night before poured over her in a warm, breathtaking wave.

She'd already made the bed earlier, so she crawled on top of the covers and laid her head against the pillows, recalling how she'd felt waking up that morning—a strange mixture of shock, worry and lingering pleasure that continued to pulse sweetly through her veins. God, the force of her reaction to him had been overwhelming, sweeping her away with a strength that was more powerful than anything she'd ever experienced.

If she were to make love with him, that would be it. Her heart would be lost for good.

Closing her eyes, Torrance snuggled her head into the pillow, knowing that if she was smart, she wouldn't let this thing between them go any further than it already had. If she wanted to keep her heart in one piece, she had to take a step back—but even as she drifted into slumber, she knew it wasn't going to be easy. None of the things that should have mattered seemed to make a difference where Mason Dillinger was concerned. Not the fact that he was a werewolf or how he felt about love and the chaos he'd caused in her life.

Despite all of it—all the logical reasons for keeping her distance—she couldn't deny that she still wanted him.

He shouldn't have touched her.

That was the painful truth pounding its way through his brain as Mason sat behind his desk, staring out his office window at the early-morning breeze blowing through the trees, scattering their leaves. The fragile bits of color performed a wild, glittering dance of chaos as they spiraled through the air, flashes of amber and rust and burnished gold, before settling softly to the forest floor. He'd always found a soothing, calming comfort in their flight, but all he could think of today was Torrance.

Last night, for the first time in his life, he'd watched a woman sleep. Watched the gentle rise and fall of her chest as she breathed—her features sleep soft and innocent. And it was a good thing she'd fallen asleep after shattering apart in his arms, because his beast had been just beneath the surface, prowling within the confines of his body, eager to claim its mate. Only, it wasn't just sex that it wanted. Even now, his gums burned as his fangs struggled to break free, eager to make the blood bond that would intertwine their lives together until one couldn't live without the other.

Touching her, feeling her pleasure rushing through her with the primal intensity of a summer storm, had been the most satisfying moment of his life—despite the painful fact that he still ached for his own release. Before it happened again, he obviously needed to set some ground rules for himself. Mating with her was one thing, but there wasn't a chance in hell he was going to let himself become some miserable jackass who couldn't breathe without his woman by his side. No matter how badly he wanted it, he was *not* making that bond with her.

And he refused to listen to the little voice in his head that continued to jeer at him, setting him on edge.

You're just afraid that she'll refuse you, Dillinger. Afraid that she'll run if she knows what you really want from her. Afraid of making yourself vulnerable…weak. Afraid of losing her forever—of ending up like your brother.

Christ, he didn't have time for this! He needed to keep his focus. Needed to keep his mind on the hunt for Simmons—and not the woman he'd left behind in his bed. And then maybe, once the threat to her life was removed, this driving urge to make a bond would recede. At least, he hoped it would. He just had to catch the bastard.

At the thought of the rogue, Mason's hands clenched atop the padded leather armrests of his chair, the tips of his fingers burning as his claws pricked beneath the thin barrier of his skin. Simmons had learned how to dayshift, and his followers had learned, as well. Mason kept trying to get his head around it, but every thought led to a new bend in the road, a fresh twist that only led to more questions. How? Why? What was the purpose? Did the strange scent on Simmons connect him to the killings that Brody and Cian were investigating? And why the hell couldn't they track the sharp, acrid aroma?

Something bad was coming. Something ugly. He knew it, deep down in his gut. And he'd trusted that feeling enough times to have faith in his instincts when it came to Bloodrunning.

When it came to Torrance…he was still at a loss.

Damn, he thought, dropping his head back against the soft, supple leather of his desk chair, staring up at the ceiling, the blank nothingness of the sandstone-colored plaster blurring before his dry eyes. His head spun with nothing but a never-ending feed of chaos, looping over and over and over.

A knock rattled the door, jerking him from his troubled thoughts, and Mason swiveled around in his chair to find Jeremy sticking his tawny head into the room. "Kid's awake. His name is Elliot Connors, he'll be eighteen next month, and he's Silvercrest. That's all he's spilled. He's pretty quiet, but I'd like to go ahead and see what we can get out of him."

"Yeah, me, too," Mason answered, leaning over to shut down his laptop.

From the doorway, Jeremy asked, "Did you get ahold of Dylan?"

Mason shook his head. "I tried, but no luck."

Dylan Riggs was the youngest member of the League of Elders and one of the few pack members Mason considered a friend. With his warm brown eyes and kind smile, many had thought the Lycan too soft to serve in a leadership role after the passing of his father, until he'd proven them wrong by defeating a string of challengers. Beneath his boyish exterior lived a hard warrior willing to fight for what he believed in.

He'd been an ally, as well as a friend to the Bloodrunners from the beginning—fighting for their cause when older members thought they could use the young half-breeds as little more than guard dogs for the pure-blooded members of the pack.

Dylan had spent the past few weeks visiting his younger sister in a remote part of Alaska. She'd moved up the year before as part of some existentialist movement—which meant no telephone. There wasn't even a cell phone tower within a hundred miles of the camp where she lived. Dylan was expected home anyday now, so Mason had given his cell a try—but there was still no answer. He hoped the Elder made it back soon, because he could use his insight, as well as Dylan's close connection to the pack. Simmons's ability to dayshift was worrying enough, but the fact that his followers possessed the ability, as well, struck a chord of terror deep in his gut.

Something was coming all right. And it wasn't good.

"Come on," he rasped, moving past Jeremy and into the hall, "let's see what Elliot Connors has to say."

Minutes later, Mason sat on the edge of the downstairs sofa, his hands clasped loosely between his thighs, while Jeremy stood with his back against the wall, the teenager huddled on one of the beds, his left wrist handcuffed to the heavy wooden headboard. Being a Lycan, he could have smashed the sturdy bed to pieces if he'd wanted, but not without making enough noise to wake the dead.

"You're Dillinger," the teenager stated in a flat, hard voice, his dark eyes cutting between him and Jeremy, as if he were waiting for one of them to attack. "I've heard about both of you. You're like legends. They say you keep Bloodrunning because you *like* to kill."

"If someone deserves to die, we have no problem taking them down," Mason answered honestly, scenting the fear on the boy; a cold, cruel sweat that covered the teenager's skin.

"But we're not here to kill you, Elliot. We *do* need you to talk to us, though. Answer some questions."

Elliot's dark gaze grew cautious, narrow with suspicion. "What do you wanna know?"

"We need to know about Simmons. Anything you can tell us about him."

"Don't you already know everything?" he hedged.

"The dayshifting, Elliot." Jeremy's voice came hard with impatience, and the teenager seemed to curl in on himself. Worry and fear were too evident in the tight lines of his expression, making him look older…run-down.

"What about it?"

"We need to know how you learned to dayshift. How Simmons learned it. And why it's screwing with our ability to track him by scent."

The teen shook his head from side to side, mouth grim with something that looked surprisingly like guilt—an uncommon emotion for a rogue Lycan. "I don't know," the boy mumbled, staring at his lap.

"Elliot, if you don't work with us, we can't…"

His head jerked up, face ruddy with color. "I don't remember. I don't want to remember! It was a freaking nightmare and I don't even wanna think about it!"

There was something here. Something that ran deeper than meat lust and evil. "You seem like a decent kid, Elliot. Why get mixed up with these assholes?"

The teenager's ragged breathing filled the room, harsh and gasping, as if he'd run uphill. "I didn't have a choice."

"We *always* have a choice," Jeremy countered.

"Whatever," Elliot muttered, his lip curling with attitude. "You gonna kill me now or what?"

"For whatever reason, you saved his mate's life," Jeremy told him, his tone dry, "so no, he's not going to kill you."

The boy eyed Jeremy with a bleak, distrustful stare. "What about you?"

"You're safe here," Mason assured him. "Neither one of us wants you dead, but we're going to need your help. You have to cooperate."

"I get it," he snorted. "You're gonna squeeze me for information or else. Right?"

The kid's animosity was blatant, in your face, but Mason couldn't blame him. He remembered exactly how it felt to be Elliot's age. Alone, full of anger, trying to find your place in the world. The teenager was a pure-blood, full pack—with all its rights and privileges. But that didn't mean he didn't have his own set of issues. Learning to deal with the animal half of your nature was difficult under the best of circumstances—traumatic at the worst.

Something told him that Elliot Connors had a good core, but had gone off course somewhere along the way. But until he knew for sure, he was keeping him under lock and key, not taking any chances.

And there was one thing more he still needed to know. "Have you gone over, Elliot?"

Dark eyes slid away, the kid's rangy body shifting nervously on the bed. "What do you mean?"

"You know what I mean. Have you fed? Taken down a human?"

Like a fragile flame snuffed out, the teenager's belligerent expression closed in on itself, leaving nothing but smoke in its wake. "I'm done talking," he muttered, barely moving his mouth. "You wanna torture me, go ahead. Otherwise, just leave me the hell alone."

Mason stood as he looked toward Jeremy, who gave a short nod of his head, both of them realizing that they'd gotten all they were going to get out of the boy for the moment. There were times when it was best to leave someone alone with their demons, and this was one of them. Elliot Connors was going to wear himself down faster than either of them could—without getting physical, which Mason wanted to avoid.

"If you'll give us your word not to cause trouble," Jeremy said, "we'll go ahead and take off the restraint."

"I'm not going anywhere," Elliot snorted, and Jeremy walked to the bed, taking a key from his pocket to undo the handcuff. Mason followed behind his partner as Jeremy headed up the stairs, but turned back on the second step, one hand on the rail. "Just one more question."

Elliot met his gaze, then shifted his angry stare to the wrinkled sheets on the bed. "Yeah?"

"Why did you save her life?"

He watched as Elliot swallowed, his Adam's apple bobbing in his throat, while his eyes squeezed shut. "I didn't know they were going after a girl," he said gruffly, opening his eyes to stare at his lap. His hands shook, and he fisted them, squeezing so tight that his knuckles turned white. "When I saw that creep Duff attack her—I didn't have any choice."

"You had a choice, Elliot. You could have let the bastard have her, but you didn't. And that's why I'm going to let you live," he told him, then headed up the stairs after Jeremy.

"I'm going to see if there's a game on and kick back for a while," his partner said, sounding worn-out, his face tight with strain as he made sure to lock the basement door. "God knows I need it after yesterday."

Feeling awkward, Mason forced himself to say, "I haven't told you thanks for sticking around here and keeping an eye on him."

A slow grin kicked up the corner of Jeremy's mouth. "No problem, man. I know you'd do the same for me. And we can't have you bunking with the boy wonder downstairs, when you've got a hot-blooded woman in your bed up here."

A short bark of laughter jerked from his throat, and he eyed the bite marks on Jeremy's neck, knowing the pain must have kept him awake for most of the night. "You sure you don't want to have Jillian take a look at you?"

"Yeah, I'm sure," his partner snorted, shaking his head. "Damn woman would probably get a kick outta torturing me. I'd just as soon save myself the pain."

Mason wanted to argue, but knew it was pointless. "I'm gonna check and see if Torrance is up yet, then take another look at my e-mail, see if anything new came up. I sent out some feelers to a few out-of-state Runners to see if they've ever heard of a Lycan being able to mask his scent the way Simmons did. Maybe someone will know something we don't."

Jeremy nodded, his expression thoughtful. "When Carter and Hennessey get here, we should try to come up with some kind of plan."

Looking at the locked door, Mason blew out a deep breath. "Maybe we'll be able to get some more out of Connors by then."

"I hope so." Jeremy sighed. "Because we've got nothing, and my gut is screaming that he's hiding something."

Like Goldilocks in the three bears' house, Torrance was sleeping in his bed when Mason found her. One touch on her arm, and she jerked awake with a start, pulling away from him the second she realized he was leaning over her, his warm hand brushing her hair back from her face. It wasn't his presence that startled her—but rather the immediate desire to pull him down on the bed with her and pick up where they'd left off in the night.

Jeez, Watson, you've got the willpower of a gnat.

Scooting a bit further away from temptation, she pushed her hair out of her eyes in time to see Mason slowly straighten away from the bed, then take a single step back, staring down at her with an unreadable expression. She watched as he ran one dark hand back through the reddish-brown waves of his hair, making her own palms itch to stroke the soft, thick strands. To tangle her fingers in their warm heat and pull him down for a scorching, breathtaking kiss.

"I didn't mean to scare you." His voice was hard, the stiff words shattering the heavy stillness that had settled between them. "After last night, I didn't think you would... Hell, not that it matters."

"I'm sorry...it's not that," Torrance whispered, pushing herself up until her back rested against the polished headboard. He didn't believe her, and she knew she was going to have to explain herself. He could have lied to her last night when she'd questioned him about how the mating thing would work, but he hadn't. He'd been honest with her, and now he deserved the same.

"I can smell the fear on you, Torrance," he stated flatly, as if he were working to hide his emotions—and she guessed that he'd had lots of practice at it.

Wrapping her arms around her knees, she pulled them into her chest and shook her head. "I know you think I'm still afraid of you...of what you are, but you're wrong, Mason. I realized this morning that I wouldn't have let you touch me like that if I didn't trust you." The steady sound of her voice amazed her, but she knew her cheeks had heated with a telling flush of color. "But after last night...I think it might be best if we just keep things...if we just stayed...friends. I don't think it'd be such a great idea if we got...involved."

The look he gave her was piercing, as if he were trying to figure her out, get into her head. "If you're not afraid, then what is it?"

Chewing on the corner of her lower lip, she said, "I'm just trying to protect myself from getting hurt."

"You think I'd hurt you?" he gritted through his teeth in a quiet snarl, clearly outraged. His brows lowered over the golden brown of his eyes, lending a fierceness to his expression that made her want to reach out and soothe him. She wanted to rub her thumb over the deep grooves between those thick brows and comfort him—but didn't dare.

"No," she told him, hating the way he was looking at her. "I know you wouldn't physically hurt me, Mason. You're a protector. But this connection between us is powerful, and I refuse to settle for less than…" She struggled for a way to explain, but all she could say was, "I just don't think it would be a good idea for us to take this any further. You're not a safe bet for someone like me."

With a slight nod, he said, "So this *is* because of what I am."

"No, it isn't," she argued, fisting her hands with frustration. "And I wish you'd stop turning my words around on me. You know what you're…like. I mean you're…you… God, Mason, all you have to do is look at me and I'm…I…"

He gave a rough laugh, the sound kind of cramped, as if he hadn't used the skill in a while. "If there's a compliment in there, Tor, I'm not sure I want to find it."

Pressing one hand to her chest, Torrance tried again. "I'm trying to tell you that this is because of who *I* am. I want more than a life built on good sex, Mason. And, yeah, it'd be good. I admit it. You touch me and I'm destroyed, okay? But that's not going to keep us happy the rest of our lives. That's not enough for me. We're too different."

"You mean you're human and I'm a nightmare?" he sneered, making a rude sound under his breath.

Her chin lifted at his tone. "I mean we want different things out of life. You don't want love, and I do."

"What the…" he muttered, shoving his hands deep in his pockets as he stood there with a poleaxed expression on his face. "Torrance, we only just met. Why the hell are we already talking about love?"

"Because this connection between us changes all the rules. I'm not trying to fight with you. I'm just trying to be honest about what I want out of life, the same way you were honest with me last night when I asked how this life-mate stuff works."

For a long moment he just stared down at her, a vein pulsing in his temple, and then he suddenly nodded again. "I get it now," he rasped. "You don't take any chances. You always push before you get pushed first. Is that it?"

"If it is," Torrance shot back, wishing she could make him understand, "all it means is that I learned a lesson the hard way. I spent my childhood watching my mother go through one pretty face after another, and when I was old enough to know what I wanted out of life, I made a decision to never settle for less than my dream."

"Your dream? What the hell does that mean?" he demanded, moving toward the foot of the bed, where he proceeded to pace back and forth, a sharp, resonating tension riding the hard length of his body. A white T-shirt stretched across his chest, muscular legs wrapped in a pair of clean, well-worn jeans, a night spent in bed making him look even better than he had yesterday—but then, Torrance was no longer viewing him with a touch of fear. Now, when she looked at him, she didn't want to run. No, all she wanted was to experience the touch of his hands, his mouth…his body.

Giving herself a sharp mental shake, Torrance searched for a way to explain something that was such a private part of her. "I'm talking about the dream of what I want in life. The kind of man that I'm looking for. One who can give me more than a pretty face and pleasure. Michaela blames it on all the romances I love to read, but…" She broke off, a sad smile twisting her mouth as she placed her hand over her heart. "It's more than that. It's something that I feel in here, Mason. Something that I need, and I'm not willing to settle for anything less. I want—"

"What?" he muttered, the word all but jerked out of his chest, brittle and snide. "A fairy tale?"

"I don't want a Prince Charming. I just… I just want my dream man."

"Yeah, and being a werewolf rules me out, no doubt," he grunted with a rough laugh, his tone bitter, while the air in the room all but skittered with the sparks of their argument—like their own little storm in the making.

"It has nothing to do with a man's physical appearance. It's an emotional thing. How he feels about me. I want a man who *loves* me, Mason. A man who…who wants me more than anything else. Not sex. Just…*me,*" she confessed with passionate conviction, willing him to understand. "Who wants to hold me as we watch the sunset. Who drinks coffee with me as we cuddle to watch the sunrise. Who holds me under the moonlight in his arms, because he just wants to be close to me. Who can smile and laugh and share his life with me, because he wants it. Because…because he loves me *most* of all."

He didn't say anything. Just stood there at the foot of the bed, no longer pacing, his hands still shoved deep in his pockets, the look on his rugged face a mixture of anger and frustration and something she couldn't identify.

"Do you understand?" she asked softly.

"Yeah," he breathed out on a rough burst of air, his jaw working. "I understand you want a goddamn paragon. When you grow up and want a man, let me know."

She flinched, his words striking her like a blow. "Well," she whispered, "if I want a man, then that rules you out, doesn't it? A real man isn't afraid to love something, Mason. He isn't afraid to open himself up and share that part of himself with someone else, no matter what his reasons are."

"Christ," he hissed under his breath, his head falling back as he glared at the ceiling. "I knew it. I knew the second I set eyes on you in that goddamn café that you were going to complicate the hell out of things."

"This is complicated with or without my help," she countered, not wanting things to stay like this between them. "It scares me, the thought of what I feel when I get close to you. This mating thing between us, it's drawing us together, and for you, that's enough. I'm trying to tell you, Mason, that for me, it wouldn't be. I can't disengage my emotions that way. I've tried before, trust me…and it doesn't work. What happened yesterday is proof of that. A few hours with you…and everything changed for me. I went from being terrified of you, to terrified *for* you, to…to what happened last night. It's never been that way for me before. And what we did was—"

"Not nearly enough," he finished in a raspy slide of words, eyes heavy-lidded as he lowered his head to stare back down at her, the sun pouring through the windows setting the auburn threads in his hair afire. "Hell, Torrance, it's never been that way for me before, either. A Lycan only finds one mate. *One.* I may not be wired for this love you're so set on having, but I can promise that I'll be faithful to you. Now that I've found you, I sure as hell wouldn't waste my time screwing around on you."

She would have loved to believe that, but she knew better. "I wish that could be enough for me," she whispered, the caving pain in her chest suddenly making her wonder if she was doing the right thing, "but it isn't. You can make promises, Mason, but without love, nothing will last, no matter how powerful. I'm just trying to save myself the heartache beforehand."

"You know what, Torrance? Life doesn't always come

packaged the way we want it. And no matter what you say, you trust me," he rasped. "You wouldn't have come last night if you didn't."

"I trust you with my body, Mason. Just not my heart. And I didn't want to fight with you. I was just trying to be honest," she said softly, gripping the pillow beside her and pulling it to her chest, as if it could protect her from the chilling look in his eyes. "You don't believe in love, and I won't settle for less. Why get into something when we already know how it's going to end?"

He cursed viciously under his breath as he turned and headed for the door. When he had one hand on the knob, he paused. "You know," he ground out, his back to her as he turned the handle, "between your goddamn dreams and nightmares, Torrance, it's like I can't win for losing."

With those softly snarled words lingering in the air between them, Mason walked out of the room.

Chapter 9

No matter how many ways Torrance ran it through her brain, she couldn't decide if she was doing the right thing by pulling away from Mason—or if she was screwing up her best chance at happiness.

Had she made the right choice, or had she panicked? She didn't know—and the connection between them made it impossible to reason things out, the driving physical need to be close to him destroying her ability to think clearly. Here they were, living in the same house, and yet so much separated them. Fears and hesitations over their pasts, as well their futures.

For the thousandth time that day, she asked herself why she couldn't just live in the present. The question drove her crazy while she whittled the hours away sorting through the boxes and suitcases that had been brought from her apartment. Thankfully, there was plenty of space in Mason's closet and empty drawers in his dresser, so she used those to store her clothes. It took forever, but she finally found her cell phone and its charger, which she plugged in beside the bed. Having nothing else to do to pass the time, she decided she'd had enough of hiding.

A quick run through her hair with her brush and slick application of her favorite lip gloss, and she headed toward the kitchen. When she stood just outside the archway, she found herself blinking in amazement, unable to believe the scene playing out before her. It was like some kind of testosterone-fest. On their own, Mason and Jeremy took up more than their fair share of space, both physical and emotional. They were just so big, their personalities so much larger than life. Always there was an air of energy, sharp-edged and powerful pulsing around them. You couldn't be near them and not feel affected... touched.

Bloodrunners were a potent hit on a woman's system—and now she was looking at *four* of them. Sometime during the hours she'd been keeping to herself in the bedroom, two more Runners had arrived.

Taking a deep breath, Torrance rubbed her damp palms against the tops of her thighs and walked into the sunlit kitchen. The intense splash of sunshine pouring in through the window had her lifting one hand to shield her eyes, while the Italian tiles warmed the soles of her feet. The low conversation that had filled the sunny room trailed off, four sets of eyes immediately zeroing in on her. Feeling like a shy, geeky child caught beneath the glaring flood of a spotlight at the annual Christmas pageant, Torrance shifted from foot to foot, managing to murmur a quiet, "Um, hi."

Jeremy flashed her his million-watt smile. "Hey, doll face."

"Torrance," Mason murmured, his tone cautious...and yet, somehow intimate. The connection between them burned electric and tangible on the air, so thick you could taste it—

and she knew the others noticed. "I'd like to introduce you to Brody Carter and Cian Hennessey. They work with me and Jeremy, and they both live here in the Alley."

She gave a little wave at the Runners, feeling awkward and self-conscious at being the center of attention.

The one named Brody was…intimidating, to say the least. He stood on the far side of the kitchen, leaning his broad shoulders against the wall, thumbs hooked in the front pockets of his blue jeans. A few inches taller than Mason, she knew she'd have to crane her neck at an impossible angle just to stare up at him, not that she was getting that close. His hair was a deep, dark auburn that fell softly to his shoulders, his almond-shaped eyes a beautiful shade of green, shades darker than her own, so that they probably looked black when the lighting was dark. Chiseled features formed a unique face, with a sharp nose and arrogant jawline. But his most distinguishing feature was his scar…or scars. Slashing from his left eyebrow, across the sharp bridge of his nose, down to the corner of his opposite jaw, three thin ridges marred the golden hue of his skin.

He looked…untouchable; and yet there was something about him that drew your eye again and again, a faint thread of vulnerability in those dark green eyes that told her he wasn't as scary as he looked.

His partner, in contrast, was a complete opposite. Lean and dark, with ink-black hair and piercing gray eyes, it was far too easy to believe Cian Hennessey had more than earned his reputation as a womanizing ladies' man. Even sitting in an arrogant slouch at the table, she could tell he was over six feet, like the others. But his body was rangier, roped with long, lean muscles, his cheekbones aristocratically crisp beneath skin a few shades paler than his friends, as if he didn't get out in the sun as often as his fellow Bloodrunners. He wore jeans and black boots, along with a dark gray T-shirt and an expensive-looking black leather jacket.

"Well isn't this a tasty little morsel," he drawled, and you could hear a trace of the Irish in his voice, his gray eyes turning smoky as he moved them slowly down her body from head to toe, then right back up again. "You've been holding out on us, boyo. For that sweet smile and innocent blush, I think I'd be willing to ignore the fact that she's your woman." He paused, eyeing her carefully as he drew in a deep breath, then softly added, "Though it seems you still haven't taken the final step. Interesting."

"What final step?" she asked, directing her question to Mason, who stood standing with his back against the counter, watching her through dark eyes that had so much going on behind them.

"Ignore him," he rasped, before turning a warning glare on his grinning friend. "Leave it alone, Hennessey."

"Touchy today, eh, Mase?" Cian murmured, arching one dark brow. "I know a bonded lass when I see one…and I know when one isn't."

Bonded? Torrance searched her brain for why that term sounded familiar, then remembered that Jeremy had used it when telling her about Mason's brother, referring to Dean and his wife Lori as a bonded couple. "What does that mean?" she asked again, noticing the curt shake of Mason's head; a wordless warning to his friends to remain quiet.

"Why don't you—"

"I'll explain it later, Torrance," Mason grunted, clearly wanting the topic dropped. "It isn't a conversation you want to be having right now, trust me."

She frowned at him, then realized that he was probably right. If it was personal, she didn't want to hear the explanation when in the company of three other men.

Tucking her hair behind her ear, she moved closer to Mason, aware that Cian continued to watch her with a heavy-lidded look in his pale gray eyes. They should have looked cold with such an icy color, but they burned instead with a raw, smoldering heat as he studied her features one by one, lingering on her mouth until she nervously chewed on the corner of her lip. Flashing her a seductive smile that had probably never failed to get him exactly what he wanted, he said, "You know, if you're not Dillinger's yet, sweetheart, then maybe you should be mine."

She should have told him to stuff his cocky arrogance up his backside, but found herself laughing softly instead, unable to hold back a wry smile at his outrageous behavior. "You really do live up to your reputation, don't you, Hennessey?"

He inclined his head with a slight, arrogant nod that should have looked old-fashioned, but somehow fit him perfectly. "Call me Cian, *mo ghrá.*"

Mason growled under his breath. "She is *not* your love, you Irish ass."

"She could be if she wanted."

"I'm afraid I'm swearing off men for the moment," she drawled over her shoulder, reaching up to grab a mug from one of the cabinets. When she had her coffee, she settled beside Mason, just in time to see Cian send him a deliberate scowl. He nodded his dark head in understanding, a lock of ink-black hair falling across the smooth perfection of his brow. "Yes, Dillinger does seem to have that effect upon the opposite sex more often than not," he remarked dryly.

Jeremy snorted softly under his breath, Mason made another low growling noise that vibrated in his chest like thunder, and, sensing that things were about to get off track, Brody spoke up for the first time since she'd entered the room. "So what did your houseguest have to say?" he asked, his low voice a little scratchy, but warm and soothing, like a fine French brandy.

Taking a seat on the countertop beside the stainless steel sink,

Jeremy said, "Well, according to the boy wonder downstairs, Simmons has been a busy little bee, recruiting more than his fair share of the brokenhearted, the downtrodden, the hopelessly—"

"Christ, just give us an answer," the Irishman grunted from his seat at the table, growing impatient.

Jeremy snickered, obviously enjoying the buttons he'd deliberately pushed. "It seems our pal Simmons has decided to start his own little gang of friendly neighborhood psychopaths, this one bent on human destruction."

"More like consumption," Torrance murmured, shivering at the thought.

"That, too," Mason added grimly.

"Yeah," Jeremy drawled. "You know what rogues say about humans being the 'other white meat.'"

"You're sick and wrong, you know that?" Hennessey muttered with a rough laugh, smiling as he hurled the insult.

"I prefer *twisted* myself," Jeremy said lightly, his head tilted at an arrogant angle, the corner of his mouth raised in an endearingly crooked grin.

"More like screwed," Mason grumbled, sounding irritated as hell.

"I wish," the blond snorted, waggling his tawny brows. "Too much damn hunting lately, and not enough time to bless the ladies with my charming presence."

"So many ladies, so little time." Cian's straight teeth flashed brilliant and white as his mouth curved in a provocative smile. Beneath his breath, he began humming a familiar tune.

"I swear to God, Hennessey, if you start singing Julio Iglesias again," Brody grated, his scowl downright frightening, "I won't be responsible for what I do."

"Looks like I'm getting on Broody Brody's nerves again,"

Cian chuckled, clucking his tongue while his gray eyes glittered with humor.

Shaking her head at their crazy banter, Torrance turned a questioning look toward Jeremy. "Are they always like this?"

"This is a good day. Normally they just don't get along," he told her, his tone dry.

"He sang that damn song for hours last night while we dealt with your mess," Brody grumbled, a menacing look on his face as he shoved one huge hand back through his hair. "I swear I thought I was going to snap."

Cian shrugged his broad shoulders in a "What are you going to do?" gesture. "You know Brody. I'm good for his blood pressure. Keeps him from brooding too much, focusing on the negative."

"Yeah," Mason remarked with a sharp snort of laughter, "you just keep him focusing on ways to kill you."

"What are friends for?" The Runner sighed, that sinful mouth curving in a wicked expression that could have given Lucifer a run for his money. "So, tell me, boyo. Now that you've met your mate, will you keep hunting?"

"Damn right, I will," he replied, shoving one hand into his front pocket, his coffee held in the other, ankles crossed as he rested his weight against the counter. "You guys wouldn't be able to find your asses without me. But Jeremy and I will be sticking close to home from now on."

Cian arched one raven brow. "Leaving us with the wanderers, eh? So that you can stay at home with the little woman. How endearing."

Mason sent him a hard grin. "Just think of it as an opportunity to broaden your bounty of women."

"There is that," the Irishman murmured, saluting Mason as he rocked the chair back on its hind legs, balancing at a precarious angle.

"Did anything new come up in Delaine?" Mason asked, brushing her arm as he reached around her to grab a cookie from the pack sitting on the counter, that simple touch leaving chills in its wake. Torrance was so wrapped up in the idea of him wanting to stay close to home now, because of her, that she almost lost the thread of conversation.

"Nothing," Cian replied, drumming the long fingers of his right hand atop the deep luster of the kitchen table. "Not a damn thing. Whatever is going on with the killer's scent, it's impossible to track."

Brody shrugged. "We've both got a bad feeling about it. And after what you told me on the phone about that strange odor Simmons was giving off, we don't know what to think. But there's no trace of rogue musk anywhere at either of our scenes to identify him. Just that noxious vinegar smell."

"It's all connected somehow," Mason said, his dark brows pulled together in a worried frown. "Simmons's scent was muted, almost covered by that acidic odor. But we could still tell it was him when we got close enough. Maybe he's only just learning how to master it."

"And maybe someone else already has," Brody murmured, carrying on with his line of reasoning.

"Yeah," Cian rasped. "And whoever it is, they're our killer."

"If this thing gets too deep, I can always call in another team from one of the neighboring packs to help you out until Jeremy and I are free. There's more than a few who owe us the favor."

"Not yet," Cian told him, shaking his head, his long hair brushing the leather-covered width of his shoulders, the raven strands looking almost blue beneath the bright glare of sunshine pouring over him. "If it gets to the point we need backup, I'll let you know. But the fewer who know about this, I think, the better. And speaking of hunts, what has Simmons had to say?"

he asked. "You were telling us about his call when this red-headed little beauty walked in."

"My name is Torrance," she drawled, rolling her eyes when he winked at her. The guy obviously got a kick out of pushing his friends' buttons, but you couldn't help but like him.

"Simmons hasn't spouted anything but bullshit," Mason muttered, shifting closer until his arm pressed against hers. "All he's done is ramble on about becoming some kind of god. His usual narcissistic crap."

"What about his number?" Brody asked. "I suppose he wasn't kind enough to give us something we could use to locate him."

Jeremy shook his head. "It came up as a private listing. He's too smart to make this easy. He's gonna make us work for it."

"What we need is a computer whiz," the redheaded Runner murmured. "You know, one of those pasty fellows who lives in his basement and only comes up for air when he needs a new hard drive."

Cian turned his head toward his partner. "And we need one of those why?"

Brody lifted one shoulder. "If we had a computer genius, maybe we could have traced the call."

"If we're going to start collecting people," Jeremy snorted, "I'd vote for a priest to save Hennessey's immortal soul."

Sharp barks of laughter filled the sunny kitchen, and Torrance couldn't help but get the feeling that she'd missed an inside joke. Still, she felt…at home. It seemed amazing that she felt so comfortable standing there drinking coffee in a roomful of werewolves, but she did. Only two days ago she'd been worrying about whether or not she should start writing the short story she'd been playing around with in her head…or focus on going back to school instead. And now those old worries seemed so insignificant, paling in comparison to this new, vivid, breathtaking reality that had wrapped around her, pulling her in, altering the way she viewed…everything. Life. Love. Friendship.

"So why Simmons?" Brody asked, pulling her out of her thoughts. "Why now?"

Jeremy took a sip of his coffee, cradling the dark blue mug in his palms as he said, "If you're going to declare a war, start at the top—and Mason has been a Bloodrunner longer than any of us. Simmons knew if he went rogue, that Mason would be the one to come after him."

Brody nodded his agreement. "They mean to cut off the head of the snake."

"The head of the snake?" she repeated, unfamiliar with the analogy.

"Military strategy," Jeremy explained. "You want to take a unit down, start at the top and destroy it from there. Mason has been a Bloodrunner the longest, which means he's probably one of the most powerful—"

"Key word there being *probably,*" Cian cut in, winking at her again.

"And anyone who's Silvercrest knows that Mase is the one who would be assigned to take him down," Brody added. "They have a…history."

Yeah, she knew all about their history.

"So the idea, then, is to draw Mase into a hunt and eliminate him, weakening our strength, while letting Simmons get his revenge for his brother at the same time. Like killing two birds with one stone. But where exactly does Simmons fit into the grand scheme?" Jeremy mused, scratching the side of his nose. "Is he heading it…or is he just a bottom-feeder?"

Brody rubbed his chin. "I think he's a recruiter. Who better to lure kids like this Elliot than someone who is willing to get them what they want? Women. Drugs. Name your vice, and Simmons can supply it."

"So you think he's just one arm of a bigger monster?" Mason grunted.

"Yeah. But then the question becomes how many arms are we looking at?"

Mason nodded, a deadly look of intent in his dark eyes. "And who's at the head?"

"Who knows?" Jeremy muttered. "The walls holding the pack together are crumbling down around us, and here we are, left in the goddamn dark."

"Maybe the boy can shed some more light on things," Cian murmured, linking his muscular arms behind his head.

"We've tried to get him to talk." Jeremy sighed. "He's definitely hiding something, but we can't get any more out of him."

"I bet Cian could," Brody suggested, but Jeremy shook his head.

"Scaring him shitless isn't going to help," the blond snorted.

Torrance didn't know what he meant by *that,* and she wasn't sure she wanted to. The irreverent Irishman was giving her another smoldering stare, and putting Mason in a royal snit, if the look on his face was anything to go by.

"That's enough, Hennessey," he growled in the next moment, obviously losing his patience.

"Not nearly," the other man drawled lightly, earning a low, sinister snarl for his taunting response.

"No fighting until we get this solved," Brody warned, glaring at both men.

Hating feeling useless and wanting to be able to help, Torrance cleared her throat and spoke up. "Why don't you let me talk to Elliot?"

"What?" The word blasted from Mason's grim mouth, as harsh as the cracking sound of his coffee mug slamming onto the kitchen counter.

"No offense," she told him, gesturing toward the others,

"but you're all a pretty intimidating lot. He might feel more comfortable spilling something personal to me than he would to one of you."

Cian nodded thoughtfully, studying her with a piercing gaze. "She has a point. He'd probably find it easier to talk to a woman, and whatever he's hiding has likely been bottled up for so long, it's just waiting to bust out."

"No way," Mason growled.

"Why not?" she asked, her instincts telling her it was the right thing to do, even though she was nervous at the prospect. After all, the kid was a werewolf—but then so were all these men, and she felt perfectly safe with them. Torrance couldn't explain it, but she wasn't going to bother denying it either. She *did* feel safe with them. And Elliot had saved her life.

"Why?" Mason repeated, running one hand through his hair in a blatant act of frustration. "Because I don't want you anywhere near him!"

"He already helped save my life," she argued gently. "What do you think he's going to do?"

He remained silent, glaring, but she didn't back down. "Please, Mason. Just let me talk to him. I'd like to be able to help."

"No way in hell," he muttered, shaking his head...but now that she'd set her mind to it, Torrance wasn't about to give up.

Moments later, Mason was grudgingly taking her down the stairs, the others waiting in the kitchen. Torrance shoved her trembling hands in her front pockets, not wanting to look nervous in front of the young Lycan, but when she walked into the warm, soothing room and he turned a pair of deep brown eyes on her, she couldn't control the small gasp that rushed past her lips. She knew that he was, in essence, one of the bad guys, one of the creatures from her nightmares, but the sight of him broke her heart.

He was...beautiful; a fallen-angel kind of beautiful. Thick, caramel-colored hair fell to his shoulders, framing a face saved from being too pretty by a hawk nose and square chin. Those brown eyes studied her from beneath heavy lashes, and there was too much pain in that solemn, watchful gaze. Too much grief and regret…too much worry and fear.

He still had the youthful lankiness of his age, hovering there on the cusp of adulthood. No longer really a boy, and yet, not quite a man. But he was obviously carrying a man's guilt, and she wanted to help him, the same way that he'd helped her. There was just something about him that drew her to him.

"Hi, Elliot," she said softly, sitting down at the end of his bed. "My name is Torrance."

"Hey." His voice was quiet, his expression guarded, haunted gaze flicking nervously from her to Mason and back again.

"I wanted to thank you for saving me yesterday. It was an extremely brave thing for you to do."

"Torrance—"

"Be quiet, Mason," she said, cutting him off, "or you can go back upstairs."

He made a low growling noise in response, which she ignored, keeping her attention on the teenager. "I know what it's like to find yourself in the middle of something that overwhelms you, Elliot. Until a few days ago, I thought I had a good grasp on everything—and then in the blink of an eye, all of it changed. Life has a way of doing that to people."

"Yeah," he rasped, the look in his dark eyes so full of pain, she wanted to cry for him—for whatever horror it was that was tearing him apart.

"I know you talked a bit to Mason and Jeremy about Simmons, but I think there's something you're keeping to yourself. There's something more, isn't there?"

He swallowed, his gaze glassy. But he didn't say no.

"Did something happen?" she asked gently. He did a kind

of full-body tremor, but kept quiet, huddling back into the corner, where the bed had been pressed up against the wall. "To someone you care about?"

"No," he said thickly. "I...I didn't even know her."

Torrance curled her leg under her body, folding her hands in her lap. "It might make you feel better, Elliot. To talk about it."

"I can't." His eyes screwed shut, voice full of anguish...and regret. "It was... I can't."

"If you don't let it out and ask for help, how do you know that it won't happen again?"

He lowered his head, cradling it between his palms, his fingers digging into his scalp so hard that she winced. "I don't want to think about it. I...I didn't mean to do it, but he told me that I might end up hurting Marly if I didn't learn control first."

He was talking, which they'd wanted. And yet Torrance knew that she didn't want to hear this—that it was going to tear her up inside. But it had to be done.

Taking a deep breath, she asked, "Who's Marly? Is she a girl you like, Elliot?"

"Yeah. She's— God, what does it matter?" he muttered, looking away, staring at the wall. "She'll never have anything to do with me now."

"Is she part of your pack?"

He swallowed so hard, she could see the movement in his throat. "I don't have a pack anymore."

Torrance waited, giving him time to work it out, watching him fiddle with a hole in the knee of the jeans Jeremy had given him. "She's human. I met her at a concert. She's small, like you," he added, flicking a quick look up at her, before cutting his gaze back to the torn fabric on his knee. "But her hair is blond, almost white, and she has big blue eyes. She's so perfect and tiny, like a little doll. God, I was so afraid of what would happen when I tried to…you know. Afraid that I might want to change in the middle of it." He blew out a rough, shaky breath, and Torrance cast a quick look over at Mason, who was watching them with a closed expression that gave nothing away. She wondered if, like her, he felt the same sense of dread twisting his insides, but turned her attention back to Elliot.

Pulling at one of the frayed edges, he started unraveling the coarsely woven denim. "I didn't know anyone to ask about how to, you know…be with a human girl. So a friend of mine said he knew this guy who could help me." He swallowed, rubbing both palms over his knees, then crossed his arms, hunching deeper into the corner as he muttered, "So I went with him."

Keeping her voice gentle, she asked, "Did he take you to Simmons?"

"Yeah. At this warehouse down in Covington. There were other Lycans there, kids I recognized from both my pack and some of the nearby ones. And this Simmons guy is there, telling us that if we trust him, he can show us how to control our beasts. That he can teach us enough control to take human girls without hurting them—even how to dayshift. All of it. So I went back a few times, and then one night, after we met, he asked me to go with him, told me that he had a surprise for me."

"Where did you go?"

"I don't even know where they took me," he rasped, shaking now. "I can't remember anything about that night except for what happened later."

"It's okay, Elliot. You can tell us, and we'll try to help you through it."

"Simmons had told me that if I joined up with him, he could teach me how to control myself, so that I could be with a girl like Marly. Like an idiot, I'd told him about her, telling him why I wanted to learn more. He said he'd help me, but that I first had to learn how to have sex with a more experienced woman while in control of my wolf."

"And so you tried?"

His cheeks were flushed a brilliant crimson within the ghostly pallor of his face, his breathing rapid and shallow. "Yeah, only…"

The room went silent, nothing but the slow, inexorable ticking of the clock on the wall to mark the passage of time. "What happened?"

He shook his head, his body beginning to rock in a gentle back-and-forth motion. "I can't tell you. You'll think I'm a monster."

"Whatever it is, it isn't your fault. I think you were set up by this Simmons jerk. Manipulated by him, Elliot, because he wanted you on his side. If you tell me, it might make you feel better."

"Yeah?" he snorted. "You won't think so after I tell you."

"Try me," she offered.

"I killed her."

The three words blasted into the room with the force of a bullet, jolting her.

"Why?" Torrance kept her voice soft and easy, even while dread twisted her stomach into a painful, churning knot.

He took a deep, trembling breath, and then the words just tumbled out of his mouth, ragged and hoarse with emotion. "She wasn't experienced, like Simmons said. I thought I had all this control, after what he'd shown me. I thought I could keep my wolf under wraps if I wanted, right? I think they must have given her something, because she was really coming on to me. She didn't act innocent. She acted like…like she knew what she was doing. But, she…she bled when I went in…and it was— I don't… I don't know how it happened. All I know is that I lost it and I changed. There was blood everywhere. On the bed, the walls, in my mouth. And she was… Oh, Jesus, it was a nightmare. I totally freaked, and someone knocked me out. Some guy named Curry, I think. When I came to, they told me that I'd killed her and I couldn't go back to the pack. That Simmons had turned rogue and I'd have to join up with them."

Reaching out to him, Torrance took his hand, his fingers cold and damp as they clutched on to her like a lifeline. "Elliot, I'm so sorry."

He flinched at the words, staring at her through red, desolate eyes. "Why are you sorry?"

"Because they used you as much as they used that girl," she told him. And then, as gently as possible, she said, "Where's Marly now?"

His eyes slid closed, fingers pulling away from her hold as he wrapped his arms around his middle. "I don't know. I think they told her something bad about me, because she stopped taking my calls and never called me back."

"Do you think you were in the mountains?" Mason asked. "Or still down in the city?"

"I don't know." He opened his eyes, his gaze haunted as he looked toward Mason. "I don't want to remember."

"So you've been staying with them," she murmured, "because you thought you had no choice."

"They told me I was one of them now. That I'd killed and had to face the consequences. The laws…"

Mason spoke quietly from his place against the wall. "Just forget the laws right now, Elliot."

"Are you going to kill me?"

He made a sharp sound of disgust. "We don't murder children."

The boy's chin lifted, his jaw hard. "I'm not a child."

"What happened, it will take time for you to get over—but it wasn't your fault, Elliot. Simmons played you, and got exactly what he wanted."

"I killed her," Elliot grated, the words raw with anger and loathing. "I murdered her. For that, I *should* die."

"That's not true," Torrance said with firm conviction. "No matter what they did, it didn't change you, Elliot. You're still a good person. You didn't let them hurt me, did you?"

"I couldn't," he groaned, his voice cracking with emotion as he moved his gaze to her face. He stared at her, the look in his eyes making her shiver, and quietly said, "You... You reminded me of Marly."

They came up the stairs a few moments later, understanding that Elliot needed some time alone. Mason had hoped to get her aside so that they could talk, but Torrance immediately headed for the bedroom, murmuring that she wanted a shower. Not that he could blame her. Elliot's horrifying story left an ugly coat of disgust on your skin that made you want to scrub yourself clean. Mason hadn't thought he had any sympathy to give to someone who'd fallen into Simmons's clutches, but something in his gut hurt for the young man who'd been so obviously traumatized by what had happened to him. The guilt was eating Elliot inside out. It was tragic and infuriating—and it made Mason want to get his hands on Simmons and wipe the earth clean of his filth once and for all.

He just had to find him.

Rubbing at the knots of tension in the back of his neck, he found the others waiting for him in the kitchen and filled them in on what Elliot had confessed downstairs. Afterward, he escaped to his office to check his e-mail again, but so far none of his sources had anything to report. He hadn't thought Simmons would head back down to Covington, but he'd wanted to cover his bases just in case. And none of the Runners he'd e-mailed had anything for him, either. He had one call on his cell from Pallaton that he returned, and then, thinking he'd given Torrance enough time alone, he headed toward his bedroom.

Before he could open the door, Mason heard her talking and realized two things at once: she was on the phone with someone. And she was upset.

"I don't know what I'm doing here, Mic. It's so confusing. I want him so badly, but I'm afraid of getting too close to him. I mean, there's no way he's going to let himself feel something for me, so I know I should step back and save myself the heartache—but this mating thing between us just keeps pulling on me, making me want to throw myself at him." She paused, probably listening to Michaela on the other end of the connection, then softly said, "I'm glad he was honest about it, too, but it still sucks. And I don't think there's any chance of him changing. It's tearing me apart, not knowing if I'm making the right choice by trying to keep my distance or if I'm just screwing everything up."

"Son of a bitch," he cursed under his breath, her words making him feel like a world-class jackass. Why couldn't she just be satisfied with what he *could* give her. Why did she have to insist on an idiotic ideal that he knew he was never going to be able to offer her? It was like trying to hammer a square peg into a round hole. No matter how hard he tried, the fit just wasn't there—and the knowledge was enough to make him want to turn and slam his fist into the wall.

Why did everything have to be so bloody complicated?

Three days ago his life had been simple. Hunt...and kill. In between, food and the occasional woman when his body needed the release. His friends and his family. Easy and straightforward, he'd known his way through every situation like clockwork. Known what to do...and how to do it to achieve the desired results. And now he couldn't even handle one delicate, beautiful little human, who just so happened to possess a bit of backbone.

With his hands shoved deep in his pockets, Mason forced

himself to walk away, moving silently down the hall. He'd heard enough. Anything else and he'd be throwing open the bedroom door and— Hell, he didn't know what he would do. What else was there to say? No, he couldn't deal with it right now. Until he got Simmons and she was safe, nothing could change. He didn't even want it to, he reminded himself with a surly growl. He didn't want to lose his heart to her. He just wanted to have her, *all of her,* and still be able to protect himself at the same time.

Mason stopped instantly in his tracks, nearly stumbling over his own feet as his mind snagged on that particular phrase.

All of her.

He played it over again, dissecting it, looking at it from every angle, until the truth finally slammed into him so hard he slumped to the side, just like a drunk whose legs wouldn't hold him up. Propped against the wall, Mason stared sightlessly at the floor, his brain buzzing with the stunning, earth-shattering revelation.

He wanted her heart.

Oh, yeah, he thought, shaking his head. He was a contrary bastard, but there was no denying it. He wanted Torrance to love him. Wanted it more than he'd ever wanted anything in his entire life—and it scared the holy living hell out of him. Needing something to calm the jittery feeling in his gut, he headed for the kitchen and found Jeremy standing at the sink, sipping from a cup of coffee as he stared out at the forest. "Want a cup?"

"No, thanks," he rasped, wondering when his voice had started sounding like a gravel pit. "Keep going the way you are with that coffee and you're going to end up a caffeine addict. That must be your tenth cup of the day."

"I'm already a caffeine addict." Jeremy laughed without looking away from the idyllic view. "Now I just feed the addiction."

"Well, I need something stronger," he muttered, opening the pantry to pull out a bottle of Jack. "Where did Brody and Cian go?"

"They headed home to get a few hours' sleep. I don't think they got much last night after dealing with the mess we left in the woods."

"They better sleep while they can." He poured two fingers into a glass and tossed back a sharp, satisfying swallow of the whiskey as he planted himself in one of the chairs. "I have a feeling things are gonna start happening fast."

Turning away from the window, Jeremy sent a critical glance at the dark amber liquid in his glass. "She driving you to drink already?"

A hard, jagged sound jerked from his throat, and Mason lowered his head, watching the hypnotic swirl of the whiskey as he rolled his glass between his hands, elbows planted on his spread knees. "Driving me outta my ever-loving mind," he muttered, before tossing back another long, satisfying swallow, enjoying the burn as it seared down his throat, settling hot and smooth in his gut.

Hitching himself up on the tiled counter, Jeremy took a slow sip of coffee. "You know what your problem is, Mase?"

Yeah, he knew what his problem was. His problem was five feet, four inches of irresistible, addictive female that had him so tied up in emotional knots, he felt like a friggin' ball of string. "Something tells me you're going to be a pal and spell it out for me," he said, the resignation in his tone unmistakable.

"That's right, because you're like a brother to me. I'm not going to stand by and watch you wreck the best damn thing that's ever happened to you because you're too chickenshit to open your eyes to what's going on." Finishing off his coffee, Jeremy set the empty mug in the sink, scratched at the golden stubble on his chin, then crossed his arms over his chest. "Did you see all those books she had in her apartment?"

"What about 'em?" he drawled, leaning back in his chair, one hand curled around the glass of whiskey as he rested it on the table, the other lying indolently across his stomach.

A small smile hovered at the edge of Jeremy's mouth. "They were all fantasies, dude. Romances."

"Your point?"

"She's a dreamer, Mase."

"Yeah," he grunted, tossing back another deep swallow of the whiskey. "And we're the nightmare."

Jeremy shook his head, his hazel eyes piercing. "That's not what I'm saying, man."

Frustration roiled through his gut, keeping company with the slow burn of the whiskey. "If you're trying to tell me something, then for God's sake, just say it."

"She believes in *love,*" his partner shot back in a rough blast of words, clearly losing his patience. "In happily-ever-afters and till death do you part. Stop selling yourself short, because the woman is already nuts for you. Hell, she was *made* for you. You think you can overcome this as easily as you've managed everything else. But guess what? You *can't.* This isn't just another asinine rule that pisses you off. This is something that grabbed you and Torrance by the throat, something deeper and more powerful than any pain-in-the-ass law the pack could ever have come up with. You can't twist it to fit your terms."

"You're not telling me anything I don't already know. And at the risk of repeating myself," he growled, "this is pretty rich coming from you."

Jeremy hopped off the counter, angry tension riding the hard lines of his body as he began pacing the length of the kitchen. "Why the hell do you think I know what I'm talking about, Mase? You need to get your head out of your butt and take some advice for a change. Let go of the past, of what happened with Dean, and grab hold of what you've been given. Don't hold yourself back, because it's going to eat you up inside. It's going to sink into your cells like a cancer and never let you go. You'll lose her, man, and then you're going to be totally screwed."

"Like you?" he sneered, irritated to be put on the spot, even though he knew Jeremy was speaking the truth.

His partner stopped pacing, the look in his hazel stare shadowed and bleak as he nodded his head. "Yeah, like me," he muttered.

"Sooner or later, Burns, you're going to have to—" The metallic tones of Mason's cell phone rang out, interrupting him.

"You better answer that."

A quick look at the screen revealed the caller's name. "Yeah. It's Hennessey. Wonder what the hell he wants." Pressing the call button, Mason lifted the phone to his ear. "Missing us already?"

"If Burns is there with you, you better put the speaker on." The Irishman's tone was grim, all business, putting Mason on instant alert.

Setting the phone on the table, he hit the speaker button. "Okay, what've you got?"

"When we left there, I got a call on my cell from Lydia Clarkson. She's a schoolteacher up in Shadow Peak."

Jeremy moved closer, jerking his chin toward the phone. "Wasn't she the pure-blood you were nailing last year?"

"Six months ago," Cian corrected him. "But believe it or not, we're still friends. Anyway, she was out hiking near the Alley, over on Clausen Ridge, when she came across something she thought we'd want to know about, so Brody and I figured we'd go ahead and come over to check it out."

"What is it?" Mason muttered, not liking the heavy feeling mixing in his gut.

"We've got another body," the Irishman said tightly. "Similar to the case we're already on."

His partner's breath made a sharp, whistling sound between his compressed lips. "Jesus! You mean the heart was eaten out?"

"Yeah, but there's more. It's an ugly scene. We're talking seriously whacked-out stuff. I know you don't want to leave the little woman right now, Dillinger, but you're really going to want to see this for yourself."

"Hell," he rumbled, rubbing the backs of his fists into his eyes so hard that sparks burned against the darkness of his mind. "Okay. I should be there within fifteen."

"We'll be waiting."

Mason disconnected the call, then ran his hands back through his hair, the uneasy weight settling deeper into his gut, warning him that this was going to be bad.

"I've got a bad feeling about this," Jeremy muttered, his voice low—seconding his own feelings. "Seriously, man," his partner grunted, his expression hard as he leaned his hip against the edge of the table, hands shoved deep in his pockets. "This is all getting a little too close to home."

"Which is why I need you to stay here, Jeremy." He knew the Runner wasn't going to like it, but there wasn't any other choice. He couldn't—he *wouldn't*—leave Torrance unprotected. And someone needed to keep an eye on Elliot.

"I don't like being the damn watchdog," Jeremy grunted, his expression twisted into a hard scowl.

Mason stood up and took his empty glass to the sink, then grabbed the bottle of Jack, stashing it back in the pantry. "Until you're a hundred percent, you're not setting foot out of the Alley. And you know there's no one else I can trust to watch over them."

"All right, all right. Whatever." He sighed. "But you owe me big-time, you bastard."

Mason arched one brow. "Don't I always?"

"Yeah," Jeremy muttered. "But this time, I'm collecting. Better watch it, or the next thing you know, you're gonna be buying me a new set of tires for my truck. Big, shiny off-roaders. Top o' the line."

"You're letting me off easy, Burns," he shot back with a gruff laugh. "You want tires, and here I was thinking of sending you to a tropical-island paradise with some half-naked beach bunnies. Might as well make use of the time you're gonna have off when this crap is over and Torrance and I can finally take our honeymoon."

Jeremy's head jerked up, a satisfied smile kicking up the corner of his mouth. "So you're gonna stop being a jackass and make a blood bond with the girl?"

Snatching up his cell, Mason hooked the phone back on its clip, then walked into the living room, pulling a heavy, brown leather jacket out of the entryway closet. Jeremy followed right on his heels, waiting for an answer. "I don't need to bond with her just to marry her," he said in a low voice. "And even if I wanted to, which I don't, do you really think she'd go for the idea of my fangs sinking into her throat? You know how she feels about Lycans. She'd probably slap my face if I even sug-gested it."

From the corner of his eye, he watched his partner shake his head in quiet regret. "Man, you really are chickenshit. You know that?"

"Watch it, Jeremy," he snorted, slipping into the jacket. "You know what they say about stones and glass houses."

"Yeah, I know," Jeremy grunted, his tone thick with frustra-tion. "But if you ask me, you're not giving her enough credit. If she loves you, she'll accept a blood bond. Hell, if she loves you, she'll even *want* it."

"And if she doesn't, she'll try to run again." After all, she hadn't said that she loved him—only that she was afraid of loving him and that love not being returned.

"It'll be a cold day in hell before you let her do that," Jeremy muttered. "Now go on and get the hell outta here. And watch your back."

Mason didn't want to go. On the other hand, the fresh air might do his head some good. Help him sort out the tangled mess screwing with his mind—all of it centered on a tempestuous little redhead he was terrified of losing.

"When you see Torrance, tell her I'll be back later," he called out over his shoulder. Then Mason grabbed up his keys and headed out into the quiet darkness of the night.

Chapter 10

The mountain air was brisk, his breath forming a white mist as Mason moved in a slow circle, studying the scene with a hunter's trained eye—while his human half raged against the injustice of the crime. Like something torn from the pages of a horror novel, complete with the blood and gore and thick, suffocating scent of blood and meat, it was a grizzly scene. And yet, strangely ordered. He'd seen death and destruction so many times, but this was different. Ritualistic, without the normal frenzy of a killing rage. He knew what happened when those of his kind let their beast's hunger for the hunt get the better of them, allowing that dark wall of rage to overcome their morality, their understanding of right and wrong. That wasn't what he and the others were looking at here.

No, this had been planned. Followed through. Executed. This had been about something other than meat lust. Something darker, even more frightening, and it scared the daylights out of him.

From Brody and Cian's grim expressions, they weren't faring much better.

Bending his knees, Mason grabbed up a handful of dirt, lifting the humid soil to his nose. He sniffed, and an acrid scent burned his nasal passages, making his eyes water. "Is this the same scent you found with the other bodies?"

Rubbing at the back of his neck with one hand, Brody waved the other toward the ground. "Not quite, but then we're dealing with a whole group here. There are footprints all over the place. All Lycan. I'd guess she's been dead for a few hours, which means she was killed sometime this afternoon."

"And that means they were dayshifters."

"Yeah, but only *one* killer." Cian leaned his long, rangy form back against the rough trunk of a pine, his gray eyes glowing eerily bright in the deepening shadows of the evening. "This wasn't an eating frenzy. This was cold-blooded butchery."

Brody nodded, blowing out a deep breath. "So the others were here for the show?"

"That would be my guess," Cian drawled, uncrossing his arms to reach for his pack of cigarettes. A few moments later he had one lit, its smoldering tip burning with a flickering orange smear of color, like an unblinking eye watching them from the fiery depths of hell. "The question is, was Simmons part of the crowd, or the main event?"

"My gut says it was Simmons." Unbending his knees, Mason pushed back the sides of his jacket, shoving his hands into the front pockets of his jeans. "Have you found any kind of identification? Her purse? Wallet?"

"Nothing," Brody grunted. "I searched the area while we were waiting for you, but I couldn't even find her clothes."

Cian's glittering gaze slipped over the brutalized remains of the woman, the usual sarcastic curve of his mouth replaced by something that looked suspiciously like compassion. "I bet she was a pretty little thing," he said softly, before pulling in another long drag of smoke.

Mason reached for his own pack of cigarettes as Brody said, "I'll get in contact with Monroe…see if he's got any new missing persons. I'm betting she was on the streets. Her arms are covered with track marks."

Monroe was the brother of one of the human women married into the Silvercrest Lycans, and he was also a federal agent with the FBI. Since his sister had opened his eyes to the wilder side of the Eastern Mountains, he'd proven to be a surprisingly helpful resource for the Bloodrunners, exchanging information when he came across a case that he believed would be of interest to them. The victims were all too often those who lived on the fringes of the law, where the rogues could hunt the easiest. Drug users and prostitutes. Easy pickings for a Lycan when he was on the hunt for fresh meat. In return, they kept Monroe apprised of their current hunts, alerting him when a rogue was on the loose. So far the relationship had proven to be highly beneficial.

"I'm going back," Mason muttered, when his cell began buzzing. He unclipped it, reading the word *private* printed across the LED screen. Frowning, he pressed his thumb down to take the call. "Dillinger."

"She was a beautiful girl. You should have seen her when she was still breathing. Breathtaking, really." The caller laughed a cruel, sadistic sound of humor. "Until her breath got taken away."

"This place still stinks of you, Simmons," Mason drawled. "You might consider taking a bath sometime."

"Ah-ah-ah," Simmons scolded. "I know this must be hard for you, but you can't save them all, Dillinger."

"Why run away, you cowardly piece of shit?" he taunted, hoping to push the bastard's buttons. "Too afraid to face me on your own?"

"And she was so sweet." Simmons sighed, ignoring the question. "Like honey on my tongue. Made me think of your own honey girl."

Mason's silence gave away more than any scathing retort or casual dismissal could ever have done, and Simmons's low, maniacal laughter filled his ear. "Ah, so she *is* more to you than just a fun piece of ass. I was hoping that was the case. It's going to make killing her that much more satisfying."

"You'll have to get through me first, Simmons. And I promise that if I go down, I'm taking you with me."

"Your confidence is going to be your downfall, Dillinger. You can't control fate, and you certainly can't control me. For all you know, she's already mine. Maybe I'm not even the one responsible for that redheaded little whore at your feet. I could be at your cabin, watching your woman through the windows. She's a tiny thing, but I bet she can act like an animal. There's something…wild about her. You know what I mean?"

The icy fear in his gut shifted, morphing into something too ugly and sharp and destructive for words. Disconnecting the call, Mason shoved his phone in his pocket, then carefully focused on lighting his own smoke, determinedly ignoring the telling shake in his fingers as he cupped his palm around the cigarette's tip, protecting the fragile flame from the wind. The sharp scent of tobacco filled his head, and he drew in a slow, deep breath, letting the smoke fill his lungs, seeking the cool, calm remoteness that he'd always been able to pull down around him. But it was gone. Shattered, ground into dust, replaced by this unstable, incomprehensible chaos of hunger and worry and gnawing uncertainty. Christ, he felt shredded. Scraped raw. And there was no denying the panic clawing at his insides, slashing him into emotional ribbons.

Taking another deep drag of the cigarette, he turned back to the others. "That was Simmons."

Brody jerked his chin at the woman, the moonlight setting the fiery strands of her long auburn hair afire, where they spread into the dark spill of blood beneath her. "Did he claim her?"

"He's playing mind games. You know Simmons—it's always some dramatic production with him. But my gut tells me he's the one."

"Wanna know what my gut tells me?" Hennessey drawled, one knee bent, black boot jammed against the tree, while he lifted his cigarette to his mouth, the filter pinched between his thumb and forefinger.

"You'll tell me one way or another, so spit it out," he growled, impatient to get the hell out of there and back home, where he could keep watch over Torrance.

"I know the significance of this brilliant red hair hasn't been lost on you," the Irishman murmured, his pale gaze sweeping over the victim's fiery tresses with a meaningful glance. "It occurs to me that with Simmons so focused on you, maybe one of us should take the girl off your hands."

Rage, perfect and pure, sparked to life. "Don't go there, Hennessey. Not now."

But the Irishman didn't look in the mood to heed the warning. "I'm just making a helpful, friendly suggestion," he drawled, taking another long, slow pull on his cigarette, before his mouth curled in a knowing smile. "If one of us were to put our mark on her, maybe he'd leave her alone, and you could go back to your lovely existence of hunting the bastard down, without having to worry about her. Isn't that the way you like things? Nice and easy, without any fussy emotional attachments?"

"Cian," Brody muttered in a low tone of warning, obviously seeing where this was headed.

"One more word," Mason rasped, flicking his cigarette into

the damp moss covering the base of the trees, "and you're going to regret it, Hennessey."

"I'm just being a pal, Dillinger. An offer from one friend to another. If you don't want me touching her, I'm sure Brody would be up for the challenge, though God only knows what she might do when she sees that beast of his. And Jeremy's still not in top form." He shrugged as if coming to a decision. "Looks like I'd be the best bet." A slow, devil's smile spread cross his mouth. "Can't say that I mind. She looks like she'd be a fun…handful."

"That's it, you son of a bitch."

Brody lunged to force his way between them, but Mason was already taking the Irishman down. They hit the ground hard, rolling across the damp earth, the silent forest suddenly filled with the brutal, battering sounds of battle.

Nearly an hour later, his body aching and sore, Mason steered the Tahoe to a stop in front of the cabin. The nighttime sky shone clear and endless, illuminated by the giant yellow sphere of the moon as it hung low on the horizon, the surrounding trees resembling giant, swaying swamp monsters beneath the hazy moonlight. It was a beautiful night, and one he'd have preferred to spend with Torrance, rather than studying a brutal crime scene and brawling with Hennessey.

Now that he was home, he'd hoped that some of his tension would ease, but as he opened his door and climbed out of the Tahoe, he still couldn't shake the worry riding across the back of his neck. Couldn't put an end to the churning unease knotting his gut that warned him he'd left something undone, unfinished. That he was selling himself short.

Locking his jaw, he turned his back on it, determined not to get sidetracked by emotion. He didn't have time for emotion. Things were going to start rolling now; he knew it.

Simmons was too on edge, his madness controlling him more than his thirst for revenge. The rogue was close to the breaking point, and when he cracked, Mason was going to be there to bring him down.

Bring him down, and put an end to the miserable bastard's existence once and for all.

But he knew that would only be the beginning. No, Simmons was only one arm of this monster. Someone was playing with him, using the rogue as a means to an end that Mason didn't yet completely understand—and he was man enough to admit that he was terrified of what they were dealing with.

Too many open ends. Too many deadly possibilities.

After the ugliness of the night, he needed something clean. Something pure. He needed Torrance. Needed her freshness, that sweet, incandescent spark that lit her up inside. He wanted her. God, did he want her. Wanted to crawl up inside of her and learn everything there was to know. What made her smile…laugh. What turned her on and what made her cry. He wanted to know all of it, every fascinating detail that made her who she was.

And someone wanted to take her away from him.

Not in this lifetime.

He found her curled up on her side in his bed, resting her head in one hand, while she held a book with the other—and the relief he felt at seeing her safe shot through him like a flame, piercing and warm. Her long hair spilled across the ivory white of his pillow, flowing over her shoulder, the soft curls gleaming a deep, dark red in the glowing light from the lamp, and a low, husky moan rumbled in his chest. She glanced up at the sound, and her green eyes went wide with horror as she looked him over. Mason winced, fully aware that Hennessey had left him battered and bruised.

"What happened to you?" she gasped, climbing off the bed

to stand nervously at its side, looking torn between running to him and keeping her distance.

Pulling off his jacket, Mason tossed it toward the wooden chair in the corner. "Had a bit of a disagreement with the Irishman."

Her head tilted at a curious angle. "You were fighting with Cian?"

"Just blowing off steam," he told her, brutally aware of the dark spill of lust rushing through him, just because she was near. Because she was beautiful and strong and his. "No big deal. I'll live."

He felt her warm gaze as it moved over the scrape burning across his left cheekbone, the swelling skin beneath his right eye, the swollen, bloodied corner of his mouth. "You call this blowing off steam?" she asked, her tone dry as she crossed her arms and arched one slim brow. "Are you both crazy?"

"Fighting is just the way we cope," he explained. "It helps keep the tension from getting to the point where we want to kill each other."

"Well at least tell me that he looks as bad as you do."

"I think Brody had to carry him home," he laughed, the words heavy with satisfaction.

"Boys and their macho trips," she drawled, rolling her eyes.

Propping himself against the dresser, Mason leaned over to unlace his boots, choking back a groan of pain from his bruised ribs. "I'm…surprised you're still up."

"Of course I'm still up," she muttered, setting her book on the bedside table, along with her glasses. "I can't sleep when I'm worrying myself to death. You didn't say goodbye and Jeremy didn't know when you'd be back and I was—"

"I'm sorry," he murmured. He could see it now, the strain and nerves she'd been trying hard to hide from him since he'd walked into the room. Something warm and satisfying bloomed in his chest at the idea of her caring about him—about what happened to him. "I didn't mean to worry you. I should've called."

"I'm just glad you made it back in one piece." An impish grin lifted the corner of her mouth. "Well, mostly in one piece, anyway."

"I need a shower," he rasped, and then, *knowing* she would say no but unable to stop himself from asking because he wanted it so badly, he said, "Wanna grab one with me?"

Her eyes went wide, then dark, lips parting the barest fraction. Feeling the heavy beat of his pulse through every inch of his body, Mason waited…and waited, the seconds stretching out like an eternity as a thousand emotions flittered across her face…until she finally gave him a shy smile and said, "Okay."

Okay. One little word that damn near took him to his knees. He blinked, acutely aware that she'd thrown him off balance again. Almost afraid that he'd jump on her like a maniac if he didn't find some control, Mason turned and headed for the bathroom. He flicked on the light, adjusting the control until a warm wave of gold washed away the shadows—painfully aware of her body following behind him, coming closer. He indulged in a brief, carnal smile of anticipation, feeling like the Big Bad Wolf luring in Little Red.

Come closer, little girl…

"I still don't know what Cian could have said that would have made you fight him at a time like this," she murmured, coming up behind him as he moved to turn on the water, setting it to hot. He flinched as her delicate hands found the hem of his T-shirt, pushing the soft cotton up his back, the coolness of her hands against his hot skin making him shiver.

"Don't you?" he asked, turning to face her as he pulled the shirt over his head, satisfaction curling heavily in his gut when her smoky gaze mapped the corded sinew of his raised arms, trailed over his chest, then snagged on the ridged muscles of his abdomen. Suddenly every single grueling hour he spent training and abusing his body seemed worth it. Just for that ravenous look on her face. She trembled, wrenching her gaze back up, until he caught her with his hot stare.

"Did it have something to do with what happened in the kitchen today? What did he mean when he insinuated I wasn't a *bonded* woman?"

"Nothing." He rolled his shoulder. "He just enjoys giving me grief."

Mason knew she wasn't buying it, but she thankfully didn't press him. "Are you sure you're okay with this?" he asked quietly, beginning to unbutton his fly. "It only has to go as far you want it to, Tor. I just want to be close to you."

"Mason," she breathed softly, a torrent of emotion flickering in her eyes.

"I'm not trying to put the make on you. I just… For tonight, I don't want to worry about dreams and nightmares. I just want to be close to you. Just want to hold the heat of your body in my arms and know that you're safe. That you're alive."

"Okay," she said again, and he watched, feeling breathless, as she began to undress.

She held him spellbound as her slim fingers went to work on the button fly of her jeans. With each individual slide of button through denim, his heart kept beat with an odd, jarring cadence, until he thought the damn thing was going to pound its way out of his chest and plop embarrassingly on the floor before her, giving a whole new meaning to the idea of laying your heart at a woman's feet.

Yeah, that'd be so smooth, Dillinger. Keep it together.

But it was impossible. He was breaking apart, breaking open. The intimate act of watching her slip her braided bracelets from her wrist, pulling off her sweater and bra, then slipping off her jeans and pale pink panties, the dark denim skimming her slender feet—they undid him. Made him ache. Made him burn. Even her toes turned him on, the cute little dimples on her ankles, the smooth, pale expanse of her calf, her thigh. He wanted to press his mouth to her everywhere. Take in every texture. Every taste.

She was everything he'd ever wanted, without even realizing it.

And she was his.

With trembling fingers and shallow breaths, Torrance bared her body before him, feeling as if she were baring her soul. She'd had plenty of time to figure out what she wanted as she'd waited for him tonight. Hours to worry about him. To let the fear that something had happened to him rip her to pieces, wondering if he'd make it back home alive.

Not knowing if she would ever see him again had cleared up her confusion with astonishing speed. The possibilities for heartbreak were huge, like a great yawning hole that stretched out across her future—yet she couldn't keep fighting it.

If it had only been this strange, dizzying hunger crawling under her skin, then yeah—Torrance figured she could have waited. It wouldn't have been easy, but she'd have done it. But she couldn't lie to herself and place the blame there. No, there was something deeper than that, stronger, its power rushing through her with the brilliance of a summer storm. It had happened so quickly—and yet it had happened. That breathtaking spark of recognition. The crystallized moment in time when you realize you're falling for another person—falling hard.

It was happening to her. Not because he was beautiful and sexy and protecting her from the bad guys. No, it was just…Mason. He wasn't perfect, but then, she didn't want him to be. She just wanted him. On the outside he was all power and dominance and strength, but on the inside he was hard and hurting…a little lost, lonely, yet strong and funny, both sweet and protective. He was all chaos and life, complex and mystifying, and she couldn't resist him. He'd reached into her chest, wrapped those long, scarred fingers around her heart—and he wasn't letting go.

Now it was up to her to reach out to him, wrap him in her arms and make things right. Taking a step forward, she lifted her hands, smoothing her palms over the rugged beauty of his chest, and with a shaky sound in his deep voice that completely undid her, he said, "I want you more than I've ever wanted anything in my entire life. More than anything, *Torrance*."

She stared up at him, mesmerized by the naked hunger he wasn't trying to hide, letting her see just how badly he *did* want her. And suddenly a stream of words was tumbling from that hard, beautiful mouth, each one drawing her closer. "I want to swim around in your head, Tor. Know your thoughts. Know everything about you, and it scares the hell out of me, because I know I'm never going to learn enough to satisfy the craving. It's like an addiction that's never going to end. It just keeps getting stronger. How the hell am I going to handle that?"

The air began to steam from the heat of the shower, and she blinked against the mist as she stared up at him, wondering how any man could look so beautiful and rough at the same time. "Do you think it's the chemistry of this mating thing that's to blame?"

"Forget the chemistry," he rasped. "It's you. You've turned me inside out."

"And you don't like it?" she asked.

"I don't like knowing that you're thinking about bailing on me the first chance you get."

Something like fear flashed through his eyes, jolting her. She would never have thought he would feel vulnerable. He was too strong and dominant and full of authority and confidence,

the most self-possessed person she'd ever known. And yet—
there was no mistaking that sharp slice of emotion she saw in
the deep, molten brown of his gaze. Fear that he'd lose her,
which meant he *had* to feel something for her, no matter how
fleeting. "Why would you think that?"

"Because you know what I am," he whispered roughly, "and
sooner or later you'll see it. I don't think a monster's going to
fit your ideal too perfectly, do you?"

"Don't do that, Mason," she pleaded softly. "Don't turn my
words around on me. You know very well that when I told you
about that, I was talking about a man's heart. How he felt about
me. How much I meant to him. And his acceptance of that. The
fact that he *wants* to love me." She shivered, pulling her lower
lip through her teeth. "That he's not afraid to admit it."

Mason swallowed, the movement thick in his throat. "What
if I can't be that for you, Torrance?"

His expression was so tortured, that for a moment she had
to close her eyes, dangerously afraid she was going to fall all
over him in a sobbing mess, melting into some kind of emotional chaos. Everything had been wound so tight inside of her
for so long, she was terrified of what was going to happen when
it all came unraveled, spiraling out of control. And this man
could definitely unravel her. In fact, he already had.

Knowing she was wearing her heart on her sleeve, Torrance
lifted her lashes and reached up, cupping his cheek in the palm
of her hand. "Then maybe it's enough just knowing that I
belong with you. That I'm yours, Mason."

I'm yours.

Mason waited, his chest tight, for her to ask if he was
hers...but she didn't. His plan to keep himself locked away
from her emotionally was working, but he felt no sense of
victory. Instead, a sharp, uncomfortable spike of panic ripped

through his gut, leaving him floundering. He'd been so sure this was what he needed, but he felt as if he'd just destroyed something infinitely precious. Like something warm and sweet and beautiful had been laid across his palm, only to have him fist his fingers and crush its tenderness, damaging it beyond repair.

Torrance would let him into her body tonight—but he wanted more. He *needed* more. Hungered for it, craved it, the way an addict felt starved for their next fix. He wanted to break her open, shatter her, until he could find what he needed. Wanted to peel away her own growing defenses, layer by layer, until she was naked and bare before him. Until he could see every thought and emotion, hear her secrets pouring from her lips. Until he could *know* her. Know everything about her.

And more than anything in the world, he wanted to hear her say that she loved him. Wanted it? Damn, he bloody craved it.

"I want to make love to you, Tor," he whispered, the words shaky and rough as he pulled off his jeans and pulled her against his body, wrapping his arms around her, groaning from the feel of her soft skin, her beautiful breasts crushed against his chest. "Want to take you under me and show you how much I…care about you."

A tremulous smile curved her lips, and Mason grabbed at the moment like a snapshot in his mind, never wanting to forget it. "Get close to me, Mason. Please. Just get close to me," she said in a breathless rush, her nails biting into the slick, hard heat of his shoulders, making him growl. She drove him completely insane.

"I'll make it so good for you," he promised, his breath rough against her temple. "I'll always take care of you. I swear it, Torrance." There was so much more to say—but that was all he could give her.

They showered together in trembling haste, eager to finish and make their way to the bed, since he refused to take her against the cold tile wall. Not their first time together. Later, yes. But not tonight.

He needed to make this first time special for her.

They stood beneath the spray of the water, and Mason watched as her russet lashes beaded with glistening drops of water—and with her next blink, one droplet fell from the corner of her eye, tracing a pattern down the side of her face, before trailing over her impudent chin and settling into the sexy hollow at the base of her throat. He swallowed, wanting nothing more than to bury his mouth right there and lick the moisture from her skin. He stared, feeling lost, until the sound of her voice reached him through the thick haze of lust curling heavily around his shoulders, something weighty and real that was pressing down on him.

"What was that?" he asked, shaking his head to clear it of the hungry fog that had settled around his brain.

"I asked if it's always like this between mates."

"I don't know. All I know is that I want you more than I want to breathe. More than I want to live." He tried to be gentle as he turned off the shower and rushed her to bed, wrapping her in a warm, fluffy towel and carrying her in his arms. But it wasn't easy. The hunger was swelling through him, grinding and urgent—the visceral need to pull her beneath him, covering her with his starved body. He wanted to give her so much pleasure. Wanted to watch her go over, her mouth open, face flushed as he thrust into her deeper…then deeper.

"I want to be so close to you," he admitted roughly, laying her down atop the cool, crisp sheets. And it was true—both on an emotional and a physical level. There was an erotic edge to the fragile beauty of her flesh—that darker knowledge that he could so easily hurt her. That her very life had been given into his hands in this precious moment. That she'd surrendered everything to him. "Tor. I promise I'll be careful, but I can't wait."

"Good, because I don't want you to." She wrapped her arms around his shoulders, her body shivering with a fine tremor as he moved over her, settling between her spread thighs, her breasts soft against his chest.

Mason breathed against the small wisps of hair curling at her temple, and with eager, shaking fingers, he reached between their bodies and spread her tender flesh, fitting the wide tip of his cock against the small, swollen opening of her body. Wet, scalding heat covered him, coating him, and the pleasure rolled up from the balls of his feet, settling heavily at the base of his spine, burning around the backs of his ears. Gritting his teeth against the exquisite sensation, he flexed his muscles and pressed inside.

He kept his eyes on her face, watching the pain blend with the pleasure and anticipation as he ground his jaw and kept pressing. He didn't stop until her flesh finally gave up its resistance and swallowed the round, bulging head, clamping down around it so perfectly that his eyes damn near rolled back in his skull. The low, shivering moan that broke past her lips made him shudder. Sweat rolled down his spine, spilling into the small of his back, and he flexed again, pushing in another inch, and the dark, dangerous ecstasy dug its claws into him.

"Torrance."

She heard him gasp her name as she tilted her head back, allowing the vivid sensations to spread through her, hyperaware of every inch that penetrated her, hard and hot and thick. He felt amazing. Huge, yes…but wonderful. And it felt so impossibly right, having him become a part of her, as if she really *had* been made for him—but as incredible as it felt, Torrance could see how hard he was trying to stay in control as she watched him through her lashes. Could see the rigid tension in his face, his shoulders and all those hard, bulging muscles as he strained to hold himself in check, because he was afraid of hurting her.

He was being so careful with her, but that wasn't what she wanted.

With a tremulous curve of her mouth, Torrance smiled, deliciously aware that she was stepping out to the edge of a cliff, something new and wondrous waiting for her on the other side. "Mason," she gasped. "Stop it."

He groaned, holding himself completely still. "What, am I hurting you?" he asked tightly, his arms rigid as he held himself over her. His broad, bronzed shoulders gleamed with a fine sheen of sweat, dark hair damp at his temples, expression grim with restraint.

"No," she said with a watery laugh. "I just want you stop holding back. Just let go. I promise you that I'm not made of glass."

He stared down at her, the rugged planes and angles of his face slowly shifting into an arrested look of raw, savage hunger, making her tremble. "You want more?" he demanded in a low rasp, his hands suddenly fisting into the bedding so viciously, she heard the sharp, sibilant sound of ripping fabric. His hips pulsed, and he thrust into her a little deeper. "Say it, Torrance. *Tell me.*"

"Yeah," she whispered shakily, smiling up at him as something warm and golden and bright seemed to burst into awareness beneath her skin, filling her up, spreading through her body in a molten rush of breathtaking emotion. "I want more. I want *you,* Mason. All of you."

His body jerked as he held himself above her. *"Hell,"* he said huskily, his voice ragged. "This is so dangerous."

"But…" she panted, the anticipation nearly killing her, "it's gonna feel really, *really* good."

"Damn right it is," he grunted, his dark hair falling over his brow as his mouth curled into one of those impossibly wicked, slightly crooked grins of his—and he pressed deeper, keeping his eyes on her face, watching every flicker of emotion as he worked more of himself inside of her, stretching her, filling her to the point that the warm glow of pleasure spilled into something darker, deeper. "I knew it was going to be different with you," he groaned, gifting her with a gorgeous, bone-melting smile. He lowered his head and stamped the impression of his mouth against her own, branding her with the force of his hunger. It vibrated through those long, powerful limbs. Tremored through the rigid strength and ropey sinew of his muscles.

She made a low, humming noise of appreciation, running her palms over the hot skin of his shoulders, lifting her hands to run her fingers through the damp strands of his hair, brushing the warm mass back from his brow.

"I'm never letting you go, Tor. *Never,*" he vowed harshly, watching her, his stare so hot she could feel its searing heat spread across her skin. His hands took her own, pulled them up high over her head, holding them there, stretching her out beneath him. His thumbs swept over the leaping, erratic pulse in her wrists…and he held her wide-eyed gaze, his jaw grinding as he finally began testing the give of her body, thrusting his hips. She was tight, but so wet that she gave way around him, and he began working her hard…harder, until she'd taken every inch and he'd completely buried himself inside of her.

His head fell forward, arms shaking as he pressed deep, just holding himself there, shoved up into her like a thick, heated pipe, solid and hard but throbbing with life. Then he pulled back, and lunged forward in another brutal, grinding motion that buried every inch of his cock inside of her all over again, slamming against her limit, and she screamed, the pleasure exploding instantaneously, as if he'd hit a switch. His eyes went wide, his expression stunned at the first clenching pull of her

.climax, and then he growled a feral, rumbling noise in the back of his throat and erupted into action, driving the pleasure into her until she didn't know how to hold it inside.

He kept pushing her, making her come over and over, like a hedonistic gear being revved higher and higher, until the intense, breathtaking spasms bled into one another, forming one huge, explosive swell of sharp, mind-shattering sensation. The relentless, provocative push of his body into hers made her crazed with it, her skin damp and flushed with violent color. Writhing atop the wrecked bedding, Torrance spread her legs wider, wavering between begging for everything he could give her and pleading for him to let her rest, the hard, relentless burn of ecstasy almost too sharp to bear.

"Not yet," he grated, his dark eyes golden, deliciously wild. "Just one more time, Tor. Let me feel it again, just once more."

"I can't," she sobbed, gasping, her back arched while her head tossed restlessly on the pillow, their bodies covered in a glistening sheen of sweat, sex-damp and burning. *"I can't..."*

"Yes, you can." His lips pulled back over his teeth, breath ragged and fast, while his eyes burned down at her with a primitive, savage intensity.

"Mason," she breathed, his name a plea, though Torrance was no longer even sure what she was begging for. She clutched at the powerful muscles in his back, feeling them shift and flex as he powered his rigid body into hers. The low glow of the muted bathroom light burned behind him, setting the bronzed skin of his wide shoulders to a warm gold, like a god come down to pleasure her, while the sensual curve of his wide mouth was pure, unadulterated devil. *"Mason..."*

"I know," he growled. "Don't fight it and just let me give it to you." The pleasure; the dark, almost frightening intensity; his swollen shaft—it didn't matter what he meant, she wanted them all. Her breath caught as he shifted position, slipping his hands behind her knees. He pushed them higher, nearly flattening them against her breasts, the tilted angle of her pelvis allowing him free access to that drenched, pulsing part of her that throbbed like a heartbeat, her sensitive skin stretched wide as he worked more and more of himself inside of her. She had no shelter, nowhere to hide.

Emotions surged, sensation building upon sensation… swelling…deepening layer by layer, like pigment building upon a canvas, creating something brilliant and stunning and new.

Something that was all hers.

Something she was dangerously afraid that she already loved.

"Torrance!" Mason shouted, the word guttural and raw as his own release roared through him, powering through his body in a thundering wave. It surged up from the very depths of his soul, destroying him at the same time all the scattered pieces of his existence seemed to finally snap into place. And when she followed him over, spasming around him in another sweet, crushing release, Mason thought the top of his head would come off. "Damn, that nearly killed me."

She laughed a soft, happy sound, her face and chest flushed a beautiful blushing pink that made him want to howl. "You're incredible," he rasped, thrusting gently into her as the last waves of the most powerful orgasm he'd ever experienced pulsed through him. "God, I think I'm destroyed, but I want it again, Tor."

I want it forever.

He released his hold on her legs and collapsed over her, a hard, exhausted grin lifting his lips as she wrapped her arms around him, holding tight, her face pressed into the hollow of his shoulder. "Just give me a second to catch my breath," he whispered.

A rough, trembling giggle shook her body beneath him, and

the grin playing at his mouth melted into a smile that seemed to bloom from somewhere deep inside of him. The sex had been so insanely good it blew his mind, but it was what happened afterward that broke him down. That destroyed him. He rested his face against her belly, his body wrapped in bliss as she stroked her fingers through the damp tangles of his hair, petting him like an animal, and he loved it. Loved breathing in the sweet, feminine scent of her passion. Loved her hands on him. Loved the sheer beauty of everything that she was, both inside and out.

"What now?" she asked softly, when their breath had returned to normal.

"I need… I need for you to trust me, Tor." He regarded her almost solemnly, lifting his head to stare up at her over the pale line of her body, her skin glowing like a pearl. "You can, you know. You're my mate."

She let her head press back into the downy pillow. "And that means that I should trust you, Mason?"

"I would never betray you," he said gruffly. "Not for anything. Not with anyone."

A small crease formed between her brows. "You mean you'd never hurt me?"

"That's exactly what I mean," he rasped, wishing she could just see inside of him. What she wanted was there—he just couldn't risk letting it out. Hell, he didn't even know how to let it out.

But he could show her. And in those dark, provocative hours, he argued his case with the touch of his skin against hers, the press of his body, the ravenous hunger of his kiss—

Again…and again…and again.

Chapter 11

Mason stood at the bay window in the kitchen, staring out at the pale stream of light struggling to fight its way into the dawn sky. The shadows of night still hung heavily over the forest, nature quiet and still beyond the window in a perfect, suspended state of grace, while chaos reigned within him.

Though Torrance had slept peacefully in his arms, Mason had been the one who'd dreamed.

He couldn't recall exactly how it began. One moment, there'd been nothing but the gently soothing darkness of sleep…and in the next, he'd found himself running through the forest, the ground damp beneath his feet, the air heavy and humid, thick enough to feel against his skin, just the way it is before a violent storm. He was tired, his body battered and bruised…aching as his muscles burned, but he couldn't stop. He had to get *there;* only he didn't know where he was running to. He just kept moving, his feet pounding at the underbrush, rocks and stones and broken twigs slicing at his soles, his body naked but for the jeans riding low on his hips.

It was night, the forest thick with shadows, his vision glowing as he used his wolf's eyes to find his way in the dark. He ran harder, faster, driven by an insane sense of urgency, until the blinding moment when a hand grasped his shoulder from behind, jerking him to a stunning, stumbling halt.

Whipping around to confront his attacker, he'd come face-to-face with his brother. Dean stood as tall and proud as Mason remembered him, his thick hair brushing his shoulders, a small scar at the corner of his mouth, a souvenir he'd carried since their roughhousing days as kids. He held a small woman in his arms, her face pressed to his chest, ebony hair streaming over his brawny arms. Her feet, so narrow and pale, looked infinitely fragile beneath the hem of her eyelet gown, the white cloth charred in places, stained with streaks of dirt and blood in others. *Christ,* he thought. *It was Lori.* She'd been found wearing that same gown the night the fire had taken her life.

His brother was holding his dead wife in his arms.

Mason squeezed his eyes shut, while anguish burned a raw wound in his chest, his body rigid with pain and fury for the horrors of the past.

"You're losing her, brother," Dean called to him, and though he stood only a few feet away, his voice reached out to Mason like a thin, metallic stream of sound traveling over a great distance.

"What?" he croaked, the word no more than a hoarse whisper, emotion choking his ability to speak as he opened his eyes.

"Mason, listen to me," Dean shouted, his features twisted with concern. "You're losing her!"

"Losing Torrance?" he rasped, shaking his head in confusion, trying to make sense of Dean's words as the forest around them began to spin. At first, it moved in a slow, revolving shuffle, gaining speed second by second, the leaves and limbs and sturdy trunks becoming a blur while Mason stood trapped in its center, as if caught in the eye of a hurricane.

"Don't feel sorry for me," Dean called out to him, the edges of his body blurred, fading into the surrounding, spinning forest. "I have Lori waiting at home, waiting for me. We're together…always. Love doesn't make you weak, Mason. Love makes you strong, and I wouldn't have had it any other way."

"Dean," he groaned, wondering how to tell him that his wife was dead in his arms. "Dean," he choked out, his throat trembling.

"Open your eyes before it's too late, Mason," he told him, walking forward. He held the woman in his arms out, offering her to him, and Mason stumbled back, his body quaking. "Open your eyes," Dean growled. "I don't want you to be alone."

Before he could react, the icy weight of the woman's body was thrust into his arms, against his chest, and Mason looked down in horror…only to see a fiery mane of red flowing over his arms, covering her face. His muscles shook as the truth crashed over him, through him, taking him to his knees, the damp earth of the forest soaking into his jeans. His breath caught as she stirred, her face tilting, a breathtaking smile of pure joy curling across the beauty of her mouth.

"I love you, Mason."

No sooner had the stunning words left her lips, than the force of the spinning forest caught hold of her body, wrenching her out of his hold. In a state of horror, Mason watched the ravaging cyclone of wind and trees carrying her away, her arms outstretched, reaching for him, but no matter how violently he struggled, his feet were rooted in place, sinking into the ground beneath him as it gave way like quicksand.

"I love you!" she screamed. *"Don't leave me! I love you…"*

The next thing he'd known, he'd jerked awake with a roar

trapped in his chest, skin damp with sweat, sounding like he'd run a marathon. Torrance's small form had been pressed against his side, her soft breath brushing against the curve of his jaw.

Now, standing at the window, Mason watched the sun crest over the tops of the trees in a burning arc of gold, and he headed for his bedroom, needing to check on her. The moment he sat down beside her hip, she stirred.

"Why aren't you in bed?" she asked sleepily, soft morning sunlight shining down on her head, setting the deep red tones of her hair afire in that way that took his breath. Every damn time he saw it.

"I had a bad dream," he said, his mouth twisting with a wry smile.

Her luminous green eyes softened, hazy with the promise of comfort. "I know all about those. If you come back to bed, I'll make you feel better."

"I have no doubt of that," he rumbled, his rough fingertips brushing gently over her temple, tucking the wayward strands of hair behind her ear. "But after last night, you need time to recover. I know you must be tender."

She blushed a brilliant shade of rose, making him chuckle, and she picked up his pillow, whacking him against the side of his head.

"I don't suppose you've put on any coffee?" she asked, the hopeful note in her sleep-husky voice impossible to miss.

"That sounds like a desperate request," he chuckled, forcing the memories of his dream away as they hovered at the edges of his mind. He didn't want to think about Dean and death and the past. He wanted to soak himself in Torrance. Wanted to fill himself up on her laughter and smiles. "I'm almost afraid to admit I haven't made any yet."

"Oh, God," she moaned dramatically. "You're cruel."

Smiling, Mason leaned down and pressed his mouth to her

temple, nuzzling her in a way that made her shiver. "After last night, how can you say that?" he teased, nipping her earlobe, breathing into the sensitive shell of her ear. "You know I only want to take care of you—keep you melting in satisfaction."

And had he ever, Torrance thought with a dreamy sigh.

When she'd seen him battered and bruised, she'd been reminded that life was fragile and fleeting, that fate could turn on you at the drop of a dime. She hadn't wanted to waste whatever time she might have with him. And the night had been perfect.

"You know," she moaned, stretching, "Jeremy was definitely right."

"Jeremy was right about what?" he asked thickly, trailing his fingertips down her side, his thumb stroking low across her sheet-covered belly, making her tremble.

"About this," she murmured, giving him a slumberous, lazy look of fulfillment. She was steeped in it. Could still feel the residual pulses and aches of pleasure humming pleasantly through her well-used body, her muscles shivery and tired from the physical exertion. "There's a heck of a lot to be said for this mate-for-life, love-at-first-sight stuff."

"What?" He squinted down at her, as if staring into a bright light, and against her side his fingers stilled.

For a moment she couldn't figure out what was wrong, and then she suddenly realized what she'd just said. "I didn't mean to say that," she laughed softly, the sound brittle, her heart already breaking at the bizarre look on his face. "I meant to say *lust,* Mason. You know. *Lust* at first sight."

An awkward silence met her words, and she shifted uneasily. She wished he'd just ignore it, pretend it didn't happen, but no such luck. His gaze no longer seemed to be burning quite so warm, as if some arctic wind had swept through him.

"I really wish you wouldn't make a big deal about this," she whispered, off balance despite the fact that she was still in bed. She may have been lying down, but her head was spinning. It was ridiculous, but she'd thought, at least for a moment, that last night had changed things. Clearly, it hadn't. At least not for Mason. It hurt. God, there was no denying that it hurt. But she wouldn't regret it.

"It's okay, Mason," she said softly, grabbing at the sheet and pulling it a little higher. "It's a physical thing, you said so yourself. I understand."

"Torrance," he groaned. "I'm sorry. I wish I could be different. I—"

"You were honest with me, so no apologies necessary. Okay?"

"Damn it, don't shut me out like that."

He wasn't the one being shut out—she was. Shaking her head, she said, "Mason, do you even hear what you're saying?"

"Christ, I'm sorry, Torrance." He sighed, rubbing one hand over his face, the bristle on his cheeks and chin making a scratchy sound against his palms.

Those were the *last* words she wanted to hear. Not after last night. Not after the man had systemically stripped her down, ripped her open and shown her exactly what it felt like to give herself to another person, fully surrendering both her body and her heart.

She'd been making *love,* no matter how breathtakingly wild and primitive their mating had been. She had been doing it with her soul—and he…hadn't.

"Last night didn't change anything." It wasn't a question, just a simple statement of fact. The words fell soft and quiet between them, and despite the sick feeling in her stomach, she was relieved at how poised she sounded.

His mouth twisted, the hard cast on his face looking almost like regret.

She'd opened her eyes to the morning, feeling reborn, ready to fling herself into the newness of love and the brilliant, somewhat frightening gift she'd been given. And even with psychotic maniacs out there waiting to take them down, she'd still felt blessed. Had known, after the loneliness of her life, that to have found something this significant was both beautiful and profound. A miracle.

We only met three days ago, she thought with a wry laugh. But this thing between them, it felt…different. Damn it, it *was* different. Real and beautiful and awe-inspiring. The stuff of dreams and dragons, of magical kingdoms and happily-ever-afters. She didn't want to kill the magic by ripping the foundation out of her dream before it'd even begun. He'd promised to be faithful, to stay by her side—but without love, how could anything last? The life her mother had lived—a life Torrance had witnessed in full detail—answered that question all too well: it wouldn't.

Throwing her legs over the side of the bed, Torrance reached down to the floor for the oversize T-shirt he'd given her last night when they'd raided the kitchen for a midnight snack, and pulled it over her head with shaking arms. The last thing she wanted at this moment was to be naked in front of him. God, she already felt stripped enough as it was, all her emotions laid bare before him, like an insect pinned in a display case.

"I need to grab a shower," she murmured, knowing she had to have some time to herself, to figure things out.

He stood, heading around the bed, but she stopped him before he could reach her, holding out her hand. Her chin lifted, but her eyes had that dry, scratchy feeling that always came before a flood of tears. Mason lifted his hand toward her face, as if he'd cup her cheek, but she stopped him with a single word. *"Don't."*

The air made a harsh sound as he forced out a short breath, and he dropped his arm to his side. "We can work this out, Torrance. I can make you happy. I know I can. What I can't do is lose you," he gritted through his clenched teeth. "I never thought I'd find this. I never even dared to think that there might be someone out there. Someone that was mine and mine alone. This thing between us, it's more than anything I've ever known. More than I knew I was even capable of. Why can't we leave it at that?"

Torrance blinked up at him, trying to fight back the salty flow of tears, wishing she could be happy with what he had to offer. But she couldn't. She was greedy when it came to this man—she wanted it all. "Because," she said softly, wrapping her arms around her middle, "no matter how much I want you, I know that without love, you'd never stay."

"You said last night that you were mine," he rasped, golden eyes blazing. "And I'm not leaving you."

"You'd never stay…*faithful*." She threw the last word down like a gauntlet, and he all but tremored with rage before her, his fury blasting against her like an angry swell of frustration, hot and beastly.

"I told you you were the *only* woman for me now, and you can call me whatever else you like, but I'm not a goddamn liar!" he growled. He turned way from her, stalking toward the door in long, angry strides, but before he got there he slammed to a stop, sending her a sudden look of surprise over his broad shoulder.

"What is it?"

He closed his eyes, cursing a long, foul streak under his breath as he brushed past her on the way to his dresser.

"Damn it, Mason. Will you just tell me what has you looking so—"

"I forgot to tell you about my parents," he muttered, pulling out a sage-green T-shirt and slipping it over his head, the muscles in his arms and chest momentarily distracting her.

A shiver of dread scurried up the back of her neck, making her shiver. "What about them?"

"They're coming over today to meet you," he grunted, avoiding her stare as he pulled on his socks and boots. "In fact, knowing them, they'll probably get here stupid early because they're looking forward to it, which means they could be showing up any minute now with breakfast. They don't live in Shadow Peak, but they're still in the mountains. Only about twenty minutes away."

"Parents?" she whispered, as if she didn't know what to make of the word.

"Yeah, my parents," he drawled, his smile tight as he cut her a knowing look, his brows raised. "You know, as in my mother and father. Believe it or not, I didn't spawn from the devil or anything."

"But why? Why are they coming *here?*"

"Because if I hadn't called and told them about you, they'd have wrung my bloody neck when they learned that I'd found my life mate and failed to mention the fact. Trust me, it's going to be a lot easier getting it over with now rather than later."

"This is nuts," she groaned, holding her head in her hands as the beginnings of a killer headache started pounding through her skull.

"I'd hurry if I were you," he told her, and without another word, he walked right past her and out of the room.

Feeling like she'd just been blindsided by a truck, Torrance collapsed on the edge of the bed, staring at the dark grain of the floor, wondering what she was going to do.

For a few brief hours hope had burned so sweet…and now it'd just burned out.

A half hour later, Torrance's rioting emotions were still keeping her company as she followed the voices coming from the kitchen. Stepping through the archway, she saw an older couple sitting at the table, while Mason was dishing up fresh-baked cinnamon rolls she assumed had been brought by his mother. Jeremy held court at his customary place in front of the sink, while the seated couple laughed at whatever he'd just said.

Mr. and Mrs. Dillinger. Mason's parents. In the flesh.

God, what more was she going to have to deal with today? Already she felt wrung dry, the past several days catching up with her in a way that made her feel wilted, like a bad head of lettuce. Not exactly the image she'd wanted to project when meeting the parents of the man who'd stolen her heart, but with the way her luck had been going lately, she should have expected as much.

She started to move forward, but then froze like a deer in the headlights, realizing that they were all looking at her now. Mason's dark eyes watched her with a cautious wariness, as if he didn't know what to expect from her.

"Mom, Dad," he said in that deep, whispery baritone that always sounded so sexy, "this is Torrance."

"It's…so nice to meet you," she said in a rush, plastering on a smile as they came toward her, his father wrapping her in a huge bear hug, then relinquishing her to his mother, who kissed both her cheeks, her brown eyes—identical to Mason's—bright with genuine warmth and delight. She'd been so worried that the moment would be awkward, but Robert and Olivia Dillinger were so wonderfully warm and accepting, she almost felt completely at ease.

Jeremy pulled in an extra chair from the living room and they all gathered 'round the kitchen table for breakfast and coffee, the conversation lively while both parents did their best to keep her entertained with stories of Mason's juvenile misadventures. There was the time when he'd climbed a thirty-foot pine to play lookout for Jeremy during a game of war, and ended up too scared to make it back down on his own—to an endearing story about the beautiful locket that Olivia wore around her neck. It had been a gift from Mason on her birthday when he was only thirteen, and he'd saved his money for months. Olivia even opened the locket to show her the pictures of Mason and his brother that she carried inside. And though it was heartbreaking to see the photo of Dean, his dark hair and chocolatey brown eyes reminding her of Mason, Torrance couldn't help but smile over the photos. There was something just so wonderfully cute about such a tough guy's mom carrying his picture in a locket.

In fact, Robert and Olivia Dillinger were an adorable couple all the way around. While his father was as handsome as Mason, just an older, slightly more distinguished version, his mother fell more into the category of cute and cuddly, with a wholesome beauty that radiated from her dazzling smile and warm brown eyes. They seemed a mismatched pair, much like her and Mason...and yet Robert Dillinger watched his wife with an avid absorption, as if she were the queen of the universe.

Eventually the plates were cleared, and Jeremy excused himself to go and check on Elliot—and just like that, reality crept back in...reminding Torrance that they were in the midst of a nightmare. Leaning back in his chair, Robert crossed his brawny arms over his gray sweater, his easy grin fading beneath a hard look of concern. "You told us you had more news when we got here, Mason. I think now's the time to tell it."

"Who's Elliot?" Olivia asked, her smooth brow knitted with confusion.

"It's a long story," Mason replied, rubbing his hand across the back of his neck.

His father gave him a sharp nod. "Then you had better get started."

For the next ten minutes Mason related everything that they'd been through during the past three days. Olivia's big brown eyes remained wide with horror as Mason explained about Simmons and Elliot, while his father's expression took on a grim cast that would have scared the hell out of her, had she not seen for herself how easygoing he'd been during breakfast.

"So they're using kids like this Elliot, all but blackmailing them into joining their ranks. Inflaming their natural meat lust, making them crave it—making them do things they would have never thought they'd do," Mason said darkly. "We're dealing with something that goes against the laws of the pack here. Jeremy and I both fought Simmons in broad daylight, and that bastard had his full wolf form. And he's got a whole little gang of thugs following him, who can dayshift, as well—whose scent can't be tracked. God only knows how he's done it, but—"

"I do," his father stated quietly, the words somehow seeming to hang heavily in the air between them. An uncomfortable feeling settled deeply in Torrance's stomach, making her wish she could get up and leave the room, but she didn't dare move.

Mason's entire body held still as he stared at his father. "What do you mean, you do?"

"I know how it's done," his father said. "How to teach someone the way to dayshift, because it's one of the first secrets revealed to an Elder. When a Lycan is taught the power of day-shifting, rather than coming into the power naturally as he nears the end of his life, as some do, it's for the purpose of using him as a soldier—as a weapon of war. The reason you've never heard of it is because it's been centuries since it was last used. When the Lycan transforms his body in daylight, he no longer produces the wolf's natural musk. Instead, he gives off an acidic odor that deflects the ability of others to track him, giving him a double advantage."

Mason shook his head, a dark look of betrayal washing over his rugged features. "You knew about this, and you're only telling me *now?*"

Robert sighed heavily. "I'm sorry, Mason, but it wasn't my place to tell you."

* * *

"No," Mason grumbled, his voice thick with biting sarcasm. "As always your loyalty was to that goddamn League, even after they turned their back on you!" Looking toward Torrance, he explained his meaning. "It's true. The man sitting beside you was once a young, powerful Elder…until the day he fell in love with my mother. Being a man of honor, he informed his peers and they rewarded his honesty by voting him off, believing that no Lycan could faithfully serve the pack when his heart belonged to the human world. And even though he knows it was bullshit, he remains dedicated to the same bastards who stabbed him in the back!"

"And you'd rather I spent my life hating the world?" his father roared, banging one beefy fist on the table so hard that both women jumped in their seats. "Why, Mason? I have love, a family—more than any man deserves. Your anger does me no honor. Not when I consider myself one of the most blessed men, be they human or Lycan, that I've ever known."

"Mason, I know it's difficult for you, but you've got to let the anger go. Enough's enough," his mother said gently. "Look at this wonderful girl. You've been given a gift. Don't waste it."

Mason stared at his mother, understanding what she was trying to tell him—but he couldn't do it. He *wouldn't* do it. "Torrance has nothing to do with this," he rasped, unable to ignore the crushing effect of his words on her.

"Wow," Torrance said with a small, tight smile. "That sounds remarkably like my cue to leave. If you'll excuse me, there's something I need to do."

"No, don't leave," his father rumbled. "Please, Torrance, stay. You're a part of this, and you need to be a part of the conversation."

"Really, Mr. Dillinger," she said awkwardly, "I don't think that's necessary."

"Don't be silly," his mother told her with a gentle smile, patting her arm. "It's obvious you're a mated pair, Torrance." Looking toward her son, she said, "What I want to know is why you're not a bonded pair. After what you've told us about Simmons, knowing her life is in danger, why in God's name haven't you made a blood bond with her, Mason?"

"Mother," he said in a low tone of warning.

But Torrance was already saying, "Blood bond?"

"He hasn't even explained it to you?" His father sighed, sounding weary with disappointment.

She shook her head, and Mason blew out a rough breath. "In the Lycan world, when a man finds his mate, he can permanently bind her to him by making a *blood bond* with her. He…bites her with his fangs, and in doing so, creates a deeper connection, a kind of metaphysical link between them that can never be broken."

"Oh," she whispered, the word heavy with awe. "I…I thought that if you bit someone, it changed them."

"Not between mates. A Lycan male can't change their human partner. But it binds them together forever, Torrance. It deepens their connection until they feel their other half even when they're not with them."

"Were you afraid to tell me, Mason?" she asked, the wounded look in her eyes crushing him. "Because of my nightmares?"

"That's part of it," he told her. "I would never ask you to do something like that, knowing how you feel about wolves."

"How does she—?" his mother started to ask.

But Mason cut her off, saying, "But it's also something I vowed a long time ago to never do, whether I ever found my mate or not. The bond creates an emotional link between the partners, one that—"

"One that's based on love. Am I right?"

He stared at her for a long moment, then quietly said, "Yes."

She made a low sound of understanding in her throat. "So that's it, then?"

"Torrance, you don't know the risk," he growled, willing her to understand. "The connection between mates becomes stronger, but not without a price. If I'm killed, then you could die, too, following me into death. I won't risk you that way. I won't do that to you."

"Jeremy, he told me about what happened to your brother. He called them a bonded pair. I just didn't— I guess I wasn't thinking. I should've figured it out…that there was something more." She looked up at him through a sheen of tears. "That's what Cian meant, wasn't it? He knew you hadn't bonded with me. They all know, don't they?"

Feeling like a total shit, Mason gave her a jerky nod. "Yeah, they know. A Lycan can just…tell."

"Not just a Lycan," Olivia murmured, sending a look of disappointment in his direction. "I'm human, Mason, and it's still clear to me that you're—"

"If you'll excuse me," Torrance suddenly murmured, looking almost ill, "I have to go."

"Torrance," he growled, but she ignored him.

"It was a pleasure to meet you, Mr. and Mrs. Dillinger," she said with a quiet grace and poise that most women couldn't have managed, considering she was not only hurt but probably furious with him for not explaining things to her sooner.

"Nice going," his father snorted, shaking his head in disgust the second Torrance had fled the room. Mason knew that he'd hurt her again, but she'd still left with her head high, and a warm wave of admiration burned through him at the same time he felt like kicking his own ass—if he could only reach it.

"I've never been so disappointed in my entire life," his mother scolded, as if he were still a child in need of discipline.

"I didn't raise you to act like an idiot, Mason. You're breaking that poor girl's heart. What's the matter with you?"

"Nothing's the matter," he gritted through his teeth, his fingers biting into the edge of the countertop at his back. "Other than the psychotic killer out there who wants to take that woman away from me! I'm scared to death of losing her."

"Fear is sometimes healthy, Mason," his father said with a sigh. "And sometimes it's just an excuse to keep us back from the things we want most in life. Admit to the truth that's in your heart. Bond with her. Make it right, son. Don't be afraid of death. It finds us all in the end. All we can do is make the most of the time we have."

"And love is what gives us the strength to overcome our fears," his mother added. "What happened with Dean was a tragedy, but don't let it hold you back from what you know is right. You're the bravest man I know, Mason, and we're so proud of you. But you have to trust in your love. If you can't learn to do that, then you don't deserve her. Don't take a thing of beauty and turn it into something ugly. The bond can help keep her safe. Love can—"

"Love isn't going to protect her!" he shouted, his hand making a cutting motion through the air, as if he could physically destroy the reality of that statement. "Love isn't going to keep her alive!"

His father stared at him, then slowly gained his feet. "Let's go home, Olivia. There's no talking any sense into him when he's like this."

His mother pressed a kiss to his cheek, her smile sad, and they left, leaving him alone in the kitchen with nothing but his lousy mood and the anxious knot of fear in his gut for company.

He cast a short look at the coffeepot, then decided the situation called for something stronger. Opening the pantry, Mason pulled out the Lagavulin and poured himself two fingers in a glass. The first slow sip hit his mouth like fire, and he enjoyed the rich burn in his eyes and throat as Jeremy walked back into the room, Hennessey and Carter at his back.

"We saw your parents on our way in. What did the old man have to say?" Cian asked, folding his long body into a chair at the table, his left eye swollen and bruised from their late-night brawl. "Any news?"

A sardonic smile twisted his mouth and he turned, propping himself up against the counter, his legs crossed at the ankles. "Oh, he had news all right. Seems that 'Dayshifting 101' is a course taught to *all* members of the League of Elders. Each and every damn one of them. And it's meant to be used as a weapon of war, the lack of a traceable scent caused by that damn acidic odor meant to give the Lycan an advantage as a soldier."

"Holy…" Jeremy whispered, his hazel eyes huge as he considered the ramifications of that statement.

"Yeah."

"Jesus. That means that whoever taught the skill to Simmons—"

"Is most likely someone on the League," Cian finished for him, propping his leather-covered elbows on the gleaming surface of the table. "This just keeps getting deeper and deeper."

"And Robert didn't tell us this a long time ago, why?" Jeremy asked, scowling as he poured himself a drink, offering the bottle to both Cian and Brody, who shook their heads no. "That seems like a helluva piece of information to keep to himself."

"Because he's still loyal to the same assholes who abandoned him," Mason grunted, unable to understand his father's fierce sense of loyalty. "I think he was hoping we'd never learn."

"Yeah, well, we did. The hard way," Jeremy muttered, running his hand over his wounded throat.

"So, did he explain how to do it?" Brody asked, speaking up for the first time.

"No, and I didn't ask. The League can have their secrets as far as I'm concerned. All I want is to track down the son of a bitch behind this and kill him."

"So if it's one of the Elders…" Cian murmured, his pale eyes sharp with thought as he leaned back in his chair, staring intently at the floor, as if he could find the answers there. "Which one?"

It was a good question, and there was no easy answer.

If war was being declared, the Bloodrunners would be all that stood between humanity and those who meant to hunt them down like prey, feeding upon them like cattle. They had to strike first. Had to put an end to this thing before it got too out of hand.

"Graham's my father's best friend," Mason said heavily, speaking of the Lycan who served as the highest-ranking member of the League. "I practically grew up with him, and he's too soft. I can't imagine him being behind it."

"Pippa Stanton is a sour old lemon, though," Jeremy snorted, speaking of the lone female among the Elders. "I could see her playing the dominatrix role of an evil mastermind."

"Watch it, Burns," Cian drawled, giving an exaggerated shudder. "That dominatrix remark about such a foul old crone is going to give me nightmares."

"Come on, Irish. I can't imagine you afraid of a little domination," Jeremy snickered, his hazel eyes glittering with humor.

"I like my women soft and easy," the ebony-haired Runner declared in a slow slide of words, while the corner of his mouth twisted in a wry grin.

Mason snorted under his breath, throwing back his Scotch in one long, burning swallow. "You two mind if we stay on topic?"

"Well, there's always old Clausen and Summers," Brody

murmured, rubbing two fingers against the end point of his scar, where it tapered across his jaw. "They're both so backward in their beliefs, I'm surprised they can even see where they're walking."

"And we can't overlook the obvious," Jeremy added, crossing his arms over his chest. "Stefan Drake is a racist asshole who hates humans. I could too easily see him in the role."

"I agree about Drake," Mason grunted. "As for the other Elders, they're too new for any of us to know much about."

"Mason's right," Cian muttered. "We don't know these people. I mean *really* know them enough to be able to determine if they'd be capable of something like this. We're too disengaged from the pack."

"You guys could always ask your precious Dylan what he thinks," Brody interjected, his voice snide. The year before, Dylan's sister had run Brody's heart through the wringer, and it was no secret that there was no love lost between the Runner and the Elder. Not that Mason could blame the man who was like his brother. Having your heart ripped out tended to make a guy kinda bitter, and Brody had already been dealt enough shit to deal with in life.

"I'm picking up your sarcasm," Jeremy drawled, "but you're right, Brody. Dylan *could* help us."

"Unfortunately, Dylan is still unreachable. And no matter how loyal he is to us, his first loyalty is still to the League," Mason said grimly. "We need another plan." He knew the reaction his suggestion was going to get, but it had to be said. "Maybe we should call in Jillian."

Just as he'd expected, Jeremy whipped around, pinning him with a hard, incredulous glare. "Over my dead body."

"If we don't get some help here, it just might come to that, Jeremy. We need to talk to someone who has their pulse on the pack as well as the League. Who knows them better than Jillian?"

"She'd never do it," his partner argued, while his face went dark, the healing wounds on the side of his throat standing out in stark contrast against the violent color of his anger. "She couldn't give a damn about helping us."

"I disagree," he countered. "Jillian has always wanted what was best for her people. There's no way she hasn't picked up on the trouble within the Silvercrest, and she's the most unprejudiced member of the pack I know, aside from Dylan. If we ask her, she *will* help us. And we need it."

Jeremy shook his head from side to side, his fingers clenched around his glass so fiercely it was a wonder it didn't shatter. "I don't like it."

"Yeah, and while you're fuming about it, why don't you think about why the idea of being near her, of having her working with us, pisses you off so badly?"

"It. Won't. Work."

"You got a better idea?" he growled.

Jeremy opened his mouth, but Cian's lazy drawl broke into the argument. "Maybe one of us should return to Shadow Peak ourselves, accept our place within the pack and hunt the traitor from within?"

Silence followed his words, thick and heavy, like something you could sink into. The three standing Runners stared at one another while the idea ran its way through their minds, arguments and affirmations battling against one another. Casting a curious glance at their hard expressions, Cian rocked back on the chair's rear legs and quietly laughed. "If you three could only see your faces. Priceless."

Brody's scowl deepened, making him look even scarier than usual. "Son of a bitch," he grunted. "That's diabolical."

"But brilliant," the Irishman drawled, his white teeth flashing in a wide smile.

Jeremy studied him through narrowed eyes. "You volunteering for the job, Hennessey?"

"Hell, no!" he barked, shaking his dark head. "I'm not *that* insane. We'd have to make it fair somehow."

Brody thought it over, nodding as an idea occurred to him. "We could draw straws for it."

"I don't like it," Jeremy argued, slamming his glass down on the counter.

"I don't like it, either," Mason agreed. "But…it might be our best shot, Jeremy. Whoever was on the inside would have complete access to the pack—to everything. They could work with Jillian, and we could get to the bottom of this thing before it explodes in our faces."

Jeremy scrubbed his hands down his face, muttering, "Oh, Christ," under his breath. "And I thought *your* plan was insane."

"It could—" Brody started to say, when a loud banging noise sounded from the living room.

"That's Elliot," Jeremy grunted, his voice grim.

Together, the group rushed into the other room, fanning out around the locked door that led downstairs, the teenager's pounding growing louder against the wood. "Dillinger! Burns!" he called out hoarsely, and Mason unlocked the door, whipping it open.

The light spilled into the shadowed stairway, revealing Elliot's slumped, sweat-drenched form curled up on the top stair, his dark eyes wild with emotion. "I—" He swallowed thickly, unable to get the words out. "I… I was asleep. Dreaming," he panted, the words ragged, "about, about that…night. I know where we were," he growled, running the back of his hand over his mouth, his upper lip dotted with beads of sweat. "There was a cliff. Water. The sound of a waterfall."

"Flat Rock," Jeremy muttered. "On the western ridge."

"Let's check it out," Brody rumbled, already moving toward the door. "There's a north and a south side that we'll need to search."

Cian nodded, heading after his partner. "Well take the north first," he called back over his shoulder, "then—"

"I'll take the south," Mason cut in.

The two Runners stopped in their tracks, turning back. "You can't go it alone, Dillinger."

"Jeremy can't go, and I need him to stay here anyway. If I run into anything, I'll give you a call before I get myself into something I can't handle."

Brody scowled. "You *better* call us," he muttered, stalking out the door with his partner.

"You did good, Elliot," Mason said gruffly, watching as Jeremy helped the trembling kid to his feet, one arm slung around the young Lycan's shoulders.

Elliot nodded numbly, his expression blank, as if he were trapped within some kind of internal nightmare, and Mason knew the teen was thinking about his dream. If Elliot remembered where he'd killed the girl, then he'd most likely *relived* the killing, as well.

"He's gonna be okay," Jeremy grunted in answer to Mason's unspoken concern. "Just get on outta here and see what you can find."

"I'll go let Torrance know that I'm leaving."

"Sounds good, man. And whatever you do, stay frosty," Jeremy called out, taking Elliot down the stairs.

Mason had just shut the door when he heard a voice say, "You're leaving?"

He turned to find Torrance standing at the edge of the living room, the hallway at her back. "We may have a lead on where Simmons is," he told her, "but I have to hurry. When Jeremy comes back up, he can fill you in on everything."

She nodded, and even across the length of the room, he could see her face go pale. "Be careful, Mason."

"I will," he promised, her concern for him evident, and that strange sense of belonging pierced through him again, making him want to pull her into his arms, take her to the floor and bury himself inside of her sweet warmth until she could thaw out the cold fear that filled him up inside. "If this wasn't so important, I wouldn't be going."

She nodded, but remained silent, slender arms wrapped around her middle.

"Elliot is pretty shaken up," he added. "It might make him feel better if you could talk to him again. Maybe even keep him company."

"Of course I will," she said, her own worry for the young man creasing her brow.

For a moment Mason just stood there, caught in indecision as his eyes moved over her face, settling on every precious feature, committing them to memory. There was so much he needed to say, but now wasn't the time. "Wait up for me?" he asked.

She hesitated for only a moment, then softly said, *"Okay."*

Chapter 12

Tick. Tick. Tick.

Torrance watched the hands of the sleek, modern clock hanging upon the wall tick away the seconds, one by one, their sluggish pace as slow and thick as molasses. God, she couldn't take this. The waiting was going to destroy her sanity. Mason had been gone for hours, and with each minute that passed, her worry and fear multiplied at an exponential rate.

She sat at one end of the leather sofa in the basement—Elliot at the other, watching the MTV countdown—while her mind chewed over her troubling thoughts, trying to make sense of the chaos that had become her life. She didn't find any answers, but her head now hurt like hell.

Then the downstairs phone rang out on Jeremy's bedside table, and she looked over her shoulder to watch him set his Clive Cussler novel aside. He answered the call, and seconds later his brow pulled into a tight grimace. "Okay, hold on just a sec. I've got him right here, honey."

"Yo, Elliot," he called out over the music, putting one hand over the receiver. "This one's for you."

The teenager looked up, reluctantly taking his dark eyes from the half-naked girls dancing in one the latest hip-hop videos. "It's for me?" he asked, frowning.

Jeremy shrugged, holding his hand over the mouthpiece. "It's some girl. No idea how she knows you're here, but she sounds pretty upset. I think you should take it."

At the mention of a girl, Elliot rushed across the room, snatching the phone out of Jeremy's hand. Wanting to give him as much privacy as possible, Torrance stood up and headed toward the stairs, thinking she'd try to find some aspirin for her head, when a loud *thwump* from the other side of the room stopped her. She spun back around, unable to believe the horrific scene playing out before her eyes. Jeremy lay slumped on the floor, blood oozing from a gash on his temple, while Elliot stood over him, the phone still clutched in his fingers…dripping with blood.

"Ohmygod! What happened?" she shouted, rushing to Jeremy and dropping to her knees beside him. She grabbed a discarded T-shirt from where it lay on the foot of his bed and pressed the soft cotton against the gash in his head.

"He's fine," Elliot panted, staring down at her. "I didn't hit him too hard. Just enough to knock him out. I didn't hurt him."

"How do you know if you hurt him?" she growled, glaring up at the pale-faced teenager. "You bashed his head in, Elliot! Of course he's hurt!"

Torrance watched as he walked to his bed and picked up the sweatshirt that Mason had loaned him, pulling it on over his T-shirt. He ran his palms up and down his thighs, then turned back toward her, his eyes all but glowing within the paleness of his face. "You've got to come with me, Torrance."

"What the hell's going on, Elliot? Who was on the phone?"

Moving slowly, she reached toward the cell phone hooked on Jeremy's belt, but Elliot rushed forward, unclipping it and hurling it toward the wall on the opposite side of the room. It hit with a sharp, metallic sound, tumbling to the floor in scattered pieces. "You can't call him!" he shouted, shoving his hands into his hair, his arms curled over his head, panic riding him hard. "You can't call anyone!"

Just stay calm, Torrance. Do not freak out.

Taking a deep breath, she went back to applying pressure to Jeremy's temple, trying to make sense out of what was happening—but it was too bizarre, like something out of a dream. "Why are you doing this?" she asked as calmly as possible, when what she really wanted to do was scream. "Was it Simmons?"

"It was Marly. Simmons has her," Elliot said huskily, looking ill. "And…and Mason's mother."

"Oh, God," she whispered, squeezing her eyes shut as she tried to think over the pounding in her head. She tried to stay calm, but panic was sinking too deeply into her system, Jeremy's warm blood seeping through the thin cotton, wetting her fingers. "God, Elliot. If that's true, Jeremy could have helped us!"

"No!" he shouted. "You don't understand. She said they're going to kill them both if we don't go to him. *Now.*"

"Like hell," she cried, lunging for the blood-covered phone that he'd tossed on the bed. Before she could touch it, Elliot had her trapped against him, her back to his front, one lean but impossibly strong arm locked around her waist.

"Please," he rasped against her ear. "Don't make me hurt you, Torrance. I swear I'm telling you the truth."

She wanted to struggle but took a deep, shuddering breath, trying to reason with him. "Are you sure it was Marly? Maybe he was just trying to trick you, Elliot."

"I'm sure. And he said to tell you that he has the bitch's necklace and her...her pictures of her boys. What's he talking about?"

"This can't be happening," she groaned, her head falling forward as the enormity of the situation pressed in on her, like a crushing pain in her chest, making it difficult to breathe. "He's talking about Olivia Dillinger's locket. She has Mason's picture in it, along with his brother's. We need to wait for them to get back, Elliot. We can't do this alone."

"No," he argued. "We've got to go now. I c-can't leave her up there with him."

"Elliot," she said numbly, reluctantly accepting what she had to do. He was too terrified for Marly's safety to listen to reason, and she couldn't leave Olivia on her own with that monster. But, God, Mason was going to *kill* her when he got his hands on her. *Furious* wasn't even going to begin to cover how he'd react when he learned that she'd allowed herself to end up in Simmons's clutches, but there didn't seem to be any other choice. She only hoped he got back in time to help Jeremy. She didn't think the wound would be serious for a Lycan, but she still hated to leave him alone.

Shoving her own terror at the thought of facing Simmons again to the back of her mind, knowing it would only make her hysterical, she said, "Okay, Elliot. Okay. I'll go with you."

"Come on," he said, his voice cracking. He released his hold on her body, but grabbed hold of her wrist, pulling her along behind him. "We've got to hurry."

They stepped out under a cloud-smothered sky, the thick covering blocking out the warmth of the late-afternoon sun, and Torrance shivered, wrapping her arms around herself. She hadn't even had time to grab her jacket, and the dark green sweater she wore was too thin for the freezing wind that made her teeth chatter. Or maybe that was just the biting cut of fear slicing through her system. Torrance knew Elliot wouldn't hurt her—but she also knew better than to think that Simmons was going to just let her walk away. No, he was going to play with her, use her and Olivia to lure Mason onto his turf, and then she was going to be forced to watch the man she loved fight for his life.

Torrance knew Mason would win. She *knew* it. But she didn't trust Simmons to fight fair. And what of Elliot? She couldn't imagine Simmons letting the young man go. No. He was too much of a liability. "Did you set them up?" she asked, dreading his answer as they hiked their way through the dense forest, the wind whistling through the higher branches, splashes of thin light making the shadows deep.

"What?" he asked, his voice gruff with fear.

"Did you lie to Mason and the others about what you remembered today? Just tell me the truth."

"You think I lied to Mason?" he rasped, cutting her a sharp look.

"Did you?"

"No," he growled. "God, Torrance, I have no desire to be torn limb from limb, even though that's what will happen now that…I've done this."

"Elliot, I know you're scared, but you've got to talk to me. I can't help you if you don't."

"Help me? Hell, Torrance," he snorted, shaking his head. "Only you would talk about helping someone who was kidnapping you."

"I know you wouldn't hurt me, Elliot. But you're going to have to work with me, or we're both going to end up dead."

"Don't waste your time worrying about me," he grunted, holding a low-hanging limb out of her way. "We both know Mason is going to kill me one way or another now."

"Elliot," she said, the sound hollow…because she believed

the same thing. "You should have just trusted them. They would have helped you."

"It doesn't matter." He hunched his shoulders, his expression bleak. "I can't— I have to do what I can to make sure nothing happens to Marly." His throat worked, and she knew he was choking back tears, the expression in his brown eyes a mixture of fury, helplessness and despair. "It's because of me that he went after her. Now it's up to me to get her out of there."

"No," Torrance murmured, determined to do whatever she could to make things right—even though they'd all gone terribly, terribly wrong. But she wouldn't abandon him. Not with Marly and Olivia's lives at stake. "It's up to *us,* Elliot. You're not in this alone."

Before Mason had reached the south side of Flat Rock, Brody called to say that they'd found evidence of another feeding in a cave on the north ridge. He'd driven straight there, and they'd picked up a faint scent trail in the surrounding woods, which they'd been tracking for hours, but the gusting easterly wind slowed their progress. In an effort to keep quiet, he'd set his phone to vibrate—nearly jumping out of his skin when it began buzzing on his hip.

"Yeah?" he rasped, lifting the phone to his ear.

"Do you know how I catch them, Dillinger? I strip away their humanity and tempt the beast with blood, with the beauty of the ultimate kill. All it takes is once, that one first sweet taste of ultimate power, and they're hooked, tighter than a junkie at a heroin banquet. It's *that* intoxicating. They never stand a chance against me…and neither will you."

"Wanna bet?"

"I'll give you a bet…but I don't think you're going to like the odds."

Something in the bastard's voice was too smug, and Mason felt the icy claws of panic dig painfully into his gut.

"You know what I like best about her, Dillinger? This fiery hair of hers. Is she that red everywhere? No, don't tell me," he laughed. "I'm looking forward to finding out all on my own. Bet she tastes like strawberries."

"Is this your new game?" Mason grunted, his heart pounding hard and fast. "Because I hate like hell to tell ya that I ain't buying it."

"You will," the rogue whispered. "See ya soon, Dillinger."

The line went dead, and Mason stood there in the middle of the woods, paralyzed while his mind raced, all chaos and emotion, instinct and reaction. The pain in his chest was so sharp, so cutting, that for a moment he couldn't breathe… couldn't move. Then he exploded into action, calling the others, ordering them to meet him back at the Tahoe. Within minutes they were speeding through the forest, while he drove like a thing possessed, nearly overturning them twice as the sky broke open with a heavy downpour.

By the time they reached the Alley, Mason was nearly out of his mind. He'd called home over and over, but there was no answer. The same went for Jeremy's cell phone, and he didn't even know Torrance's number. The Tahoe was still grinding to a slippery stop when he threw open the door and ran for the cabin, shoving the front door open so hard that it bounced three times against the wall.

"Torrance!" he shouted. "Jeremy! Goddamn it, somebody answer me!"

There were no signs of a struggle, nor was there any sign of his woman or his partner…or Elliot. A primal roar of fury surged up from his chest, but he choked it down, determined to use his head and not let the panic take hold of him. But, God, it wasn't easy.

Where the hell are they?

The door to the basement was open, and he rushed down the stairway, nearly dying when he found Jeremy sprawled on the floor, a dark pool of blood under his head, a wicked-looking gash on his temple.

"Jesus Christ," Mason growled, dropping down beside his slowly stirring partner. "Jeremy, damn it, wake up! Where's Torrance?"

Jeremy groaned, the sound rough with pain, and turned his head toward Mason, squinting up at him. "Mase? Oh shit…gotta go…get her."

"What the hell happened?"

"Phone call…for Elliot. Some girl. Don't know who," Jeremy muttered, wincing as his fingers probed around the edges of his wound. "He freaked…hit me when I wasn't looking. I can't remember anything more, man."

"It's got to be Simmons," Mason grunted, his breathing loud and harsh. "They… God, that bastard must have her. Did you hear anything about where they might have gone?"

"I wish I had, Mase," Jeremy hissed, his features pulled into a tight grimace as he sat up. "But he was only on the phone for a few seconds before he lost it."

Cian's low voice came from the other side of the room. "I hope you got smart and bonded with her while you had the chance, Dillinger. The rain is already letting up, but any trace of her scent is gone by now. Your only chance is to use the blood bond connection to find her."

"What the hell are you talking about?" he rasped, the dread in his gut turning into something ugly and dark. His beast paced within the confines of his body, restless with fury, ready to break free then and there. "I thought that only worked with emotions or feelings or whatever the hell you call it."

Cian nodded. "Yeah, but I know of Lycans who claim that

the blood bond can be used for physical locations, too. If you open up the link, you should be able to pick up her signal like some kind of metaphysical radio beacon. Just stop panicking and focus. You'll know where she's gone."

A sickening wave of guilt and shame slammed through him; so strong it would have taken him to his knees—if he wasn't already on them.

"Now, there's a thought," Jeremy grunted, holding the blood-soaked T-shirt against his head as he glared at him. Unlike Cian, who hadn't seen Torrance since yesterday, Jeremy had spent the day with her. His partner knew damn well that he still hadn't bitten her. "Use the bond. Why don't you do that, Mase?"

The admission stuck in his throat like a boulder. "I…can't."

"What do you mean, you can't?" Brody scowled, standing beside his partner. "Don't tell us you still haven't made a blood bond with her," he muttered with disbelief. "She's had a goddamn rogue after her and you didn't bond with her?"

"Of course he hasn't. Because he's too afraid. Isn't that right, Mason?" his father called out from the bottom of the stairway, looking as if he'd been through hell and back. His salt-and-pepper hair was matted on the left side of his head, gray sweater torn on his right shoulder.

Moving to his feet, Mason shook his head in disbelief. "What the hell happened to you? Where's Mom?"

"I'm betting the same place they have your woman," his father growled. "You going with me to get them back?"

"You know where they are?" he asked, feeling like the one who'd been knocked on the head.

"One of us isn't too afraid to follow his heart. Of course I know where they are!"

Ripping his hands through his hair, Mason struggled to control his temper. "Do you want to explain what happened—or just keep shouting at me?"

"Your mother had some things she wanted to bring Torrance, so we were on our way back to the Alley when they shot out the tires on my truck," his father muttered. "Damn thing rolled over on its side, and by the time I made my way out, they'd already taken her away. And that's enough with the bloody questions. Right now we need to get our women!"

"So where are they?" he growled, the fear in his gut so vicious, he felt ill.

"I'll tell you as soon as somebody gets me a map."

"I'll grab the one out of the Tahoe," Brody called out, already heading up the stairs. Mason offered a hand to Jeremy, helping his partner to his feet, and Brody came running back in with the map. They laid it out over the end of Jeremy's bed, his father's dark eyes roaming...searching...and then he jabbed his forefinger at a specific point, nearly ripping the paper. "There. That's it. That's where he's got them."

"Holy shit," Jeremy rasped. "I'd heard, like Cian, that a blood bond could be used like this, like some kind of internal tracking system, but never really believed that it would work."

"Of course it works," his father grunted, shaking his head at their stunned expressions.

Looking at Jeremy, Mason asked, "Can you make it?"

His partner sent him a dirty look. "I'd like to see you try and stop me," he muttered.

"Then let's move out."

"We can drive part of the way," his father grunted, studying the map. "But then we're going to have to make the last bit on foot."

"I don't care how we get there," Mason snarled, already heading for the door. "Let's just make it fast."

The air sighed through the trees, soft and silent, like a whisper weaving quietly through a room. The fear that had been riding Mason since Simmons's phone call had a chokehold on him, churning his insides into a mass of rage and stark, shredding terror. Sweat dripped from his face, slipping down his spine, palms damp as he clenched and unclenched his fists while they hiked their way through the woods. His father led the way, as he'd earned the right, considering it was his instincts that had led them this far. And they knew they were on the right path. A couple hundred meters back, they'd found one of Torrance's colorfully braided bracelets among the leaves scattered over the damp forest floor. The sight of the woven hemp had damn near brought Mason to his knees in anguish, as well as relief.

She was still alive…but for how long? Christ, if anything happened to her, he wasn't going to be able to deal with it. And suddenly he understood the depth of his stupidity with perfect clarity.

He'd wasted all this time struggling with his fears, battling his hungers, blind to the fact that his heart was already hers.

He loved her.

God, he was such a blind, raging idiot for not realizing it. And now that he had, all he wanted was to take her in his arms and bind them together for always. He wanted to sink his teeth into the fragile column of her throat, drink from the rich spill of her blood, and complete what was already an unbreakable claim on his heart.

He was willing to lay down his life to keep her safe—but what he wasn't willing to do was lose her.

Not now. Not ever.

The group stopped at the exact point where the dense forest tapered into tall grass, just before meeting the rocky face of a sheer wall of granite. There was a shadowed entrance carved out like a gaping mouth into the stone facade, the warm glow of a fire flickering inside, like a dragon preparing to expel his fiery breath.

Mason lifted his head, nostrils flaring as the wind rushed

over him, and there, on the air, was the most beautiful scent in the world. It was perfect and sweet, because she was *his*—and yet, heartbreaking in its revelation of his failures. Torrance was terrified. He could scent her fear, her sheer horror, and the wolf inside of him snarled a sinister sound of outrage, ready to charge ahead and storm the entrance.

As if reading his mind, his father shot out his arm, blocking his path as he surged forward. "Not yet, Mason. We're going to do this according to the laws of our people."

"Like hell we are. They're *your* people, Dad. Not mine."

"Mason, let it go," his father rasped, his deep voice urgent and low, one powerful hand clutching at his arm. "The longer you harbor the anger, the longer your heart will remain locked up in that miserable knot you've created. Let it go…and accept that you've been blessed."

"And what about Torrance?" he hissed, jerking free of his father's grip. "What about her? This is some blessing, isn't it, Dad? I promised her that I'd keep her safe from the monsters and look what's happened. Thanks to me, she's in there with that bastard!"

Cian moved beside them, his gray eyes burning like twin pale flames of fire in the lavender twilight. "Simmons and the boy are the only Lycans I can scent on the air. He's in there alone, with the women and Elliot."

"Not for long he isn't." Unable to wait any longer, Mason rushed forward, breaking through the line of the trees at the exact moment the sun dipped to the edge of the horizon, the sky a mesmerizing smear of pink and purple and gold. The rushing wind surged around his body, bitter and cool against his face, catching at his scent.

"Don't bother to knock," Simmons called out when he reached the dark mouth of the cave. "We've been waiting for you, Dillinger. Come in and join our little party."

With his heart in his throat, he stalked forward, his wolf's eyes adjusting to the darker, firelit interior of the dank cave, his father and the Runners at his back, fanning out at his sides. An unbelievable rush of relief nearly floored him at the sight of Torrance wrapped in his mother's arms to their right. Her skin shone as pale and luminous as a ghost, head buried in his mother's shoulder, but she was whole and dressed and, amazingly, untouched.

Thank God.

His mother appeared just as shaken as his mate, her dark eyes hollow with fear. Elliot lay slumped against the ground, unmoving, a few feet away from the women, and on the far side of the cave, Simmons sat upon a massive boulder, his elbows resting on his bent knees. The rogue's arms and face and bare torso were covered in blood, his jeans streaked with more of the dark crimson, the tangled length of his long brown hair slicked back from his narrow face. Beneath his sharp brows, his eyes were sunken, lifeless hollows.

Keeping one eye on the Lycan, Mason moved toward the women, pulling Torrance into his arms, cradling her head to his chest, aware of his father embracing his mother beside them. He wanted to crush her in his arms and tell her that everything was going to be okay, but he couldn't get the words out.

"Just look at them, Mason," the rogue called out, a satisfied smile curling the sinister line of his blood-smeared mouth. More blood dripped down his chin, matting in the thick pelt of hair covering his chest. "The two things you care about most in this world, and they're all mine."

"Like hell they are," he snarled, tightening his arms around Torrance until she groaned softly against his chest, her face buried against him, and he forced himself to relax his hold.

"Oh, I'll fight you for them," the Lycan laughed. "And then, while you lie dying, I'll enjoy them both…while you watch."

"You've overstepped the bounds of depravity, Simmons," his father growled, his deep voice guttural with rage. He had said they were going to handle this "according to the laws of their people," and Mason knew that meant a proper, ceremonial Challenge fight—or, in simpler terms, a fight to the death. Before Robert Dillinger could utter the words Mason knew were coming, he said, "Consider yourself Challenged, Simmons."

"Oh, goodie," the Lycan laughed with a smile, rubbing his bloodstained hands together. "This is going to be fun."

Mason grunted, then pulled Torrance with him as he moved toward the wall of the cave, wanting her as far from the rogue as possible. He was aware of the others following behind them, while Brody stayed in place, keeping a careful eye on Simmons, who watched them with an amused expression. "You're both...unharmed?" he asked hoarsely, barely able to force the words past the tightness in his throat, his gaze moving swiftly between the two women.

His mother nodded, while Torrance stared up at him, their terror so stark and raw it made him want to rush at Simmons and tear the bastard's throat out with his fangs. The only thing that stopped him was the knowledge that his father would hold him back, demanding he handle the situation according to the rules. "What happened to Elliot?"

"Your woman happened to him, Mason," his mother told them with a small, sad smile. "He was ready to Challenge that monster himself, so she brained him with a rock. She saved the boy's life."

"Not for long," he muttered. "I'm killing him for this, as soon as he's awake to fight me."

"You can't do that," Torrance whispered brokenly, sagging against the rough wall at her back. "None of this is his fault, Mase. He only wanted to save Marly, but when we got here,

Simmons was—" She swallowed convulsively, her face too pale, and he knew what she couldn't say.

A deep, guttural slash of sound rumbled in his chest, full of anguish and pain. *"He killed the girl?"*

Torrance nodded, blinking slowly, her green eyes red and swollen with her grief. "I had…I had to stop Elliot. He was going to get himself killed, so I did the only thing I could think of."

"You knocked him out?"

"Yeah," she said shakily, wrapping her arms around her slender body, as if she were trying to hold herself together.

"You're amazing," he breathed out on a husky groan, so proud of her that it hurt.

Crouching down beside the teenager, Jeremy pushed the thick caramel locks back from Elliot's temple, checking the injury. "Looks like the night for getting your brains bashed in. But who knows? Maybe she knocked some sense back into him," he muttered. "I still can't believe he was stupid enough to try this on his own."

"He didn't have a choice," she whispered, trembling, staring at Jeremy with tear-drenched eyes. "It was Marly on the phone. She told him that Simmons had her and Olivia, and that he was going to kill them if Jeremy didn't bring me to him. Then we found Simmons…and he…he…"

"Don't think about it," Mason grunted, hating that she'd witnessed something so terrifying and evil—something straight out of her nightmares—and he hadn't been able to stop it.

Torrance rolled her lips inward, lifting one shoulder. "I couldn't think of anything else to do, so I hit him. It wasn't even that hard a blow, but I think I might have struck where he got hit before."

Moving to Mason's side, Cian cast a long, heavy look toward the rogue waiting across the cave, watching them with feral anticipation. "He's going to be damn near impossible to take down, Dillinger. He's still riding high on the rush."

"What do you mean?" Torrance asked.

"For a Lycan," the Runner explained, "eating human flesh is almost the ultimate high. It jacks you up like pure adrenaline."

"Then he'll be even harder to defeat," she gasped, panting as she began to panic. "You said it was almost the ultimate high, Cian. Wh-what's better?"

"Bond blood," Jeremy muttered grimly, glaring at his partner.

"Bond blood?" she repeated, grabbing on to Mason's arm with a biting grip. "If that's all you need to make yourself stronger, then do it, Mason. My God, you *have* to do it!"

He shook his head, cupping her face in his hands, catching at one glistening tear with his thumb as it slipped from the corner of her eye. "I won't do this to you, not after what you've been through tonight. I won't use you, Torrance."

"Damn it, don't do this," she cried, gripping his wrists, her lips trembling as her voice cracked. "You have to do it, Mason! I don't want to lose you. *Please.*"

"I can't," he growled, the irony of the situation not lost on him. He'd been so sure that she would refuse his bite out of fear if the moment ever came where he found the courage to ask her, and now that he'd finally stopped being such a blind jackass and realized he was head over heels, crazy in love with her—now that she was standing before him, proud and courageous, willing to accept the most primal act of his beast—he couldn't. After what she'd been through tonight, seeing a young girl consumed by Simmons, there was no way Mason was going to make her stand there and take his fangs in her throat. No way was he going to risk binding her to him, then leaving her to follow him into death if he couldn't defeat the bastard.

He had everything he wanted standing before him, and he couldn't take it.

Because he loved her.

"I know you don't love me," she whispered, her heartbreaking words husky with pain as she stared at his throat, "but don't do this, Mason. Don't let him kill you. *Please.* I'll release you afterward, I swear it. We'll find some way to have it reversed, canceled, anything. Just don't…don't let him kill you. I can't watch that, Mason. I can't live through that."

"Torrance, baby, look at me." She lifted tear-drenched eyes the color of the forest in the height of spring, and his heart rolled over, filling him with so much love, he couldn't hold it all inside. "I love you," he said on a harsh breath of air, grinning at the vision of her eyes going completely round, her mouth opening into a perfect *O* of surprise.

"Wh-what?" she gasped, tears spilling down her cheeks like tiny rivers, wetting his hands as they cradled her face.

"I love you," he said fervently. "Love you so much that I don't even know how to explain it. All I know is that you're in my heart, my mind, the air that I breathe, every part of me. *I love you.*"

"Then you'll do it? You'll make the bond with me?"

He shook his head, leaning forward to press a tender kiss to the corner of her eye. "I won't do it, sweetheart. Not like this. Not after what you've been through, not—"

"Who cares what I've been through?" she cried, gripping handfuls of his shirt in her hands. "I'm alive, Mason. But if you die—"

"If I died, you'd die, too," he growled, pressing a hot, hungry kiss against her trembling mouth. "And there's no way I'm letting that happen."

Mason released his hold on the woman he loved, and turned toward Simmons. As he walked to the middle of the cave, the bloody remains of the girl became visible on the far side of the boulder where the Lycan remained sitting. The closer he moved toward the rogue, the thicker the scent of blood and sex grew, making him ill at the thought of what his mother and Torrance had witnessed. And yet, Torrance hadn't faltered. If ever he were given proof that his little human was a warrior, it was now. She was all fire and strength and courage. A woman who would stand by his side as an equal, and help him meet any challenges that life threw at them.

Cian moved to his side, placing a cigarette between his lips, then dug deep in his pocket for a lighter. "Robert," he said around the slim roll of tobacco clasped within his white teeth, "it should be your honor to make the circle."

His father moved to stand before them, reaching down to dig his right hand into the moist earth, clutching a handful of soil. He stood, calling out the ancient ritual words of Challenge as he sprinkled the dirt upon the ground at four points—north, east, south and west. The points served as markers for the wide circle he then proceeded to draw in the ground with his hand in four connecting arcs. As he closed the circle, he completed the ritual with the words, "So the Challenge is raised. May justice be done when victory falls to the last wolf standing."

Waiting at the circle's edge, Mason pulled off his shirt and dropped it to the ground. He shook his arms out at his sides, bouncing lightly on the soles of his boot-covered feet as he watched Simmons move to the opposite side, across from him. "Shall we go whole or half forms?" the rogue drawled, a hard, ruthless energy all but burning from his body, pulsing around him like a fiery glow.

"Half," he grunted, wondering how Torrance was going to react to his change—and half-terrified that she'd never want to come near him again if he survived.

"I thought you might say that," Simmons laughed, looking past him to wink at the women.

His father placed a hand on his shoulder, giving an affectionate squeeze, his dark blue eyes full of pride and concern. "Any words of advice?" Mason asked roughly.

"Yeah. Torrance may be scared of our world, but what woman in her right mind wouldn't be? She's also strong and fiery and protective as hell of you. If you're in love with her, she deserves your faith."

"She's my mate."

"Which takes care of nature. But sometimes a union comes along that truly sets the metaphysical world on its ass. I was lucky enough to find it with your mother. It's time you completed the bond. Don't blow your chance, son. Life's too short."

He snorted, shaking his head at the old man's audacity. "I promise you that if I make it out of this cave alive, sinking my teeth into her is going to be at the top of my list. But I'm not doing it now."

Those dark eyes narrowed with a hard truth. "You may not win otherwise, Mason."

"But if I do, I've got a helluva good thing to look forward to."

Cian snuffled a quiet chuckle at his side and then he felt her heat at his back, followed by the soft touch of her palm against his spine. Spinning around, Mason pulled her against him, kissing his way into her mouth.

"I won't risk you that way," he growled against her lips, kissing her deeper…harder, before gently pushing her away. He sent a silent message to Jeremy, who came forward and wrapped his arm around her shoulders, securing her at his side.

"I love you, Torrance. Whatever happens, don't forget that," he said in a low rasp, and before she could respond, he turned back around, trusting his partner to watch over her. Taking a deep breath, Mason bowed his head, then stepped within the circle, ready for the battle to begin.

Chapter 13

With her heart in her throat, Torrance watched the man she loved and the murderer who'd made their lives a living hell face off against each other. Her breath caught, a hard, painful knot churning in her chest...because she knew what was coming.

Oh, God...oh, God...oh, God.

His mother grabbed her right hand, holding it tightly, his father flanking Olivia's other side. Jeremy stood at her left, and Brody moved into place beside him, while Cian stood beside Robert. It was a show of support, for both her and Mason, as well as a sign of strength.

If Mason died, they weren't going to let Simmons have her without a fight.

Oh, God, please. Please don't let him die.

Torrance forced herself to take a deep breath, then another, the sound whistling past her compressed lips as she watched both men throw back their heads, arms held out at their sides, feet braced firmly against the damp, fetid ground of the cave.

And then it began.

Like an earthquake riding under the earth's crust, Mason's wolf rolled beneath the surface of his skin. His muscles flexed, skin dark and damp with sweat, the air humid and sharp with animal musk—and it broke through. One second he was her lover, her mate, the man who possessed her heart—and then he wasn't.

He became something she didn't know, didn't recognize, foreign and unfamiliar. Thick, chestnut fur covered the upper half of his body, his hard musculature expanding, bulging with power and strength. Gnarled, deadly claws formed at the end of his powerful arms, while his head took on the hulking shape of a wolf. Only his lower half remained unchanged, the fur tapering, blending into golden skin at his waist.

Ohmygod, she thought, knowing that she should be terrified, but she wasn't. His massive head turned, glowing golden eyes finding her, holding her with the intensity of his gaze, and a smooth, melting warmth poured through her. She'd been wrong. This was no stranger. It was *Mason,* and he was beautiful, no matter what form he wore. She could see the traces of the man in those mesmerizing eyes, the worry and fear that she would reject this side of him. She wanted to run to him and hold him, tell him what a fool he was for thinking she could ever think of him as anything less than perfect. She tried to express her emotions with a warm, tender smile of love, her breath catching when the heat in that golden stare blazed, fiery and bright.

Time held, silent and heavy, and then he slowly turned back toward Simmons, and in the next breath they exploded into action. They came together with a harsh, meaty sound, their bodies slamming into one another with preternatural power, snarling and gnashing at each other with white, gleaming fangs.

Torrance pumped her fist in the air when Mason knocked Simmons onto his back, then winced as the black wolf countered with a roundhouse that whipped Mason's head to the side, blood spurting from his nose.

The two combatants moved apart, dancing on the balls of their feet the same way she'd seen boxers do, their movements light despite the muscular, bulky forms of their wolves.

"Finish him quickly, Mase!" Jeremy called out, his deep voice guttural and raw.

"Yeah," Cian rasped around the cigarette wedged between his lips. "Kick his ugly ass and make it hurt. The pathetic bastard deserves the pain."

They went at each other again in a volley of slashes and kicks, the choreography of their movements oddly beautiful, at the same time it horrified her with its violence. Biting and sharp, their rage radiated through the moist, firelit cave like a noxious vapor that coated the skin. Torrance rubbed her chilled palms against her arms, as if she could rub off that thick, cloying film of hatred, but it was too strong.

She'd never truly understood how powerful the vile emotion could be until now. And it made her admire Mason all the more, for the fact that he could face such evil and survive without the encounter blackening his soul.

The fight escalated, and she watched as Mason landed a powerful side kick that made Simmons stumble, but the rogue countered with a slash of his claws that ripped across her lover's chest, making him snarl with pain. "Come on, Mase," she whispered beneath her breath, but Simmons kept coming. Harder. Faster. Like something impossible to take down.

And her fear nearly choked her.

Simmons landed another powerful roundhouse, and Mason's head spun, the edges of his vision going dark, and in that stark, vivid moment, he realized the rogue was almost too powerful to beat.

Almost…but Mason had something the rogue didn't have. *Torrance.*

He had the promise of a future with the most amazing woman who wanted to share her life with him. Who would grow old with him; give him a family and a lifetime of love and laughter and smiles.

Simmons's claws slashed at his left shoulder, ripping through skin in a scalding flash of pain, the rush the rogue had gained from killing Marly making him too fast, too powerful. When another kick came at the right side of his head, he went down, his knees slamming into the ground with a bone-jarring impact. Sweat and blood streamed into his eyes, while relentless waves of pain rolled through him, threatening to take him under, sucking him down into that crushing state of darkness.

"Get up, you ass," he snarled at himself, and he could hear Simmons circling him, feel the suffocating blackness of the rogue's hatred and rage lashing against him.

He shook his head, struggling to gain his feet, when a sweet, perfect sound broke through the disorienting haze of pain that surrounded him. It seemed so far away, like someone shouting at him through water, and he couldn't make out the words. Then it came at him again, louder this time, battering against his consciousness with a blinding urgency—and suddenly he heard Torrance calling out to him, the sound of her voice making his blood surge. "Kick him back, Mason! Damn it, don't you dare die on me! You have to fight. You have to, because I love you, Mason! I love you!"

"Torrance!" he hissed, blinking his eyes as he tried to find her through that blanketing fog of pain. He lifted his head, searching through the faces at the edge of the circle, and the moment their gazes connected—her eyes tear-drenched and so

full of love—an intense, explosive energy surged through him, charging him up, revitalizing him, hitting him like an emotional shock to his system. Mason drew on it, on the love and life that he wanted to share with her, feeling the magnificence of it pour through his body.

God, he'd been such a fool. All the time he'd wasted thinking he'd be sucking wind, incapacitated by fear if he gave in to this emotion, when he couldn't have been more wrong. It wasn't fear that filled him; it was love—its power more potent than anything he'd ever known. Loving her didn't make him vulnerable. That's what Dean had been trying to tell him. It made him strong, and hearing her say she loved him only intensified that power until it was rushing through his veins like a life-giving force, making him all but invincible.

"I've been waiting for this day," Simmons growled at his back, the garbled words dripping with satisfaction, and he thought, *Finish it, Dillinger. Finish it now.*

Swiftly twisting to his feet, Mason turned and immediately went on the attack, his claws striking, ripping through fur and skin and muscle, and he watched as the rogue's eyes went wide with fear. With a roaring battle cry, Mason kept advancing, swiping at Simmons's head with one set of claws, slashing at his furred gut with the other, landing blow after blow, while the rogue tried to retreat. But Mason was too fast, too strong. With a husky, bellowing shout, he swung his right leg into a powerful roundhouse that slammed into the side of Simmons's skull, breaking his upper jaw and sending him crashing to the floor of the cave.

The Lycan lay facedown in the dirt, until Mason nudged him over onto his back with one booted foot.

Simmons was still alive…but not for long. Blood bubbled on the rogue's black lips, even as he motioned Mason closer. "You can't stop it, Dillinger." Mason stared down at him, and the rogue smiled, his teeth smeared with streaks of crimson. "You're going to find more bodies. Like the redhead. Like the pretty little blondes your friends keep finding. It's never going to end."

"It'll end," he grunted. "Just like this."

"Won't matter." The rogue laughed, sputtering as blood filled his mouth. "You'll see. There'll be…more killings. More rogues. There are so many pieces of this puzzle that you don't even know about. But it was fun making that kill. I knew it would screw with your head, seeing all that pretty red hair." Simmons's mouth twisted, eyes red with the glittering burn of hate. "You can't win."

"I already did," Mason rasped, his chest heaving. "I'm the last wolf standing, you miserable son of a bitch, and you're out of time."

"My death is only the beginning," Simmons gasped. "You have no idea what you're up against. When they make their move, you *will* die, Dillinger. All of you will."

"Not if they die first." And bending down beside the body, he took Simmons's head into his claws, and ended the Challenge once and for all.

Mason had no so sooner turned away from Simmons's body than he found Torrance launching herself into his arms. With a choking sob, she buried her nose in his thick fur, clutching at him, her body shaking with a fine tremor of relief, and something vibrant exploded in his chest, the searing emotion nearly bringing him to his knees.

Though he was more wolf than man, she embraced him. Accepted him. And she'd told him that she loved him.

Oh, God, please. Let it be true.

Drawing a deep breath into his lungs, he allowed his wolf to pull back into his body, the change spilling over him like a warm, smooth wave of water, and he lifted her into his arms, crushing her against his chest. Catching Jeremy's eye, he said,

"I'll buy you a whole case of Lagavulin if you'll take Elliot home with you tonight."

His partner gave him a two-fingered salute and a smile. "Not a problem, man."

Nodding a goodbye toward his parents and friends, Mason walked out of the cave, heading into the autumn night, carrying his mate into the dense forest, driven by the need to get her home before he lost the tenuous hold on his control.

"Mason," she said quietly, her voice still husky from the tears she'd cried. "Are you sure you're okay to carry me? I know you must be in pain." Her head rested on his uninjured shoulder as she gently brushed her fingertips over the pounding of his heart, carefully avoiding the angry-looking wounds left from Simmons's claws.

He pressed a kiss to her temple, urging his legs to move faster. "I don't feel a thing," he told her, and it was true. Though his body should have been steeped in agony, he felt amazingly good, riding an emotional high that blocked out any discomfort from his injuries. And for the first time in years his heart was at peace. The wind blew through the trees, shaking the fall leaves from their branches until they fell gently to the ground, crunching beneath the soles of his boots as he navigated his way through the moonlit woods. After the evil they'd survived, it felt so good, so right, to be surrounded by the peaceful sounds of the forest, holding the woman he loved in his arms.

"I meant every word, Mason. I *do* love you, and I'm so proud of you," she told him in an aching whisper, lifting her head from his shoulder. With her raised hand, she brushed his damp hair back from his temple in a tender gesture of caring. His arms trembled, holding her tighter, and she grinned, a spark of wicked excitement burning in her eyes. "Now that it's over, where are you taking me?"

"Home," he grunted, wincing at the primitive hunger roughening the edges of his speech. "Then I'm taking your sweet little backside straight to bed, and I'm not letting you out of it for at least a week."

"I'm good with that." Her gaze lowered, following the movement of her fingers as they stroked against the warm skin of his throat. "Are you going to make a bond with me?" she asked.

Hanging on the verge of something feral and violent—something beyond his control—his gaze dropped to her mouth. "You believe that I won't hurt you, Tor?"

It made Mason's heart do some weird skipping thing, the way her tender smile bloomed like a promise—something fragile and sweet and beautiful. When she lifted her gaze, her eyes glistened with breathtaking emotion. "I believe you're the most wonderful thing that's ever happened to me. Of course you won't hurt me."

"Torrance, I'm sorry for being such a blind jackass these past few days," he muttered in a rough, breathless rush of words, his heart pounding in his chest to a violent, thudding rhythm. "I just couldn't let go of the fear, sweetheart, like it was locked up inside of me. And then, when I thought I'd lost you, everything broke open. I...I knew then that I loved you, that I'd been falling in love with you from the moment I found you, and I couldn't stop it. I didn't want to stop it."

"I wanted you to make the bond in the cave," she admitted, her voice velvet-soft as it stroked his senses. "I still do."

Mason closed his eyes as the hunger swept through him like a hot wind, bringing with it the piercing eagerness for what was to come. "I *need* it, Tor. I need that connection to you."

She pressed her mouth to the corner of his jaw, the touch of her lips so innocent and yet wildly evocative. "I need it, too, Mason." Then she shifted in his arms, tilting her head to the side, away from his body, and with trembling fingers she pulled the long waves of her hair over her shoulder, exposing the delicate line of her throat.

With burning eyes, Mason stared at the tender vein pulsing sweetly beneath the fragile skin…the most tempting thing he'd ever seen. His human half raged at him to keep walking, to get her home and into his bed, where she belonged—but the dominant hunger of the wolf could no longer be denied. "Torrance," he breathed against her temple, halting beneath the silvery moonlight, the swaying trees and rustling wind coming to a strange stillness, like captivated spectators. "I… I can't wait any longer."

"I don't want you to wait, Mase." She turned to look up at him, staring deeply into his eyes as she cupped the hot side of his face in her palm, her fingers cool against the burning heat of his skin.

"Do you know how I won tonight, Tor?"

"You kicked his ass," she said, giving him a mischievous grin.

"I thought of *you*," he told her, smiling with the joy of everything that he held in his arms. "Of everything I want with you. Want to be for you. Of the life I want to share with you. Thinking about how much I love you, regretting like hell that I hadn't told you sooner. And then you gave me the words, and it was like something coming to life inside of me. After that, there was no way I could lose."

"Mason…"

He kissed the corner of her mouth, the smooth arc of her cheekbone, the delicate line of her jaw. "I love you, Tor. The human half of my soul loves you. The wolf half loves you just as strongly. I love you because you're my heart, and simply because you're you, so beautiful and perfect and strong, inside and out. I know you deserve more than a nighttime forest," he growled, even as he panted against the delicate, milk-white length of her throat, his gums burning as razor-sharp canines began to slip free—the need to bite her pulsing through him like a raw, angry wound. "But I *can't* wait."

"Haven't we already waited long enough?" she asked, and he could have sworn there was a smile in her voice.

"I needed you to see what I'm capable of becoming," he grated, his chest heaving. "I needed you to see that, before you accepted this."

"Mason…" She sighed, and he could hear the desire thickening her words. "Don't you know I think you're beautiful, no matter what skin you wear?"

Groaning deep in his throat, he let her feet slip to the ground, his hands shaking as he ran them down the front of her body, her back to his chest. She shivered when his head lowered, his tongue flicking out to taste her skin—and, unable to wait a second longer, he sank the sharp points of his teeth into her sweetly yielding, vulnerable flesh.

Torrance cried out a sharp, sobbing sound of excitement, and his arms clutched at her with desperation, one wrapped around her hips, the other across her chest, his fingers cupping the perfect weight of her breast in his hand, her nipple swollen and hard against his palm. He stiffened against her, shuddering with pleasure as the breathtaking sensations rolled down his spine. It was too good, the rush of ecstasy so dark and sweet as her taste filled his mouth, warm and wildly exciting, and he pulled her hips tighter against him, his hardened shaft thickening to the point that he ached. He drank her in for as long as he dared, then pulled his fangs free with a gasping breath, nuzzling the small marks he'd made in her tender skin.

"I love you," he whispered, his voice shaking as he put the words into the warm curve of her throat. "God, Torrance, I'll love you forever."

She made a soft sound of satisfaction, and he lifted his head, watching the hard, evocative pleasure she'd experienced from the bite slowly drain away, leaving her drowsy and replete. "It felt so right," she murmured, a small smile of wonder on her lips.

"And perfect," he rasped, pressing a tender, reverent kiss to the hollow of her throat, the trembling curve of her jaw—and then he was cradling her against his chest again, his long legs eating up ground, aware of the need to get her home… *now*…before he ended up taking her right there in the forest. He carried her straight to the bathroom when they reached the cabin, stripping her before pulling her into the shower with him, quickly washing away the evidence of the nightmarish evening they'd survived.

And then finally…*finally* he was laying her down on his bed, covering her with the heat of his body—and everything in his world was right.

Lying on the cool, crisp sheets, Torrance gasped, lost in a heightened state of pleasure as Mason pressed a damp kiss to the curve of her breast, just before he took the nipple into the scorching, vivid heat of his mouth, suckling her with strong, deep pulls that made her writhe. He laughed a low, sexy rumble of sound as he moved to the other breast, pressing a kiss to the sensitive tip before sliding lower, his fingers biting into her hips—and she squeezed her eyes shut so tightly that brilliant, glittering sparks of crimson burned on the backs of her eyelids.

When his wicked tongue flicked against the tender indentation between her hip and thigh, she fisted her hands in the sheets, a low moan shivering in her throat as the rough slide of his palms pressed her thighs wide.

For one heart-stopping moment, she could feel the hungry, provocative press of his gaze—and then he touched her with his tongue.

"Your taste is unreal," he groaned in a broken rumble, his voice guttural and raw with unmistakable lust…and something darker. Deeper. Something surging from the animal side of his nature that called to her fragile humanity and made it melt. "I can't get enough of you."

"Please," she sobbed, begging, not even sure what she was begging for, but knowing that only Mason could give it to her. *"Please."*

"Come for me," he growled, the deliciously graphic words spoken against her tender flesh, pulling the pleasure up out of her. "I want to feel it, taste it. Come on, angel," he whispered, the erotic tickle of his breath adding to the overwhelming sensations rushing through her, making her crazed. *"Come for me."*

She couldn't have stopped it even if she'd wanted to. One second she was strung out on the painful, desperate edge of need, and then everything pulled tighter...closing in on her, hard and hot and brutal, and she went crashing over. The harsh, aggressive rush of ecstasy pushed her into a star-kissed, pulsing, blinding unknown, where nothing existed but the perfect, beautiful spasms rolling through her with vicious intensity. Deep and hungry and erotically intimate, his tongue thrust into her with carnal demand, taking everything he wanted—everything she had to give.

"Mason!" she gasped, arching and crying out as the pleasure consumed her, drowning her in wave after wave, until everything went black and still and warm in her mind.

When she came back, strands of hair stuck to her damp cheeks, her lips raw from the bite of her teeth as she'd tried to keep from screaming the roof down. She was destroyed, both inside and out, and yet he stared down at her as if he thought she were the most beautiful thing in the world. Gone was the dark, delicious brown of his sexy gaze—his eyes shining the golden color of his wolf once more.

She licked her swollen lips, blinking up at him while her body hummed, tingling sweetly from her temples down to her toes. *"Wow.* I hate to say it, but that was so amazing, I don't think there's any way you'll be able to top it," she taunted him playfully, her voice husky with satisfaction.

The warm line of his lips curled the barest fraction, making him appear endearingly boyish for a moment. "We'll see about that," he whispered against her mouth...and then there was no more breath for speaking. No more air. Nothing but Mason. He was everywhere. In her reeling senses, in the thoughts spinning deliciously through her head. The animal wildness of him slipped beneath her skin, intoxicating her, making her feverish with renewed desire. She groaned as his tongue stroked deep, conquering her mouth, his breathing violent and harsh as his hands clutched at her, their bodies damp with sweat, writhing against each other, unable to lie silent and still.

"Torrance," he whispered, and there was no mistaking the aching emotion in the roughness of his voice. "How do you do this to me?"

"Because you do the same to me. You know, all this time I thought I was waiting for a man who could match my ideal," she panted, working to get the words out over the thundering of her heart, wanting him to understand. "Someone who existed only in my mind, because it was safer that way. That way no one could let me down and drag me down with them. But really, all along, I was just waiting for *you*. Dreams are nothing but a way of passing the time until we find what we really want, Mase, until we realize where we're really meant to be. For me, that's here with you, and trust me when I say you're so much better than any dream I could have ever had."

Mason groaned from the surge of emotion that rushed through him at her words and lowered his head, sharing the air between their parted lips, aware of every decadent point of contact between their naked bodies. With a smile on his lips, he kissed his way into her mouth, and it was too good, too hot—

deliciously wicked and yet poignantly reverent. He wanted to worship her, love her, take care of her. Cherish her. He wanted to make a life with her—and he wanted to make a life *inside* of her. Plant his seed and make a baby that had her fiery hair and beautiful green eyes. Hell, he wanted a whole horde of them. He wanted the warmth and love and miracle of being surrounded by the ones he loved—more than anything in the world.

He smiled, knowing she could see his wolf in it. The sharp points of his teeth. "I love you, Tor." Her lips formed the words as he braced his weight on one arm, watching her eyes as he pushed inside of her, loving that sharp flair of awareness, as if he were reaching into her soul.

"It's gonna be hard this time," he warned huskily…and it was. His body powered into her, deep and thick and hot, pushing the pleasure up into her until she was sobbing out raw, choking cries of ecstasy, pliant and flushed, his to do with whatever he pleased. And when the star-studded darkness of release crashed over them, they clutched at each other, their hands slipping across the damp heat of their skin, struggling for a hold.

The hours flowed together in an endless whirl of pleasure, their limbs tangled, bodies coming together again…and again. They twisted and turned, investigating every angle, rolling across the bed, shoving at each other in a battle for pleasure that had them sweat-slick and panting, the intensity so much greater for the love that bound them together. And when they finally collapsed in exhaustion, their bodies drowsy with satisfaction, Torrance snuggled against his side. "Hold me," she whispered, laying her hand over his heart.

With loving reverence, Mason wrapped her in the possessive hold of his arms…and pressed his mouth to the tender marks on the column of her throat. *"Forever."*

* * *

The cry of a hawk pulled him from sleep, or maybe it was simply his internal alarm that warned him his mate was no longer by his side. Rolling to his right, Mason ran his palm down the empty space beside him and closed his eyes in quiet regret. He had hoped that being held in his arms would keep her nightmares at bay—and he couldn't help the twinge of regret in his gut that she hadn't turned to him in need. He knew he was being unfair, but old doubts prickled at the back of his neck, making him swear foully under his breath. He rolled out of bed and grabbed his jeans, hitching them up over his hips as he set off toward the door.

With one hand on the knob, Mason found himself wondering if he could actually use the blood bond they'd made to find her. Closing his eyes, he breathed deeply in and out, then reached out for Torrance with his mind, with his heart…and realized he *knew* exactly where she was.

"Cool," he laughed under his breath, a foolish smile playing at his lips as he set off for the kitchen. Seconds later he found her perched on the counter, a bowl of Neapolitan ice cream in one hand, a spoon in the other.

"Hey, there," she said the moment she set eyes on him. Grinning, she scooped up a heaping spoonful of chocolate ice cream and held it out to him. "Wanna share with me?"

Moving toward her, Mason placed his hands on her knees and opened his mouth for the spoon, enjoying the sugary burst of flavor on his tongue as he swallowed. "I was afraid that you'd had another nightmare," he told her as she set the bowl on the counter, one of the straps of her cotton tank top slipping off her shoulder.

"No, I was just hungry." She laughed softly, a mischievous twinkle in her big green eyes. "I think all this physical activity must be good for my appetite." Lifting her hand, she touched the heat of his face with cool fingertips as her expression turned gentle. "And I doubt I'll be having any more nightmares. I think they've been put to rest, Mase. Thanks to you."

"In that case," he rasped, forcing the words past the lump of emotion in his throat as he scooped up a dollop of the three-flavored dessert on his fingers, "I think we should celebrate, sweetheart."

Then he dribbled the ice cream onto her shoulder.

"You fiend," Torrance gasped, the breathless sound turning into a shivering moan as Mason leaned down and lapped the freezing cream from her skin with his tongue. "I can't believe you did that!"

"Are you really going to complain about it?" he asked, his dark eyes glittering with laughter as he licked a bit of chocolate from his bottom lip, then stepped between her legs, his big hands resting on her bare thighs.

She narrowed her eyes at him, but the corners of her mouth were twitching with humor. "I guess there's not much point," she admitted. "After the way we met, I should have known you'd turn out to be a devil."

"I'll show you devilish," he whispered in her ear, his long fingers curving over her hips as he pulled her against him, the evidence of his arousal impossible to miss.

Torrance trembled, moving restlessly against him, amazed that desire could burn again so quickly. "D-did I mention insatiable?"

"I'll show you insatiable," he growled playfully, nipping her throat, making her gasp at the same time he pushed forward, thrusting against her, the rough denim of his jeans creating a decadent friction against the soft cotton panties she'd slipped on before heading out of the bedroom.

"And sinful," she moaned, her breath catching, deliberately egging him on.

He grunted a provocative sound of hunger against her shoulder, teasing her with his teeth. "I'll show you sinful, woman."

"And delicious," she giggled, thoroughly enjoying their game.

"I'll show you how delicious *you* are," he warned, one hand pulling down her tank top while the other smeared strawberry ice cream over the swollen tip of her breast, the cold shocking against her sensitive nipple. When he closed his warm mouth around the chilled tip, Torrance screamed, arching her back, the intensity of the sensations shooting straight to her core.

"Grab the bowl," he rumbled moments later, in a slow, wicked slide of words. When she had it clutched in her fingers, Mason pulled her off the counter, his hands under her bottom, her legs wrapped around his lean hips, and to their mutual delight, they spent the remainder of the night in playful, erotic splendor…discovering that ice cream is so much sweeter when enjoyed by two.

By the time they opened their eyes the following day, the noontime sun was climbing on the horizon, bathing the glade in saffron shades of sunshine beyond the high windows. Squinting against the brilliant light, Torrance lifted her face from the warmth of Mason's shoulder and tried to make out the blurry numbers on his digital alarm clock.

"What time is it?" he asked, his deep voice still scratchy from sleep.

"Heck if I know," she laughed tiredly, dropping her head back onto his firm shoulder, nuzzling closer so that she could press a kiss to the warm column of his throat. Drawing in a deep breath, Torrance wanted to purr like a jungle cat, his scent was so delicious. So masculine and warm, going straight to her head. There was a sense of rightness, of peace, in her heart that had never been there before. A sense of completion, heightened by a breathtaking feeling of hope for the future. "You know I'm blind without my glasses, and I'm too comfy to look for them."

Stretching the long, lean lines of his beautifully muscled body, he asked, "No nightmares last night?"

"Nope, not a single one." She lifted her right leg, pressing her bent knee against the swollen, steel-hard length of his erection, smiling against the curve of his whiskered jaw when a low, rumbling growl of arousal vibrated in his chest. The moment was perfect and warm, lackadaisical…while at the same time sweetly provocative, knowing that he wanted her. That all she had to do was say the word, and he'd be on her in a heartbeat. "I think we've found a cure for what ails me," she teased.

"I like the sound of that." He pulled her closer, against the hardness and heat of his body, sounding endearingly nervous as he said, "So, how do you feel about spending the day together…planning?"

"Planning what?" she asked, still drifting in that dreamy state of haziness that came after a deep, exhausted sleep.

He lifted his dark head from the pillow to gaze down at her, managing to look entirely too sexy, with his shaggy hair and dark whiskers. Watching her through heavy-lidded eyes that glittered with a mix of lust and love, he said, "I was thinking about a wedding."

"A wedding?" Suddenly wide-awake, she sat straight up in bed, completely stunned.

"Yeah," he said, cupping her cheek in his warm hand. "I love you, Tor. As far as the Lycan world is concerned, we're already married. But I want to have a wedding with you, sweetheart. See you in a beautiful white gown, your hair flowing over your shoulders like a flame, holding flowers in your hands. No way in hell am I gonna miss out on that. Whaddya say?"

"I say yes," she practically squealed, throwing herself into his arms, pressing playful kisses over his face and his chest, both of them shaking with happiness and laughter. "Yes and yes and yes!"

"Thank God," he rumbled, pulling her fully on top of him, his big hands on her bottom, anchoring her in place. "Let's try to make it happen this weekend."

"This weekend?" Torrance stared at him in shock. "That's impossible! Nobody can plan a wedding in four days. We'll need a few weeks at least."

"I'm not waiting *weeks* to make you my wife," he grumbled, holding her tighter.

"Mason!" she laughed. "There's no possible way to organize anything faster than that."

"We'll see," he murmured silkily, giving her a pirate's smile as he pulled her down for a hungry, eating kiss…

And they were married four days later.

Epilogue

Despite the fact that the bride and maid of honor had only a handful of days to prepare, it was a storybook wedding worthy of any magical fairy tale. The ceremony and reception were held outdoors, in the center of the Alley, as was tradition when a Bloodrunner married. There was thankfully no rain, but to compensate for the chilly autumn weather, the Runners had gone into the city and purchased some beautiful stone fire pits. They'd been placed among the tables, the towering blazes adding to the romantic atmosphere while providing necessary warmth.

Torrance was radiant in the ivory sheath that Michaela bought for her in Covington, the groom so in love, there was no doubt in anyone's eyes that they were meant to be together. And Dylan had arrived back home in time to help celebrate the momentous occasion, graciously offering to give away the bride.

Sitting beside his wife, who was busily chatting with her

best friend, Mason took a sip of his champagne, conversing quietly with the Elder. "It's time to keep your friends close and your enemies closer," Dylan told him. "It's someone who's pack, Mason. You can't trust anyone."

"It's someone *you* work with," he replied in a low rasp, looking out over the dancing, laughing guests. "It's someone on the League."

Dylan breathed out a heavy sigh. "Whoever it is, I have no doubt that you'll find him."

"Damn straight we will," Mason grunted. And then, shaking off his unwanted tension, he turned to smile at his friend, knowing there was one more order of business to take care of before he could whisk his new bride away to the privacy of their cabin. The day after Simmons's death, the Runners had drawn straws, choosing the one who would return to the pack to hunt the traitor from within. "I think it's time we made our announcement."

"This should be entertaining," the Elder drawled with a grin, though his eyes revealed the strain he was under. As a member of the League and friend of the Runners, Dylan was trapped between opposing sides of what was sure to turn into a bitter conflict.

Standing, Mason picked up a spoon to clink against the side of his champagne glass, careful not to hit too hard and shatter his mother's favorite crystal. "Excuse me," he called out. "If I could have everyone's attention for a moment. It's my honor and privilege to be the first to tell you that our own Jeremy Burns has gone before the Silvercrest's League of Elders and submitted his count."

As expected, the Alley, which had been transformed into a flower-filled paradise, fell completely quiet, even the natural sounds of the forest and the gentle breeze of the wind falling into an eerie state of silence.

"And now," he continued, lifting his glass in a toast to his best man, who sat at the end of the table beside a smirking Cian, "my partner will be accepting his place among the pack. To Jeremy, a braver man than I."

Cheers went up from every guest, every glass lifted in salute to the tawny-haired Runner who reluctantly grinned, bowing his head in thanks.

Every glass—except for one.

On the far side of the crowd, Mason watched as a lone blond female slipped quietly into the shadowed forest.

* * * * *

Be sure to watch for Jeremy and Jillian's romance,
coming only to Silhouette Nocturne
in April, 2008.
For a sneak preview of
LAST WOLF HUNTING,
just turn the page...

The cool eastern breeze snaked its way through the swaying trees, ruffling Jeremy's hair as the wind caressed his face and arms with another eerie stroke of warning. *Go back,* it seemed to whisper across his skin. *Go back, while you still can.*

Hell, like he needed any warnings. He was on his way back to the pack of werewolves who looked on his half-human heritage as a stain, an aberration, something that made him less than worthy. The last place he wanted to be was in Shadow Peak, living among the Silvercrest Lycans—but he'd drawn the shortest straw among the Bloodrunners and now the mission of ferreting out the traitor who was tempting Lycans to turn rogue, hunting innocent humans as prey and teaching those same rogues to dayshift had fallen to him alone.

Trying to shake off the unsettling sensation, Jeremy Burns moved deeper into the woods, the sounds from the clearing finally reaching his ears. A Challenge Night—just as he'd been informed earlier that day.

He lifted his head and sniffed the air. It was thick and heavy with tension, all but cloying against his skin. Tonight's fight must be an unusual one, he thought with a wondering frown. Male agitation rose sharp on the wind, but with the women…it was sizzling and swift, like a lit fuse.

Jillian Murphy was near. The woman who was meant to be his life mate. The woman who was meant to make him complete.

As if, he silently snarled. Instead, she'd never been anything but a thorn in his side.

He wished he could just ignore it—the knowledge that Jillian's presence screwed him up inside like a knot—but how could you ignore something that was so much a part of you? This dark need inside of Jeremy was as vital as his heart and lungs, which is why he'd spent the past decade like the walking dead, going through the motions of life without really experiencing it.

Now Jillian's scent grew sharper the higher he and his fellow Runner, Cian Hennessey, hiked. The scent revealed her powerful emotions at the same time it screwed with his head. She was scared tonight, on edge, filled with an overwhelming sense of dread, but Jeremy knew she'd be putting on a brave face for the pack she considered hers, though she was a witch, not a wolf. The women of her bloodline had served the Silvercrest werewolves for centuries, gifting them with their powers. When her mother, Connie, stepped down from her place as Spirit Walker, Jillian had assumed the vital role of healer and spiritual leader of the pack. He knew they loved her, respected her…looked up to her, though she was still a young woman of twenty-eight. And why shouldn't they? She'd given her entire life to them. Hell, she'd even turned her back on him for the sake of her precious pack of wolves.

"That sounds like one hell of a fight," Cian murmured.

Jeremy grunted in agreement, his sense of foreboding growing stronger, adding to his restless agitation.

A high-pitched cry rent the air in the next instant, echoing through the thick forest, and that same female voice snarled, "You're mine now."

Jeremy scowled. "It's Danna Gibson."

Cian sent him a comical look of disbelief, then chuckled softly under his breath. "Your luck can't get any worse."

Jeremy had to agree. He'd dated Danna a few times when he was younger, before Jillian had come home from school and he'd felt the call of a life mate. And it'd been Danna whom Jillian had accused him of fooling around with the same day he and she had shared their first kiss—the day Jillian had told him she was finally ready to give them a chance.

"I wonder what the hell's going on up there." He cut Cian a questioning look from the corner of his eye, but the Irishman lifted one shoulder in a "hell if I know" gesture, his attention warily focused on the lights up ahead.

"Whatever it is, I've got a bad feeling about it," Cian said.

"Yeah. Me, too."

When a new voice, soft and smoky and lilting, rang out through the night, Jeremy nearly tripped over the gnarled root of a sprawling oak tree. "For the last time, Danna, I did *not* touch your mate."

Oh, hell. The voice behind those words knocked the air from his lungs like a kick in the chest. Jeremy slammed to a jarring stop, not even breathing, while senses, already sharpened to precision, revved into overdrive. His mind didn't want to accept it, but his body knew the truth.

It was her.

Jillian.

He was close enough to scent the damning details now, everything narrowing into a concentrated focus that had him sucking in angry gulps of air, his traitorous body greedy for every drop he could take in. The sensory intake was shocking and almost painful in its intensity, the heat of her lush little body, all hot and angry from battle, nearly doubling him over, while panic had him moving faster.

Even though Jillian had the blood of a wolf flowing through her veins, the fact she was a witch made it impossible for her to shapeshift. Danna was twice Jillian's size and as vicious as a pit-bull, not to mention underhanded—no doubt the Lycan was cheating like hell.

And what in God's name was Jillian doing fighting one of her own wolves?

Vaguely aware of Cian at his side, Jeremy's feet moved faster with the speed of his thoughts, until he finally broke through the last yards of the forest at a full run. Then he nearly staggered to his knees, his legs all but crumpling beneath him as he took in the scene playing out in the clearing like some kind of grotesque nightmare.

Jillian Murphy stood in the center of the Challenge Circle— beautiful, brave and bleeding.

And she was about to die.

* * * * *

Look for
LAST WOLF HUNTING
By Rhyannon Byrd
In April 2008
From Silhouette Nocturne
Available wherever books are sold

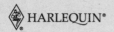
HARLEQUIN®

INTRIGUE®

WHITEHORSE MONTANA

No matter how much Nate Dempsey's past haunted
him, McKenna Bailey couldn't keep him off her mind.
He'd returned to town to bury his troubled youth—
but she wouldn't stop pursuing him until he was
working on the ranch by her side.

Look for

MATCHMAKING WITH A MISSION

BY

B.J. DANIELS

*Available in April
wherever books are sold.*

www.eHarlequin.com

HI69320

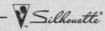

SPECIAL EDITION™

Introducing a brand-new miniseries

Men of
Mercy Medical

Gabe Thorne moved to Las Vegas to open a
new branch of his booming construction
business—and escape from a recent tragedy.
But when his teenage sister showed up pregnant
on his doorstep, he really had his hands full.
Luckily, in turning to Dr. Rebecca Hamilton for
the medical care his sister needed, he found
a cure for himself....

Starting with

THE MILLIONAIRE
AND THE M.D.

by *TERESA SOUTHWICK,*

available in April wherever books are sold.

HARLEQUIN®
Super Romance®

Celebrate the joys of motherhood!
In this collection of touching stories,
three women embrace their maternal
instincts in ways they hadn't expected.
And even more surprising is how true
love finds them.

Mothers of the Year

With stories by
Lori Handeland
Rebecca Winters
Anna DeStefano

*Look for Mothers of the Year,
available in April
wherever books are sold.*

www.eHarlequin.com

HSR71482

REQUEST YOUR FREE BOOKS!

2 FREE NOVELS PLUS 2 FREE GIFTS!

Silhouette®

n o c t u r n e™

Dramatic and Sensual Tales of Paranormal Romance.

YES! Please send me 2 FREE Silhouette® Nocturne™ novels and my 2 FREE gifts (gifts are worth about $10). After receiving them, if I don't wish to receive any more books, I can return the shipping statement marked "cancel." If I don't cancel, I will receive 4 brand-new novels every other month and be billed just $4.47 per book in the U.S. or $4.99 per book in Canada, plus 25¢ shipping and handling per book plus applicable taxes, if any*. That's a savings of about 15% off the cover price! I understand that accepting the 2 free books and gifts places me under no obligation to buy anything. I can always return a shipment and cancel at any time. Even if I never buy another book from Silhouette, the two free books and gifts are mine to keep forever.

238 SDN ELS4 338 SDN ELXG

Name _____ (PLEASE PRINT) _____

Address _____ Apt. # _____

City _____ State/Prov. _____ Zip/Postal Code _____

Signature (if under 18, a parent or guardian must sign)

Mail to the **Silhouette Reader Service:**
IN U.S.A.: P.O. Box 1867, Buffalo, NY 14240-1867
IN CANADA: P.O. Box 609, Fort Erie, Ontario L2A 5X3

Not valid to current subscribers of Silhouette Nocturne books.

Want to try two free books from another line?
Call 1-800-873-8635 or visit www.morefreebooks.com.

* Terms and prices subject to change without notice. N.Y. residents add applicable sales tax. Canadian residents will be charged applicable provincial taxes and GST. This offer is limited to one order per household. All orders subject to approval. Credit or debit balances in a customer's account(s) may be offset by any other outstanding balance owed by or to the customer. Please allow 4 to 6 weeks for delivery. Offer available while quantities last.

Your Privacy: Silhouette is committed to protecting your privacy. Our Privacy Policy is available online at www.eHarlequin.com or upon request from the Reader Service. From time to time we make our lists of customers available to reputable third parties who may have a product or service of interest to you. If you would prefer we not share your name and address, please check here. ☐

SN08

Inside ROMANCE

Stay up-to-date on all your romance reading news!

Inside Romance is a FREE quarterly newsletter highlighting our upcoming series releases and promotions.

Visit

www.eHarlequin.com/InsideRomance

to sign up to receive our complimentary newsletter today!

IRN1107

HARLEQUIN® *Romance*®

presents

The Wedding Planners

Planning perfect weddings...
finding happy endings!

Amidst the rustle of satins and silks, the scent of red roses
and white lilies and the excited chatter of brides-to-be, six
friends from Boston are The Wedding Belles—they make
other people's wedding dreams come true....

But are they always the wedding planner...never the bride?

Who will be the next to say "I do"?

In April: Shirley Jump, *Sweetheart Lost and Found*
In May: Myrna Mackenzie, *The Heir's Convenient Wife*
In June: Melissa McClone, *S.O.S. Marry Me*
In July: Linda Goodnight, *Winning the Single Mom's Heart*
In August: Susan Meier, *Millionaire Dad, Nanny Needed!*
In September: Melissa James, *The Bridegroom's Secret*

*And don't miss the exciting wedding-planner tips and
author reminiscences that accompany each book!*

www.eHarlequin.com   HRI7507

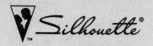
Silhouette®

Romantic
SUSPENSE

**Sparked by Danger,
Fueled by Passion.**

The Taken

Tierney Doyle is used to being criticized for
her psychic abilities, yet the tough-as-nails—
and drop-dead-gorgeous—detective has no doubt
about what she has uncovered in the case of a
string of unsolved murders. And Tierney is slowly
discovering that working so close to her partner,
detective Wade Callahan, could be lethal.

Look for

Danger Signals
by Kathleen Creighton

Available in April wherever books are sold.

Silhouette®

nocturne™

COMING NEXT MONTH

#37 MIND GAMES • Merline Lovelace

Mark Wolfson was an expert at influencing women's
thoughts. Special Agent Taylor Chase knew the doctor's
psychic powers all too well—and she'd had enough of
being toyed with. But she'd need his mind and body to
complete her vital mission on a forgotten island, where
instincts were best kept sharp—and inhibitions let go.

#38 LAST WOLF HUNTING • Rhyannon Byrd
Bloodrunners

The hunt meant more to Jeremy Burns than
dominance—it meant facing the woman he'd left behind.
Once Jillian Murphy had belonged to Jeremy. Now she
was the Spirit Walker to the Silvercrest wolves, and the
most desirable female of the pack. It would take more
than the rights of nature for Jeremy to renew his claim
on her—and she would not go easily once he had.